REVEREND RANDOLLPH
AND THE WAGES OF SIN

Reverend Randollph

Charles Merrill Smith

and the Wages of Sin

G. P. Putnam's Sons, New York

This is for John and Margaret,
Dear friends and interesting people

God of my life, what just return
Can sinful dust and ashes give?

—from the hymn numbered 366
in *Hymns for the Use of
the Methodist Episcopal Church
(1870 edition)*

REVEREND RANDOLLPH
AND THE WAGES OF SIN

1

DAN GANTRY inspected the passengers debouching from the ramp connected to flight 417 out of San Francisco. He had a name and a sketchy biography but no description. The game was to match one of the passengers with this meager profile.

"He should be one of the first off," the bishop said, more to himself than to Dan. "I've never known C.P. to travel other than first class—at least not when someone else is paying the bill."

Some passengers came out of the chute smiling, soon to clutch their waiting families. Others, heads down, plunged doggedly ahead as if into some joyless future. Dan considered and discarded a short, fat man with a pimple on his chin. Clergymen are often short and fat, he knew, and their calling did not exempt them from pimples. But successful clergymen didn't wear brown shoes with a blue suit. Remembering that Randollph was more a teacher than a preacher and that teachers will wear anything, he was about to reappraise the blue suit and brown shoes when the fat man, hesitating briefly, joined an eddy of passengers floating toward the terminal of O'Hare International Airport. A large brown pinstripe eliminated himself as he clasped to his white-on-white breast a youngish blonde who might or might not have been his wife. Dan tabbed him for a salesman of earth-moving machinery with large alimony obligations. A homburg and black topcoat with velvet collar facings was costumed for the part, but he was too old (a class A undertaker?) A nifty, blue houndstooth Norfolk jacket over a navy turtleneck was too casual and too young-looking, even though there were specks of gray in the dark hair that came well over the collar of his jacket. Probably a TV actor, or maybe a director. Dan was estimating a somewhat frayed tan plaid with a hairpiece when the Norfolk jacket stopped and grasped the bishop's offered hand and the bishop was saying, "It's been a long time," and the jacket said, "Freddie, it's good to see you again."

Dan verbalized his chagrin. "Good Lord, when you came out of the chute, I pegged you for an actor. How big a mistake can a guy make?"

The jacket responded with a chuckle which sounded like a series of suppressed coughs. "No mistake. We're all actors, aren't we? Especially preachers and teachers."

The bishop cleared his throat. "Perhaps we can ponder the significance of that profound remark while I take care of the formalities." He put a hand on Dan's shoulder. "C.P., this is Dan Gantry who, despite his rather bizarre attire, which is a style I am told is referred to as mod, is one of the pastors at the Church of the Good Shepherd. His field of responsibility is to direct the church's programs for youth and young adults, but is not limited to that. Dan, this is my former student, former faculty colleague, and very dear friend, Dr. C. P. Randollph, who will be your boss for the next year."

"Freddie," Randollph complained, "do you have to introduce me as Doctor? Sounds so solemn."

The bishop smiled. "I see you haven't changed, C.P., at least in your distaste for pretentious titles. Would you prefer that I introduce you as Reverend Randollph?"

"Horrors, no! That makes me feel like a sacred object. No one should think of himself as wrapped in a mantle of conferred holiness. Bad for the soul. Besides, Reverend isn't a title. You know that, Freddie."

"I know that, C.P. But I'm afraid that is a lost battle. The world finds it convenient to call its pastors Reverend, and what the world finds convenient, it does. I've always felt that for a clergyman, the chief virtue in possessing a doctor's degree was to escape being called Reverend." The bishop turned toward the tributary corridor which carried tides of passengers around the clock. "And now let us be on our way. I spend enough time in airports to wish to be quit of them as rapidly as possible."

2

"I find them stimulating, airports, that is," said Randollph.

"I can't imagine why," the bishop flung back at him as he nudged a large woman in a floppy hat who had managed to block the way out of the passenger lounge.

"Because," Randollph answered him, "I've never been able to decide whether a large airport is a better vision of heaven or hell. It can serve quite well for either."

The three men made their way abreast down the corridor. Past glass cases of newspapers with headlines: CONVICTED COUNCILMAN ASKS NEW TRIAL. Past an advertising poster for a life insurance company showing a happy family picnic with a black X drawn through the father and a legend, "Where would they be with you out of the picture?" Past a bank of telephones and a man angrily jiggling the receiver arm. Past forlorn young women carrying fretful children like punishment for forgotten ecstasies. Past tired janitors listlessly sweeping up the litter of people long gone.

"You're a big guy," Dan said to Randollph. "I have to look up to you."

"Bigger than average," Randollph answered, "but not big big."

The bishop suddenly swerved toward a sign which read 42ND PARALLEL. "I rather like this place," he announced. "Let's pause for a small libation. I'm sure the sun is over the yardarm by now."

They followed him into a noisy high-ceilinged room with a glass wall looking out on the hustle necessary to the nursing of great planes ceaselessly arriving and departing. The bishop artfully staked a claim to a momentarily vacant table before a covey of businessmen with briefcases could descend upon it.

"Be with you in a minute, gentlemen," a waitress said in passing with the weary cheerfulness of a woman who had too many tables and too little time. Outside a man beckoned a silvery 707 into its berth, and an electric tractor pulling a string of baggage carts tried and failed to make a sharp turn into the unloading dock and backed up to try again.

"What'll it be, gents?" The waitress vigorously swept the table of dirty glasses and a quarter tip.

"For you, Dan?" the bishop asked. "It's on me, of course. I shall

3

put it on my expense account, although as our treasurer is distressingly censorious of strong drink, I'd best list it as lunch."

"Chivas Regal on the rocks," Dan informed the waitress. "A double."

"I'll have a dry sherry," the bishop said. "I became quite fond of sherry when I was up at Magdalen, you know."

"A proper drink for a bishop." Randollph remarked. "Please bring me a very dry martini up and with a twist. Make it with Bombay gin, please."

"We ain't got Bombay."

"Pity. Tanqueray?"

"Yeah."

"Tanqueray will be fine."

"C.P.," the bishop said, "I expect I'd better explain a little more fully why I was so urgent about you taking on this interim assignment."

"I expect you had, Freddie," Randollph answered. "I gathered there were things to be said which were not said in your letters and phone calls."

The bishop plucked a blue silk handkerchief from the breast pocket of his neat black suit jacket and wiped his bald forehead. "Hot in here. C.P., one has to be careful what he commits to paper, especially when he is a bishop. And as for phone calls, who knows who might be listening these days?"

The waitress brought the drinks. Randollph fished the lemon peel out of his martini and twisted it over the glass. "They never really twist a twist at the bar," he explained. He sniffed at the pale liquid. "And the smell of lemon oil on gin is one of the world's most pleasant odors." On the other side of the glass wall a light snow had begun to fall, coating the week-old slush with a temporary patina of purity.

"Now where was I?" the bishop asked.

"You were telling us what a wicked place the modern world is," Randollph reminded him. "Bugged telephones, intercepted mail, evil people seeking to thwart the righteous purposes of good bishops."

"Well, it is," the bishop complained. "You've always said, I remember quite well, that you took a dim view of the world."

"Like any sane and observant man, I am not sanguine about the world's long-range prospects. But day by day, I love it, I love it." Randollph took an appreciative sip of his martini.

"Hear, hear!" Dan said. "I couldn't have put it better myself."

"The Scriptures warn us against worldliness," the bishop said.

"The Scriptures warn us against falling in love with the values of the present age," Randollph replied. "It's not the same thing at all. A bishop should not be guilty of faulty exegesis."

"Better guilty of faulty exegesis than guilty of some other things bishops are frequently guilty of," the bishop said cheerfully. "But let's get on with the business at hand."

"Let's."

"Ostensibly you are here to serve for a year as interim pastor of the Church of the Good Shepherd while the church conducts a search for a permanent pastor—"

Randollph interrupted. "Why in the name of seven saints do they call it the Church of the Good Shepherd, Freddie? As I understand it, the church is in the bowels of a high-rise office building in the heart of a city. How many of the people who belong to the Church of the Good Shepherd have ever seen a sheep—except maybe as a rack of lamb? I'll wager not one of them has ever seen a shepherd."

"Probably not," the bishop said. "Prosperous urban types cherish their bucolic myths. They all think they want to retire to a farm. But they don't, of course. Anyway," he continued, "our publicity has stated clearly that your interim assignment is to give Good Shepherd ample time to select a successor to the recently retired distinguished and beloved Dr. Arthur Hartshorne."

"Was he?" Randollph asked.

"Was he what?"

"Distinguished and beloved."

"Our publicity said he was."

"Come now, Freddie," Randollph chided him, "you haven't gotten to the place where press releases from the episcopal public relations department are turned out on stone tablets. Your handouts are probably the usual muck of polite lies and half-truths."

"Well, I admit we don't tell all." The bishop was unperturbed. "Beloved and distinguished are, after all, elastic terms. He certainly was beloved by Good Shepherd's board of trustees. It didn't want him to retire. Neither, I might add, did he want to retire."

"Then why did he?"

"He had reached the age of mandatory retirement." The bishop grimaced as if at an unpleasant memory. "The trustees petitioned me to make an exception, and Hartshorne heartily concurred in it. I had to be quite firm."

"So I am to serve under a hostile board of trustees and with a disgruntled ex-pastor hanging around. You failed to mention all this in your importunities. Is there more?"

"Well, there are other problems, which is why I wanted you. You are a problem solver by nature. Although you apparently choose to use the gift sparingly."

"Aren't many problems to solve in my corner of academia."

"A good enough reason to entice you out—you should be grateful, C.P. Also, what is more logical than for me to name a distinguished theologian who is on sabbatical to serve as interim pastor of my most prominent church?"

"Historian," Randollph corrected him. "Not a theologian, a historian—church history, or Christian history if you prefer. And I'm not distinguished."

"Theologian, historian, who knows the difference?"

"I do."

"The parishioners won't," the bishop said. "And to laymen anyone who has written a book they haven't read is distinguished. Dan, why don't you fish the car from that ocean of vehicles out there while C.P. and I retrieve his luggage?" He stacked four quarters next to his sherry glass and rose to depart. "It will be a miracle, of course, if your bags got on the same plane with you. But then, the clergy is supposed to believe in the possibility of miracles."

Randollph and the bishop found the sign FLIGHT 417 and joined the clot of passengers watching the conveyor belt dump suitcases into a chute like upright citizens suddenly plunged into a life of sin.

"There's more, isn't there, Freddie?" Randollph pressed the bishop. Passengers were snatching luggage as soon as it came to rest, hunting hawks pouncing on unwary prey. "You haven't come clean yet, have you?"

6

"Are those yours?" The bishop pointed to two large taffy-colored pigskin bags rumbling along the belt. "They look like you."

"So they are." Randollph plucked them from the pile as soon as they banged out of the chute, disappointing a hovering redcap. "Let's go. There will be a trunk along tomorrow or the next day. You can answer my question in the car."

Dan was waiting with a plain-looking blue Ford. "Church leases it for me," he told Randollph as he stowed the bags in the trunk. "They'll lease one for you, too."

"Not if I can avoid it," Randollph said as he got in the back seat with the bishop. "With taxis, trains, and planes available, I don't plan to do any driving. Man takes his life in his hands driving in a place like this."

Dan shot the Ford into the lanes leading to the Kennedy Expressway, aggressively competing for space. Randollph revived the interrupted conversation. "As I said, Freddie, there's more, isn't there?"

"I'm afraid so, C.P."

"So?"

"Bishops, C.P., are accustomed to facing stoutly the necessity of revealing unpleasant facts. We have to face it almost daily. What we do, it's a prerogative of the office, is to permit others to be the bearers of bad news. Whenever feasible anyway. I'm going to ask Dan to fill you in. He's been on the Good Shepherd staff for three years. He and I have talked about this situation many times. Dan."

"Where do you want me to start?" Dan, minding his driving, spoke to the windshield.

"Remember that our good bishop has been very stingy with information," Randollph told him. "Give me a full picture."

"OK." Dan was watching a silver Porsche tailing them impatiently. "I'll try to condense it. Old Arty—that's Hartshorne—sat on his prat at Good Shepherd for twenty-six years, gassing away with his corny stories, and playing distinguished city pastor, and speaking for every hick Rotary Club in seventeen states, but letting the church go to hell. By going to hell, I mean he let Stinky Smelser and the trustees run everything and do nothing. Downtown like we are, there's people everywhere, and lots of problems. The church's got money, and it's

7

got opportunities to do great things. But you can't get the lousy trustees to spend a dime."

"Who is Stinky Smelser?" Randollph asked.

The bishop chuckled. "Sometimes Dan requires a little translating. O. Bertram Smelser—I don't know what the *O* is for—"

"Obadiah," Dan said. "I have looked it up."

"Biblical anyway," the bishop said. "He is nominally the number two pastor at Good Shepherd and has been for twenty years."

"We don't call him Stinky to his face." Dan had to talk over his left shoulder as he kept an eye on the Porsche, which suddenly downshifted and shot abreast of them in the next lane, its motor sneering. "I call him Bertie, and that irritates him plenty."

"Smelser has always devoted himself almost exclusively to the business side of the church's operation," the bishop explained to Randollph. "Somebody had to. Arthur Hartshorne had no interest at all in it. And at Good Shepherd the business side of the operation is a very big side. Very big indeed."

"You make it sound like General Motors or ITT," Randollph said. "I never pastored a church, as you know, Freddie, but I thought churches were always hard up, had to scramble to make ends meet."

"Most of them are poor enough. My worries as a bishop can be stated in dollar signs. But once in a while you come across a rich church like Good Shepherd."

"What makes it rich?"

"Endowments, leases on the hotel and office space which constitute most of the building." The bishop ticked them off in the reverent tone administrators reserve for tangible assets. "All this means building maintenance and insurance problems and, of course, personnel to be hired, and, I suppose, fired. It all adds up to quite a responsibility."

"Bastard!" Dan muttered as the Porsche dived for an opening in front of him, flicking its tail insolently.

Randollph absently contemplated a billboard touting a television evangelist which queried in three-foot red letters ARE YOU READY FOR THE JUDGMENT DAY?

"And this Smelser chap, he's very good at the business side of Good Shepherd, I take it?" he asked the bishop.

The bishop took time to select his answer. "I wish I knew, C.P. He's reported to be very good at it. That's not quite the same thing as being very good at it, is it?"

"It all depends on who's doing the reporting," Randollph said. "What are you trying to tell me, Freddie? That you suspect Smelser of ineptitude? Or of chicanery with the church's assets? Or of what?"

"No, nothing specific, C.P. Call it a hunch. Call it a vague feeling that things aren't all they seem at Good Shepherd. Put it down to a dark conviction that even the best of men become ethically confused when exposed continually to very large and accessible sums of money. I'm just not comfortable with this situation at Good Shepherd."

"Come now, Freddie," Randollph prodded him. "You didn't go to all the trouble to get me out here just because you believe in the doctrine of original sin."

"No," the bishop said. "No, I didn't. My nature is to look on my fellowman as essentially righteous, even though, I confess, my daily experience with him tends to blow gaping holes in this perspective. I am always reluctant to impute wickedness to anyone when irrefutable evidence is not in hand. But there are, ah, hints I can't ignore."

"Such as?"

"Well, C.P., I'm sure it won't add to your comfort, but the trustees didn't like the idea of an interim pastor. They didn't like it at all. Nothing against you, of course," he added hastily. "After all, they don't know you. It's just that they had decided on Hartshorne's successor and wanted him named with what I thought was unseemly haste."

"Well, well, you didn't mention this in your letters, Freddie," Randollph chided him. "Now let me guess. The trustees are unanimous in their request that you name Smelser as permanent pastor."

"It wasn't unanimous. The vote was five to one. It did make me wonder, though. They were overanxious for a man who is not fitted for the job."

Dan, maneuvering for an exit, caught the silver Porsche pinned between two trucks and managed to splash it with the accumulating slush. "Hah, gotcha!" he exalted. Then, revenged, he said to the bishop, "Don't you think we ought to come clean?"

"I think you had better," Randollph said.

"Oh, all right," the bishop answered. "I wasn't going to tell you this because it may have, probably does have, a perfectly reasonable explanation." He leaned forward and said, "Dan, I have a dinner engagement at the Blackhawk. If it isn't too much trouble would you drop me there?"

"You were going to come clean," Randollph admonished the bishop.

"It's this, C.P." The bishop began his story with obvious reluctance. "We receive—that is, my office receives—a very substantial amount of money from Good Shepherd's annual assessment for benevolent causes. That amount, while still substantial, has been dropping steadily. The trustees explain that expenses are up and return on investment is down. Their annual reports bear this out. But then, they make out the reports, don't they?" It was not a question.

Randollph laughed. "Freddie, Freddie, such deviousness! You got me out here on the pretext that I was to be a cure of souls, but actually you want me to find the leak through which your rightful revenues are disappearing. Should I remind you what the Scriptures say about the love of money?"

"It's not my money." The bishop sounded testy. "It's the church's money. You'll be protecting the many benevolent agencies of the church which depend on this revenue."

"Don't be pompous, Freddie, it doesn't become you," Randollph told him. "At all events, I'm in it now. If there's more, tell me."

"I have probably told you more than there is to tell already. A mélange of coincidence, suspicion, personal ambition, and falling income doesn't necessarily add up to a conspiracy. I've already told you too much for you to be entirely objective. I surely don't want to be unfair to Smelser or the trustees." Then, primly: "A bishop should always be fair."

"Well spoken, my friend! You have your values unusually straight for a bishop. I would give precedence to fairness over every other quality to be desired in bishops. Even," he added wickedly, "even over piety."

"I try, C.P., I try." The bishop sighed. "At any rate, my episcopal bosom will be soothed to know that nothing is amiss at Good Shepherd, which I devoutly hope is the case. It takes years for a church to recover from any kind of scandal. Here's the Blackhawk."

"Is there anything more I can do for you, Bishop?" Dan asked.

"No, you've done quite enough as it is," the bishop replied. Then, turning to Randollph, he said, "I asked Dan along for more than his ability as a chauffeur. He is filled with the uncomplicated righteous fervor of the idealistic young, and he is often tactless, and he will frequently irritate you with the, ah, forthrightness of his speech." The bishop looked at Dan to see if this was sinking in, but Dan was smiling. "However," the bishop continued, "he is honest, and he is bright, and he is trustworthy. I hope you'll rely on him."

"I think those are refreshing characteristics," Randollph said. "All of them. We'll get along."

A few snowflakes drifted down halfheartedly. The wet pavement reflected the neon signs fighting the gathering darkness. Overhead an El train clattered off into the night.

The bishop, out of the car now, paused to search his memory for anything to add. Randollph got out too. "I think I've told you enough for starters," the bishop said. He hesitated briefly, then clapped Randollph on the back.

"Go get 'em, tiger," he said, and walked briskly into the restaurant.

2

THE CHURCH of the Good Shepherd had preceded the existence of Chicago. Originally a wooden hut dedicated to the conversion of Indians, it had progressed to a respectable frame structure devoted to the spiritual needs of white merchants and professionals. A more respectable frame structure succeeded the one destroyed by the Great Fire, which in turn was succeeded by a large and gloomy Romanesque brick edifice suited to the stern theology of a burgeoning prairie aristocracy. The gloomy brick was good for at least a hundred years, but as the street on which it occupied a generous corner began sprouting the first generation of skyscrapers and frontage prices were quoted by the foot, the trustees took counsel. Godly men all, they agreed that a Divine Being who abhorred waste would want them to convert this vastly valuable space into something more remunerative than a Sunday offering. After all, God is everywhere, they reasoned, and therefore just as accessible from lower-priced sites farther out as from prime tracts in the business districts. Plans were made to move and sell the old church when one trustee conceived the idea of combining a commercial building with a church. "Why should we sell out to the real estate boys when we can make the money ourselves and still have our church right here?" is how he put it.

"But how will anyone know this is a church?" one of the especially pious trustees objected.

"Why, we'll stick a church tower on top of the building, that's how."

Thus, the present Good Shepherd was a masonry finger rising some forty vaguely Gothic stories into Chicago's sooty sky and with a definitely Gothic tower perched like a duncecap on top. Known locally as the Shep Building, it contained a luxury hotel (leased, because it would be improper for a church to be engaged directly in retailing spiritous liquors), business office space, and incidentally a church.

The next morning C. P. Randollph was in the Gothic tower chewing on the bishop's revelations and underdone bacon. Some years previously a trustee with an acute abhorrence of waste had calculated the amount of empty and unproductive space in the church tower and proposed that the church construct in it a penthouse apartment for the use of the pastor. "It'll lower our parsonage costs," he explained, "and besides, it'll keep the pastor on the job twenty-four hours a day." The Good Shepherd board agreed that surely the Lord would want it to minimize costs and maximize pastoral service.

The night before, when Dan had loaded Randollph and his bags on the hotel elevator and punched the button marked *P,* he said, "It's the damnedest place you ever saw." They got off into a small hallway and walked up three steps to a large metal door. Dan unlocked the door, stood aside and said, "Enter your humble quarters."

When Randollph stepped in, he had the impression that he was out of doors. Even though it was dark outside, the lights of Chicago's Loop flooded through the walls of glass. The sight was as spectacular as it was unexpected.

"This thing's an octagon," Dan explained. "It's in the base of the tower. They just knocked out some masonry and put in glass so it would be light and cheerful, I guess. Nifty, isn't it?"

Randollph agreed that it was nifty. The octagon had been bisected by a wall, leaving half the floor as a huge living room. It was carpeted wall to wall in a deep-pile grassy green. The furniture looked to Randollph to be the kind you see in the display windows of expensive stores. Some of it was green, and some was blue, and some was gold. It had the correct look, which suggested the work of a professional interior decorator. There was a real fireplace in the middle of the bisecting wall.

"Come on," Dan said, "I'll show you the rest of the place." He pushed through a door. "Here's the dining room, and then here's the kitchen. There's also a study or a den and a lavatory in this half.

13

Makes the rooms kind of pie-shaped the way it's laid out. Different anyway."

"Where do I sleep?" Randollph asked.

"Upstairs. It's two floors. I'll show you." He led Randollph up a corkscrew stairway with open treads. They came out into a wide hallway that ran from glass wall to glass wall. "This whole side's the master bedroom and bath and dressing room," Dan said, opening a door for Randollph. "The other side's two bedrooms with a bath in between."

The big bedroom looked more like a parlor than a place to sleep. It was carpeted in a soft gold. At one end was an oversized bed with a bookcase headboard. There was a moss-green sofa with a long coffee table in front of it. There were two easy chairs upholstered in white with a design worked in gold thread.

"Somebody liked green and gold," Randollph commented.

"Aunt Matilda," Dan said.

"Who?"

"Mrs. Hartshorne. Everyone called her Aunt Matilda. Sweet motherly type that ran things with an iron hand."

The bathroom, slightly smaller than a handball court Randollph estimated, was splendid with blue and white tile, a sunken tub, and separate glass shower stall. There was a stool and a bidet. A telephone hung from the wall by the stool.

"Somebody spent some money on this place," Randollph said.

"Aunt Matilda again. It was built about five years after they came. The church would have cheap-johned it, or so I hear, but Aunt Matilda supervised everything. Story is that the trustees all had coronaries when they saw the bill."

"It's sinfully opulent for the Lord's servant," Randollph said, "but of course I shall enjoy it. Especially the view. Is it the church's thought that I'll do my own cooking?"

"No. Mrs. Creedy, the church housekeeper, will come in to fix your breakfast. Other meals, we thought you'd be eating out. You could have stuff sent up from hotel room service."

So, Randollph reflected, I'm beginning my first day on the job with a magnificent view of Lake Michigan, an unsatisfactory breakfast,

14

and the hatful of problems the bishop handed me last night. Actually, he admitted to himself, he wasn't disturbed by the possibility of a Byzantine tangle in the affairs of the Church of the Good Shepherd. True, he had chided Freddie for not telling him early on, but Freddie was the bishop. It made a difference, of course, that Freddie had been his teacher at the seminary, and his dean when Randollph had come back to teach, and his good friend. But bishops will be bishops, Randollph knew. If he needed episcopal help in cleaning up what promised to be a fair mess—and he suspected that, sooner or later, he would—that help would be easier to extract from a Freddie who felt guilty for not coming clean with him at the beginning.

He watched the scene in the streets below, miniaturized by height and distance. There was a frenetic quality to the push and bustle of people and vehicles entirely absent from his serene Pacific campus. He enjoyed the airs of academe, but they did become stifling with their petty departmental power struggles and spinsterish intellectual bickerings. He felt positively exhilarated at the prospect of fraud and conspiracy and misdeeds blacker than the lecturer in systematic theology calling the professor of sociology of religion a spiritual ignoramus. He realized he would be terribly disappointed if O. B. Smelser and his trustees turned out to be guilty of nothing more than bungling and reprimanded himself for this ignoble thought.

But how best begin?

"There's more coffee on the stove, Dr. Randollph, if you should want it, although you've had two cups already." His invigorating reverie broken, Randollph ignored the implication of sinful self-indulgence and replied, "Yes, I'll be wanting more, thank you, Mrs. Creedy."

Mrs. Creedy, in sepulchral and unmodish black, instructed him. "I've got to be about my other duties. There's a guild tea to look after this afternoon, and today's my room inspection day. I wish to speak to you about the janitors, Dr. Randollph, such ideas of cleanliness they have, but that can wait, of course, until you've settled in a bit—"

Randollph thought it best to stem this tide of housekeeping woes before it became a flood. "I'm sure your duties as church housekeeper are many and exacting, Mrs. Creedy," he said, "and I do thank you

15

for adding me to your burdens. Has the church arranged to compensate you for looking after me?"

"No, they haven't." Mrs. Creedy's thin mouth tightened. "That would be Mr. Smelser's responsibility. Mr. Smelser is very close with expenditures."

"Be assured that you will be compensated," Randollph told her, noting that the prospect of added income produced, if not a look of pleasure, at least an indication of satisfaction. "And by the way, Mrs. Creedy, I'd appreciate somewhat larger portions in the future. I'm a man who cannot face the day without an ample breakfast." He smiled engagingly, hoping to defang the modest rebuke.

But Mrs. Creedy's mouth retightened.

"Gluttony is one of the seven deadly sins, as you must know, Dr. Randollph."

Randollph thought she must be joshing but decided that a jocular Mrs. Creedy was unthinkable.

"In any case," he replied, smiling weakly, "larger portions. The sin will be mine, not yours. And stronger coffee, please."

Mrs. Creedy disposed of, however unsatisfactorily, Randollph returned to plotting his course as temporary captain of a ship with a potentially mutinous crew. Randollph's experience in running a church was nonexistent. But then, he was certain, running a church would not differ in essentials from running a corporation or an army or a professional hockey team. Establish lines of authority. Survey the operation for weaknesses and strengths. Isolate the palace intriguers and keep an eye on them. Find out where the money goes. Especially find out where the money goes.

One school of thought dictated a cautious, beguiling approach. Be charming to subordinates and officialdom. Win them over to you. Get everyone in the palm of your hand before moving. This method had merits, he reflected, but it was unlikely that O. B. Smelser would ever come in voluntarily and say, "C.P., I like you so much I think I'll tell you that we've been cooking the books." It would take more than affection to pry out that information, assuming it was there to pry.

No, a vigorous offensive would be better. Seize authority. Disrupt long-established routines. Tamper with cozy internecine relationships.

16

Keep the other team off-balance, as any competent quarterback would strive to do. Probe for weaknesses. Make them play your game.

C. P. Randollph felt the juices of decision and determination rising in him like mercury in a thermometer. Giddy with anticipation, he took the down elevator to his office.

3

DAN GANTRY intercepted him as, ears ringing from the plunging descent, Randollph got off the elevator.

"There's a lady waiting to see you, and I thought I ought to brief you first," Dan said.

"Oh?"

"I know it's no way to start your first day, but Sam Stack's important."

"I thought you said a lady was waiting. Sam Stack's a lady?"

"Sure is," Dan grinned. "You'll see. Her name's really Samantha. She has a TV show called *Sam Stack's Chicago*. I had to sneak her past Addie—that's Adelaide Windfall, the church secretary. Addie is waiting to descend on you and tell you what's what. Addie's a good old girl," he explained, "but bossy. Been here so long she thinks she's the head honcho—which, come to think of it, she probably is. Let's pop in and introduce you to Sam. Sam's a good friend of mine."

Sam turned out to be very obviously a lady.

"Dr. Randollph, this is Sam Stack. Isn't she gorgeous? For an older dame, that is," Dan said, as Randollph's rapidly appraising eye took in a tallish woman groomed in a soft beige and blue plaid suit that hadn't come off a plain pipe rack. About thirty, Randollph estimated. She had flaming red hair.

Samantha Stack gave Dan a withering look. "Dan, you ruined my entrance line," she scolded. "I was going to say, 'Dr. Randollph, I presume?' "

"How nice of Dan to start my first day here with you, Miss Stack, or is it Mrs. Stack? It must be Mrs."

"Thank you sir. I go by Ms. Actually it is Mrs. I'm divorced. The louse was a lush. But being a liberated woman, I go by Ms. Oh, I know what you're thinking," Samantha rushed on. "Don't let this designer original or all the nylon I'm showing fool you. My business requires that I dress this way. I like to dress this way. And why should I throw away my best ammunition? Are you married, Dr. Randollph?"

Randollph, awed, managed to answer, "Not presently." Then, somewhat recovered: "Perhaps we should all be seated."

"I know you are going to be busy doing whatever a pastor does," Samantha launched out again. "Incidentally, so you'll know where I stand, I'm an atheist."

"Atheist isn't a bad thing to be," Randollph said. "The early Christians were often charged with being atheists."

"What?" a startled Samantha exclaimed. Score one for me, Randollph thought.

"An atheist by definition is a person who refuses to worship the popular gods of contemporary culture," he said.

"Is that so?" Samantha asked Dan.

"He's a professor of church history, he ought to know," Dan said.

"Oh, hell, that's too respectable, that takes all the fun out of being an atheist," she said. "I guess I'll just have to be an agnostic."

"Sorry," Randollph said.

Samantha paused to survey him. "If you're not married, and you're a good-looking, healthy man, what do you do for sex? Have you taken a vow of celibacy? You aren't gay, are you?"

A number of pictures which would have been of interest to Samantha Stack flashed across Randollph's mind. Forcefully shutting them off, he said, "You have not exhausted my options, Ms. Stack."

"Zing!" she said. "I'm sorry if I've offended you." She didn't sound sorry. "I should be nicer, especially when I want a favor, which I do want from you."

"You didn't offend me." Randollph smiled amiably. "And as for a favor, I expect you find most men anxious to do favors for you. I am unlikely to be an exception."

"You do put things neatly," she said. "I have this television show; maybe Dan has told you about it. It's a local talk show. I want you to be a guest on my show."

19

Randollph thought it a splendid idea that he should grace a television show, if only a local one. It would be something to brag about, discreetly, of course, when he returned to the obscurity of faculty life.

"But why me, Ms. Stack? I'm not a celebrity."

"No, you aren't," she replied frankly. "But the Church of the Good Shepherd is. An old community institution. Socially prominent members. And money. Lots of money. People are interested in things like that. You coming for only a year—what do you call it, an interim?—that's a little different. You ought to make a good guest." She cocked her head, looked him over carefully, and said, "You'll come through OK on camera, too."

She named a date. Randollph agreed, smilingly admonishing her not to question him about his sex life on camera.

She rose, shrugging herself into a chic green leather coat before Dan could help. "Oh, don't worry, there isn't any sex in Chicago. At least not on television. Mayor Daley wouldn't like it."

As Dan held the door for her, she patted him on the head. "Be a good boy, Danny, and maybe mama will have you on her widely popular TV show. Well, peace."

With Ms. Stack's distracting presence removed, Randollph was able to take a close look at the room Good Shepherd provided its pastor-in-charge as study, office, and working quarters. It fell, he decided, far below the standard set by the parsonage in the sky. Not that the church fathers had spared expense, originally, in furnishing it. It was the kind of room they—or more likely the pastoral incumbent at the time—thought a proper pastor's study ought to be. The fumed oak paneling of the walls was slashed on the street side with tall mullioned windows of opaque colored glass, effectively shutting out the sights and sounds of the commercial activity outside. There was a massive brown desk, large brown leather furniture suitable to a gentleman's club, and a huge table that might once have served in the refectory of an English abbey, all on a once-rich and now-dingy beige carpet. On a wall opposite the windows were four engravings which, at a distance, appeared identical. Inspection, however, showed them to be Lincoln, Durham, York, and Salisbury cathedrals—as if the decorators wished to make sure no one could forget that this room was the sanctuary of a cleric. The one concession to the twentieth century was a huge reproduction of the most popular and, to Randollph, the most insipid modern head of Christ, arranged on the wall opposite the desk so that the pastor, whether fumbling for an uplifting thought to include in Sunday's discourse or needing patience to endure a windy visitor, could not miss it. A depressing room, Randollph decided. Perhaps he could do his successor a favor and redecorate it.

"Dan, would you ask Miss Windfall to step in?" Protocol demanded that the veteran secretary be dealt with immediately. "Then fetch Mr. Smelser. But keep him waiting for about five minutes." Randollph wanted an edgy O. B. Smelser.

"Right, boss." Dan, unable to maintain the use of formal titles beyond a day's acquaintance with anyone, had selected "boss" as the best compromise between the proper "Dr. Randollph" and the familiar "C.P." employed by the bishop.

Expecting a desiccated virgin, Randollph was astounded when the head honcho sailed into his office. Miss Windfall was enormous, her fifteen stone or so straining a girdle not quite up to its job analysis. Virgin she may have been, but not desiccated. There was plenty of juice in her.

Miss Windfall barely acknowledged the formalities of introduction and frowned disapprovingly at Randollph's cerise-striped shirt.

"I must have your sermon topic by Monday," she said sternly. "Your editorial for the *Spire,* that's our weekly church newsletter, by Tuesday, keep it to five hundred words, nothing controversial—the trustees don't like the pastor to be controversial—Dr. Hartshorne wrote usually about prayer and family devotions—"

Randollph began to see why the beloved and distinguished Dr. Hartshorne spent his time speaking to hick Rotary clubs.

"Miss Windfall." He interrupted firmly, not at all sure that Miss Windfall could be interrupted. "You surely aren't telling me that I am to write in the—what did you call it—the *Spire* according to the dictates of the trustees' collective conscience instead of my own?"

Miss Windfall's pace was altered, but she was not derailed.

"The trustees expect me to see that nothing gets into the newsletter that shouldn't be there," she retorted grimly. "They hold me responsible. And," she added unnecessarily, "I try to discharge my responsibilities."

First Mrs. Creedy, and now Miss Windfall, Randollph thought. So much devotion to duty was becoming oppressive, and he hadn't seen O. B. Smelser as yet. He smiled benignly and said, "I shan't be needing any help at the policy level, Miss Windfall. I'll be responsible for what goes into the newsletter. You may tell the trustees that you have been relieved of what must have been an onerous task."

Miss Windfall was momentarily stunned by this bold challenge to her authority. Grabbing the opportunity, Randollph rose. "We'll set aside some time soon to go over office routines, but I won't keep you from your work any longer." He stepped briskly to open the door for her before Miss Windfall could crank up again.

"Oh, by the way," he said, pausing, "would you ask the custodian to remove this picture?" He indicated the insipid head of Christ.

"Why, what, oh, we couldn't do that! that was a memorial gift, it was Dr. Hartshorne's favorite, he said—"

"De gustibus non est disputandam," Randollph said, certain that Miss Windfall would think he was swearing at her. "The picture offends me. I simply will not spend a year staring at a marcelled Christ. Have it out of here by tomorrow, please."

While Randollph was having a fine time upsetting the formidable Miss Windfall, Dan was not doing so well. Sent to summon O. B. Smelser, Smelser was stubbornly refusing to budge from his office.

"I have no time to see Dr. Randollph this morning," he told Dan petulantly. "I can find time this afternoon, perhaps. Tell him that."

Dan, conscious that this monstrous ill manner was a gauntlet thrown down to Randollph, an effort to put a mere interim pastor in his proper place, said, "I think you're making a mistake, Bertie."

"Well, it's my mistake," Smelser replied rudely, "and I'll thank you not to call me Bertie."

Randollph received the news of Smelser's recalcitrance with irritation. His first impulse was to issue a summons for Smelser to hotfoot it up to his office, but he decided against it.

"Well," he said pleasantly, "if Mahomet won't come to the mountain, then the mountain will have to go to Mahomet. Show me the way, Dan."

O. B. Smelser, it turned out, had his own little kingdom in another part of the building. They took the elevator to the third floor, then down a corridor to a large room cluttered with mimeographs, addressing machines, and banks of filing cabinets. There were two girls working, one at a posting machine, the other fiddling with a balky mimeograph.

"Hi, Dan, you again?" the girl at the mimeograph said. "Maybe you can make this bugger work. It keeps squirting ink over everything."

"Don't know a thing about them," Dan said. "This is Dr. Randollph, Emmy."

"Oh, hello," she said.

"And that's Roberta there toting up the collection or something," Dan said. The girl nodded and went on with her posting.

"Happy to know you, ladies," Randollph said. "We'd like a minute with Mr. Smelser."

Emmy, wiping her hands with a paper towel, looked serious. "He told us not to disturb him." She looked at a closed door with "The Reverend O. Bertram Smelser" stenciled on it. "I don't think he's in a very good mood today."

"At all events, I must have a word with him," Randollph said. He knocked twice on Smelser's door before Emmy could protest further and entered, closing the door behind him. "Mr. Smelser, I'm C. P. Randollph," he said to a startled little man sitting behind a huge table-style desk. Smelser's study, Randollph noticed, was as large as the cluttered outer office but was neat and tidy. The only item on the table was a ledger in which Smelser was making notes.

"No, no, don't rise." Randollph raised a restraining hand. "Mr. Gantry informs me that you are very busy this morning, and I can see that you are. A commendable sense of responsibility to your duties, I'm sure. This will only take a minute. I'm only here for a year, you know, so I must familiarize myself as rapidly as possible with the operation of Good Shepherd. To do that, I'll need a full statement of the church's financial position for the year to date, including how the endowments are invested, rate of return, operational costs, salary schedules, details of lease and rental income—in short, the whole works, Mr. Smelser."

23

O. B. Smelser sputtered.

What Randollph was able to distill from Smelser's strangulated reply was that this was highly irregular, that it couldn't be done, that only the trustees had authority to release financial information. His eyes glittered behind the gold-rimmed glasses he had adopted as a young man to make him look older and which the unpredictable winds of fashion had made stylish once more.

"Come now, Mr. Smelser." Randollph gently rebuked him. "You must have this information at your fingertips or I have been misled by reports of your competence. I'll expect it by tomorrow."

"No," said O. B. Smelser, with the dogged obstinacy of the meek.

Randollph looked at the obstinate O. B. Smelser with what he intended to be a friendly gaze. Smelser glared back.

"Well, now, we seem to have reached an impasse, haven't we?" Randollph said pleasantly. "How shall we resolve it? Perhaps you'd like to reconsider your refusal, Mr. Smelser."

"No," Smelser said.

Randollph was thoughtful for a moment, then said, "Would it help clarify the situation for me to remind you that I'm the pastor-in-charge and that you work for me?"

"You're only here for a year. I've been here for twenty years." O. B. Smelser's petulance was rising to the level of outright hostility. "There wasn't any need of you being here in the first place if the bishop hadn't gone against the advice of the trustees. I've run the business of this church for twenty years. Dr. Hartshorne never asked for a report from me. Why should I give you one?"

"Because I'm not Dr. Hartshorne." Randollph spoke mildly, as to a stubborn child. "You refuse my request then?"

"Yes."

Randollph sighed. "Suit yourself. I'll not coerce you."

A tiny smile of victory played across O. B. Smelser's lips. "I'm glad you see it my way, Dr. Randollph," he said. There was a note of elation in his voice.

Randollph got up to go. "You may expect the auditors of my choice to be taking over your books the day after tomorrow, Mr. Smelser," he said. "That is, unless you could find it convenient to supply me with the information I want by tomorrow."

"You wouldn't! You couldn't!" An aghast Smelser sounded like an engine that couldn't quite catch. He came out of his chair.

"I could and I would," Randollph said crisply. "Read the constitution of the church, Mr. Smelser. An unusual document. Gives the pastor-in-charge extraordinary powers. Among them, it permits him, in case he is dissatisfied with the accounting of moneys contributed or earned for the preaching of the Faith and the due administration of the sacraments—that's the way it puts it, Mr. Smelser—permits him to take such steps as he sees fit to clear up the situation. The steps I propose to take are to bring in outside auditors."

Randollph paused a moment to let this sink in on the crushed and beaten little pastor-business manager. Smelser slowly sat down again.

"Would you like to reconsider your decision?" Randollph asked. Smelser, a hand over his eyes as if to hide from unpleasant realities, slowly nodded his head.

"I'll look forward to the reports tomorrow then." Randollph spoke as though he were concluding an amicable discussion with a fellow executive. "And bring them in yourself, if you will, Mr. Smelser. We can go over them together. I'm sure your explanations will be invaluable."

A little ashamed of himself for winning an easy battle against a defenseless antagonist, Randollph corralled Dan Gantry and took him out to lunch.

4

THIS WOULD be his first specifically religious duty in the six days he had been pastor-in-charge of the Church of the Good Shepherd, Randollph reflected, as he zipped himself into a long black pulpit gown with scarlet doctor's bars flaming on the sleeves.

On the whole, he was quite pleased with his progress to date.

Mrs. Creedy, muttering something about waste not, want not, had grudgingly been providing, if not bounteous breakfasts, at least portions adequate to sustain.

Miss Windfall had been making a heroic effort to curb her predisposition, born of untrammeled years running the day-to-day operations of Good Shepherd, to tell the pastor what to do—although he imagined that the restraint was impairing her digestion no little.

And an apparently penitent O. B. Smelser had found the time to be Randollph's first appointment the morning after his mutinous refusal to visit his new boss.

"Dr. Randollph, I must apologize for my inexcusable behavior yesterday." He began the task of eating crow, anxious to have it over with as rapidly as possible. "You see, I've been working awfully hard, and one is not at one's best when under heavy pressure—" He left the statement hanging, removing the gold-rimmed granny glasses and wiping them carefully.

Randollph made encouraging sounds.

"And I may as well confess that I resented you. Oh, not you personally, I'd never met you. I would have resented anyone in your place. I may as well be honest—you'd find it out anyway. I had every expectation of being in your place. Dr. Hartshorne had promised me

I'd succeed him. The pastoral selection committee and the trustees recommended that I be named. But the bishop—" He shrugged, as if to say, who could understand the ways of bishops.

Randollph felt sympathy for this harmless-looking little man. He could imagine how in the long years of drab service he had been sustained by the vision of the day when he would be number one instead of number two and be in the public eye instead of a bookkeeper's office and lunch with city councilmen instead of anonymous peers. Encouraged no doubt by a wily Dr. Hartshorne who promised what was not his to give in order to ensure subordinate loyalty and faithful service, Smelser had come to look on his succession as a right. Mrs. Smelser had probably already speculated extensively on refurnishing the pastoral penthouse. Smelser would not be the first man to go to his grave confident that he was qualified for a position which any objective assessment said that he was not. Had it not been for the bishop's nagging sense that two and two didn't quite add up to four at Good Shepherd, he no doubt would have bagged the job he had been tasting in anticipation all these years. From Smelser's viewpoint, it was a tough break, Randollph had to admit. No doubt Smelser still clung to hope, but he must know that the naming of an interim pastor-in-charge diminished his chances. If the bishop were not ready now to name him incumbent, would he ever be?

Thus mellowed, Randollph made charitable noises about understanding.

"Thank you for accepting my apology, Dr. Randollph." An obviously relieved O. B. Smelser, now that absolution had been granted, shoved a sheaf of papers at Randollph like a peace offering. "Here are the figures you requested. I think you will find everything in order. Dr. Hartshorne relied on me entirely in the business management of the church. I hope that you will do the same." He paused to polish his glasses again, then said gravely, "It is an exacting task."

Randollph agreed that it was an exacting task and said kind but noncommittal things about needing Smelser's help in the business management of the church. Thus restored, Smelser went back to his accounts.

The bishop, who had deemed his presence essential to Randollph's premiere appearance in the pulpit of Good Shepherd, was nudging

27

a few stray episcopal hairs into place before the robing room mirror.

"C.P.," he said, "you seem uncharacteristically pensive this morning. Scared?"

Randollph, suddenly conscious of a twitch or two in his stomach, replied, "Maybe a little bit. I haven't been in a pulpit for ages. Right now I'm wondering why I ever allowed myself to be ordained."

The bishop chuckled. "I know the answer to that one."

"Then please enlighten me."

"Because you are reenacting the parable of the prodigal son."

"Oh, come now, Freddie!" Randollph, startled, exclaimed.

The bishop looked quite pleased with himself. "Of course you are, C.P. The church is your home. You were reared in what I imagine was a suffocatingly pious small-town congregation. You attended an equally oppressive conservative denominational college. There was your sojourn in a far country, wasting your substance in riotous living—"

Randollph interrupted. "I didn't waste it. I still have most of it, soundly invested."

"A tribute to the Protestant ethic drilled into you by Sunday school teachers, no doubt," the bishop said, "but irrelevant. You had your share of the fleshpots, if the gossip columnists were even fractionally accurate."

Randollph opened his mouth, but the bishop held up a hand. "No, don't interrupt. Because you have a sound spirit, you abandoned that whole scene. And because you have a good mind, you rejected the simplicities of small-town orthodoxy. But the church was still your home. Your perspectives were altered by experience, as they should be. And your theology had to be rethought. But emotionally, the church was still your home. And that is why I encouraged you to take orders, although you did not need them to be a teacher. Your orders are a symbol that you are safely returned to your father's house, and welcome. And you need that."

"Well, I'll be damned," Randollph said.

"And furthermore," the bishop went on, "while we are on the subject and I'm still enchanted by my own eloquence, let me point out that no one with your spiritual history ever escapes the conviction that helping and serving others are life's best occupation and true purpose. That's the good part of what otherwise may be a dreary and unstimulating religious upbringing. You cultivate a cool, even skeptical exterior, C.P., but underneath is a passion to be of some use in the world. And that's why you are here this morning wearing a clerical collar."

"Whew!" Randollph exclaimed.

"An appropriate response, C.P. And now to change the subject, you have had an uncommonly busy first week at the job, haven't you?"

"Oh. How so?"

"You have managed to stir up an extraordinary amount of commotion in these rather sedate halls."

"How would you know, Freddie?" Randollph asked. "Do you have spies?"

"There have been rumblings," the bishop announced solemnly, "and yes, I have spies. All modern corporations have spies, although we prefer to refer to them as intelligence sources. But," he said, turning from the mirror satisfied with the drape of his purple rabat, "I didn't need any undercover agents to inform me this time. I've had phone calls. Sputtering phone calls," he added ominously.

"From whom?"

"From Mr. Torgeson, Mr. Robert Torgeson, for one. He is, as you probably know, president of Good Shepherd's trustees. I believe that he is sometimes called Little Bobbie," the bishop said, "perhaps affectionately, although I am inclined to doubt it."

"Did he sputter?"

"He surely did." The bishop winced as he recalled an unpleasant time-wasting half hour on the phone with Little Bobbie. "But then," he mused, "I suppose that isn't too significant. Mr. Torgeson is by nature a sputterer."

Arnold Uhlinger, attached to Good Shepherd for a year's internship before the denomination would certify that his piety, wisdom, and pastoral skills were sufficient to bore country congregations with disquisitions on nuances of process theology and the hermeneutical problem, approached with the diffidence proper to a seminarian about to interrupt a bishop.

"Perhaps," he squeaked in a nervous soprano, "we ought to be

29

going." He explained, as if he might be banished unless he produced a sound reason for his presence, that this was his scheduled Sunday to assist in the service and that in any event he was the only one of the pastoral staff available as Mr. Gantry was at this hour bringing the Gospel to the mission Good Shepherd maintained in a benighted northwest area and Mr. Smelser was confined to his apartment in Rogers Park with a touch of the flu. Randollph thought that Arnie, his tall, bony frame enveloped in folds of black, looked like a nervous buzzard.

Where they were going, it turned out, was down a flight of stairs which led to a subterranean choir room. This room, Arnie explained like a professional tour guide, had been equipped and soundproofed at considerable expense so that the choir could hold its weekly practice and warm up on Sunday morning without disturbing anyone.

As he opened the heavy steel door for Randollph and the bishop, they were hit by a blast of sound. Mr. Agostino, a handsome and cheerful young Italian, was harassing the choir into a few more decibels on the "hallelujah!" which capped the morning's anthem. This was a professional choir, Randollph had discovered by rummaging through the figures extracted from a reluctant O. B. Smelser. Some were members of Good Shepherd, but most were Roman Catholics, or Jews, or nothing at all. What they were were trained voices good enough to demand substantial pay for praising the Lord—and getting it.

"I'm afraid you'll find that Good Shepherd isn't a normal church," the bishop had briefed Randollph. "You see, it doesn't have a very large membership—perhaps a thousand—and most of them seldom attend. They mostly live in Winnetka or Lake Forest," as if this adequately explained why they didn't go to church.

"Then who does attend?" Randollph asked.

"Conventioneers, weekend visitors," the bishop patiently explained. "On any given week in Chicago the hotels around here are full of people in town for business purposes. It has become quite the in thing for the visiting firemen, so to speak, to top off their visit by attending Good Shepherd. The place will be packed, every Sunday, with people who have never been here before and probably never will be here again—or at least not until their particular trade holds its annual convention here again."

"Then I would need only one sermon, wouldn't I?" Randollph had asked jokingly.

"That's not as funny as you obviously intended it to be," the bishop replied, frowning slightly. "Hartshorne grasped this early in his ministry and for more than twenty years preached substantially the same sermon every Sunday morning. His topic was 'The Life and Works of Arthur Hartshorne,' although," he added, "he had different titles for it, and he did change the illustrations. But anyway," the bishop went on, consigning the newly retired Dr. Hartshorne to the dust of history, "you will find the Sunday morning program as much an extension of a trade convention as a service of Christian worship. A scholar such as yourself may find parts of it distasteful—I find it distasteful—" the bishop wrinkled his nose.

"Freddie, get it through your head that I am not a scholar," Randollph scolded. "I'm a journeyman teacher. And I have vulgar tastes. I watch television all the time."

"Well, that will help." The bishop brightened. "I just wanted you to know what to expect."

Randollph saw that the choir room had, indeed, been constructed and furnished at considerable expense. It was quite large and was divided into two sections by a heavy maroon velvet curtain, now partially open. He could see a grand piano, rows of chairs, and an entire wall of handsome wooden cabinets and lockers, presumably repositories for choir robes, libraries of sheet music, and other paraphernalia incident to the production of a joyful noise unto the Lord. A door at the far end led, he supposed, to a stairs and eventually an exit to the ground level.

The other half, the part they were now in, was furnished with a desk, no doubt for the lively Mr. Agostino. There was an ample supply of easy chairs and a large sofa, all in institutional plastic, placed there for the repose of choir members exhausted by the exactions of rehearsal but not yet ready to go home. There was also a lectern where, his place in the anthem book marked by a long purple brocade ribbon, Mr. Agostino was frantically waving his arms in an attempt to pump a little more steam into the valves of his choir.

31

With a final swipe with his right arm, like a man swatting an attacking wasp, Mr. Anthony Agostino cut off the exploding sound, checked his watch in the sudden silence, and said, "OK, Arnie, eight minutes to curtain time." Clearly, Mr. Agostino agreed with the bishop that Good Shepherd's Sunday morning program was more of a production than a worship experience.

Arnie, in his high girlish voice, presented the bishop and Randollph to the frank stares of curiosity from the blue-robed choir. "Now let me present the choir, which no one questions is the best in Chicago and suburbs," Tony said to Randollph and the bishop. "Do it while I line 'em up. Got to do that anyway." He began to rattle off names, the women first. He put his arm around each woman as he presented her and said something complimentary about her.

"This is Revata Diogenetti, good wop Catholic girl, been to mass already, comes to sing for the Protestants 'cause she loves old Tony. . . . Here's Helmar Jackson—maiden name's some Swede handle—best alto in seven states. . . . Meet Queenie Smith"—this is to a short, heavy black girl with enormous jutting breasts. "Queenie keeps talking about dieting, but I won't let her, it might ruin her magnificent lungs, she's opera caliber. . . . Here's Marianne Reedman." He gave a tall, strikingly beautiful brunette in her mid-thirties an extra hug. "Gotta be nice to her. She can't sing, but she's rich, and her husband's a trustee of the church. I'm just kidding, darling." He kissed her on the cheek. "Rich or poor, there isn't a better soprano to be found, and she knows it. She's kind of our choir den mother."

Marianne Reedman said coolly, "Tony, all that blarney. You're an Irishman disguised as a spaghetti eater."

But she seemed to like it, Randollph thought. A girl who could take care of herself. A girl worth knowing.

And so it went. When the last of the men had been presented, also with complimentary remarks from Tony, Arnie cleared his throat and announced that the bishop would lead in the customary preservice prayer. The bishop briefly but unctuously implored the Holy Spirit to touch the vocal chords of each choir member in order that the holy sounds they were about to make would be pleasing to the ear of the Almighty. With the "amen" scarcely uttered, Mr. Agostino barked,

"OK, gang, let's get the show on the road, and watch that hallelujah! Fortissimo! Fortissimo!"

As the service droned on through a lugubrious Lenten hymn and a litany of remarkable dullness, Randollph tried to size up the audience, for it could not rightly be called a congregation, to which he would soon be dividing the word of the Lord. These were the burghers whose shops and stores and offices kept the cash flowing in their various communities. There was no bespoke tailoring or Balenciagas to be seen, but they were far from dowdy. They could be counted on, Randollph knew, for confident solutions to problems which baffled statesmen and experts and selfless devotion to the good works to which every American community is addicted. They were, by and large, the middle class, which owned every socially respectable American denomination, lock, font, and pulpit.

And they were here, listening at the moment to Arnold Uhlinger read from the Gospel according to John, for a variety of reasons, some commendable and none, so far as Randollph could discern, entirely disreputable. They were here to worship the God of Abraham, Isaac, and the American way of life. They were here to squeeze the last drop of experience from a festive venture, fully deductible, to the big city. They were here, some of them, shaky with hangovers and guilty thoughts of indulgences unthinkable in Grand Forks or Ottumwa, for some supposed process of atonement (which accounted for the astounding number of twenty-dollar bills in the offering plate). They were here because it was Sunday morning, and going to church was what they customarily did on Sunday morning.

Randollph was astonished at the professional ease with which Arnie Uhlinger carried out his assignments. The piping voice was modulated to a pleasing range suited to public persuasion. He read the Holy Scriptures with a skill bespeaking many hours of voice lessons and amateur theatricals. When he conducted what was hyperbolically listed on the worship bulletin as "The Ritual of Friendship," which consisted of identifying visitors from various states by asking them to stand and be recognized, he performed this dubious rite with warmth and dignity. Clearly, here was a lad with a future in a profession which called for and rewarded a magnetic pulpit personality.

After the anthem, the choir banging out hallelujahs with throttles open, Arnie introduced the bishop, and the bishop introduced Randollph. Although most of the good people here were visitors, the bishop said, he knew they would be interested to know that this was a significant day in the life of the Church of the Good Shepherd. After a quarter century, the beloved Dr. Arthur Hartshorne had entered a well-earned retirement. So as to give those responsible enough time to make a wise selection of a permanent successor, they had been able to persuade Dr. C. P. Randollph to serve as interim pastor. The bishop spelled out Randollph's pedigree as if he were being entered in the Westchester Kennel Club show, and Randollph was fairly launched.

Randollph was innocent of experience in the role of pastor, but as a preacher he was on familiar ground. He reflected that he had been speaking to audiences of one kind and another almost constantly since he had been a college student.

Since he was new to this position, he told them, he thought it would be appropriate to preach to them on the idea of newness as it related to the Christian Gospel. Jesus, he said, thought of his message and ministry as something new. The Gospels are full of the word "new." The new wine is not to be put into old leaky wineskins. We hear of a new commandment, a new teaching, a new covenant. He could never understand, he said, why so many Christians put a premium on the word "old." The old book, the old faith, the old-time religion. That was what the people who opposed Jesus did. Jesus was trying to get them to think in new ways, to open up to the possibilities in life which they could never know so long as they classified all aspects of life by old and meaningless and repressive rules. Randollph found it a very heady experience speaking to the thousand or so people out there in front of him. They might not agree with what he was saying, many probably didn't, but they listened. This, he knew, was because he had an authoritative voice and compelling manner. He could be putting out the most astrocious twaddle, and still, they would listen. He ended up with an appeal to all of them to open up their own thinking, admit that perhaps their ideas about God and love and sin and guilt and the religious life were ancient, porous wineskins that couldn't hold the fresh and novel wine of the Gospel. Eighteen minutes flat, he noted as he sat down.

"A most commendable sermon, C.P.," the bishop said after they had clasped hands with several hundred departing grocers, furniture salesmen, and pharmacists and had divested themselves of their pulpit finery. "A bit cerebral perhaps for the ordinary churchgoer, but most commendable."

"What's wrong with being cerebral?" Randollph was defensive.

"Heavens! Nothing's wrong with it," the bishop hastened to assure him. "I wasn't being critical. It's just that the average churchgoer is fed a steady diet of bland piety, and his intellectual digestion isn't up to handling anything stronger."

"But I'm not interested in bland piety. I'm interested in ideas," Randollph said.

"So you are. So you have been ever since I've known you. And speaking of ideas, I understand you will be having your initial meeting with the board of trustees this Thursday. Do you have any ideas as to how you are going to handle it?"

"Not yet. I'll have some by Thursday."

"I think, C.P., that I shall cancel the dedication of a new baptismal font at the Minnie B. Hatcher Memorial Church and an inspirational address to the Society of Deaconesses in order to be present at that meeting."

The offhand manner with which the bishop tossed out this surprising tidbit of information put Randollph immediately on guard. He was sure that the bishop expected no serious impairment to the visible Kingdom of God on earth issuing from a temporarily unblessed font or deaconesses missing a dose of episcopal holiness. He was also sure that this would be an unusual departure from the bishop's appointed rounds.

"Freddie, whatever for? Not that you won't be welcome, of course. But I do not require a nursemaid. Do you expect trouble?"

"Don't bristle, C.P.," the bishop said, putting his pulpit robe into its carrying case. "No, I don't expect trouble." He took his time folding over the case and snapping the fasteners which secured it into what looked very much like an overlarge handbag. "And I'm not going to be your nursemaid, a part I would play very badly I'm afraid. However, trouble—should it lurk in the hearts of some of your trustees—can be neutralized or at least minimized by a show of strength on your

35

part. Bishops are not always loved, but the bishop—or the office—is respected. Trustees of churches, especially wealthy churches, respect the bishop because they know that if he has to, the bishop can tell them what's what and make it stick."

Randollph pondered this for a moment, then said, "All right, Freddie, I have a feeling I'm going to need all the moral authority I can muster and maybe then some if I'm to find out what you want me to find out and do something about it. How will it be if you present me to the board, say a few flattering things about your confidence in me, then duck out? You can plead the press of other duties."

"You have described almost exactly the program I had in mind," the bishop said. "And by the way, could you ask your trustees to meet at nine thirty instead of their customary eight forty-five? The executive secretary of our denomination's Board of International Missions is passing through town and wants a word with me at nine. He's a pest, but board secretaries are not so easily fobbed off as deaconesses, I'm afraid."

"Consider it done."

"And now, C.P.," the bishop said, picking up his robe case and heading for the door, "though it is the Lenten season of self-denial, let me lead you to a gentlemen's club to which I belong—at a drastically reduced membership rate accorded distinguished clergy—and introduce you to a twelve-ounce steak."

5

THE BISHOP, arrayed in charcoal flannel, purple rabat, and pectoral cross, appeared in Randollph's office several minutes ahead of schedule.

"My, my, Freddie, you look every inch the bishop," Randollph said.

"I intended that I should," the bishop answered, collapsing into an oversize leather chair. "Normally I wouldn't even be wearing this dog collar, let alone this flamboyant silk and this ridiculous cross. But it will do your trustees no harm to be reminded of the weight of my office. The accoutrements of rank do occasionally serve a useful purpose."

"Still worried about the trustees, are you, Freddie?"

The bishop made a church steeple of his fingers and rested his chin upon it before answering.

"No, not worried, C.P. A mite anxious perhaps. These are all men of standing and authority in the business community. They are strong-willed and accustomed to telling other people what to do. On top of that, they have run Good Shepherd substantially without interference. Hartshorne hardly ever attended a trustees' meeting. Smelser always attends, but it is doubtful that he ever takes exception to anything—which, I suppose is why the trustees are so enthusiastic about promoting him to pastor-in-charge. Now you propose to interfere with what these chaps have come to regard as their normal procedure. . . ." The bishop paused, half-hopeful that Randollph would contradict him.

"Of course I'm going to interfere," Randollph said, scuttling the bishop's faint hopes for an amiable strategy which would at the same time unravel Good Shepherd's tangled affairs and make everyone happy about it. "Look, Freddie, I'm not upsetting the cozy routine around here just for the hell of it," Randollph continued, wondering if this was actually true. "We're going to have to flush out the miscreants, if miscreants there are, and throwing a little sand in the machinery is the only way to do it, if I may mix a metaphor."

The bishop stretched his legs and inspected his well-polished black pebble-grain oxfords. "I know, C.P. I have known all along that some disruption here is inevitable. However, the administrator's heart always longs for pleasant solutions to nasty situations. Probably why we accomplish so little. I'll back you, of course, in anything short of murder. I'll continue to hope, though, that any explosions you ignite won't reduce the church to rubble." He heaved himself out of his chair, tugged his jacket into shape. "Well, it's time to throw you to the lions. Let's go."

The trustees' room, which served as a meeting place for committees devoted to everything from missionary support to the Christmas decoration of the nave, duplicated the worn elegance of Randollph's study. Mrs. Creedy was placing ashtrays, disapprovingly, Randollph felt certain, on a massive table which could have accommodated twenty diners. Briefly inspecting a coffee urn which gurgled on a side table, she announced, "Coffee will be ready in five minutes," and disappeared.

"Well, now," the bishop said with professional bonhomie, "since we have to wait for coffee, let's improve the time by getting to know your new interim pastor." He paused while the men scattered about the room had time to collect themselves into a group.

"I only count seven." The bishop surveyed them. "Who's missing?"

"Ward Reedman's not here yet." The speaker was a slight man, probably in his mid-sixties Randollph guessed. He wore an unrumpled dark-brown herringbone tweed, white shirt, and a brown and gold patterned tie. A thin sandy mustache and slightly bulging pale-blue eyes bracketed a long, thin nose. The man looked to be in a perpetual bad temper, Randollph thought. He felt certain this would be Robert "Little Bobbie" Torgeson.

"Isn't Reedman coming tonight?" the bishop asked.

"Far as I know," the little man said.

"Well, let's get on with the introductions," the bishop said. "Dr. Randollph, this is Mr. Torgeson, Robert Torgeson, the president of Good Shepherd's board of trustees."

"A pleasure, I'm sure," Torgeson said, offering a brief handshake.

"And this is Mr. Harold Bailey, secretary, Mr. James McNutt, Professor Donald Miller, and Mr. Harry Craft." The bishop rattled them off like a train announcer. "Mr. Smelser and Mr. Gantry you know, of course." He shot an immaculate white French cuff to check his watch. "Nine forty. I think we shan't wait for Mr. Reedman. Mrs. Creedy's coffee is ready, I think. Why don't we all get a cup and get comfortable around the table?"

Randollph sipping Mrs. Creedy's coffee, found it as thin as her smile. The bishop was rumbling out banalities about Randollph's high qualification for the office of interim, that he had the bishop's complete confidence, and how he was certain this would prove a felicitous arrangement of tremendous benefit to Good Shepherd. Then, like Mrs. Creedy, having fulfilled his role for the evening, he vanished.

Mr. Robert Torgeson, his mustache twitching, offered the briefest welcoming speech Randollph had ever heard.

"Ha, humph, sure we're all glad to have you at Good Shepherd, Dr. Randollph. Ha, humph, if you have any questions, we'll be glad to answer them. Otherwise, we won't need to detain you. Dr. Hartshorne never stayed for the business session. Said we could count the money and he would count the souls. Ha."

Randollph was not prepared for this sudden and blunt dismissal and was grateful for a brief stay of execution when the door opened abruptly.

"Sorry, fellas," said the man who came through the door, peeling off a camel hair topcoat and tossing it on a chair. "Unavoidably detained." He seemed out of breath.

"Ha," Torgeson said. "Ward Reedman, meet Dr. C. P. Randollph. You're just in time. Dr. Randollph was about to leave. Humph."

"Pleased to meet you," Reedman said, nodding to Randollph as he took a vacant chair down the table. "Anything happened yet?"

"No, just getting started," Torgeson said. "Well, Dr. Randollph, nice to have you here. Feel free to drop in at any time on our meetings."

Randollph, assuming what he hoped was a gracious smile, said well, since he had a few questions, he thought he would stay awhile. Since most of his questions related to the business of the church, he probably would stay for the duration of the meeting. As a matter of fact, he announced, he planned to make it a practice to attend all their meetings.

Randollph learned what Freddie had meant when he said that Little Bobbie was by nature a sputterer.

"Well, humph, perhaps, somewhat unusual, Dr. Hartshorne didn't, ah, well, um. . . ." His eye caught Dan Gantry. "Ha, well, we can excuse Mr. Gantry. We won't be needing him."

"I'm afraid we can't do that, Mr. Torgeson," Randollph said pleasantly. "You see, I requested his attendance. As one of your pastors, he has a right to be here." Randollph noticed that Professor Miller was smiling. "And since I have requested that he attend all the trustees' meetings during my incumbency, he has a responsibility to be here, doesn't he?"

Little Bobbie was speechless.

Now that he had grabbed the initiative, Randollph plunged ahead.

"The constitution of the Church of the Good Shepherd—in many ways an amazing document—invests the pastor-in-charge with extensive powers and responsibilities." He paused to see if he had their undivided attention. He had.

"Among these responsibilities," he continued, "is the certification to the bishop each year that the temporal affairs of the church are soundly administered and all revenues strictly accounted for." He let this sink in, then added, "The pastor is not limited as to the methods he chooses to employ in determining these things."

Little Bobbie was still speechless, but Ward Reedman was not. The eyes in his almost pretty face narrowed. "What's all this about? You come in here, don't know a thing about us, and start accusing us of mismanagement? Who do you think you are anyway?" His belligerence, Randollph thought, was probably genuine enough, but it was also cover for a case of nerves.

"I'm not accusing anyone of anything, Mr. Reedman," Randollph said. "I was just pointing out that I am obligated to certify to the bishop that *I know* everything is in order."

"Well, I'm the fourth generation of my family to serve as trustee," Reedman said truculently, "and you are the first pastor to be so particular about it. When the trustees of Good Shepherd say everything is OK, the pastor takes their word for it."

"They shouldn't have." Professor Donald Miller spoke so softly that it took a moment for the words to register.

"I think you'd better explain that, Miller, and you'd better have good reason for saying it, ha," Little Bobbie growled.

Miller was reaming the bowl of a large meerschaum with the air of a surgeon making carefully calibrated incisions. "You know my reasons, Robert. I bring them up annually. We pay too much for our services—insurance, the janitorial and window-washing contracts for the hotel and offices, auditing, supplies—and we receive too little from our leases and on our investments—"

"Miller, you son of a bitch, are you accusing me of—"

"Oh, don't be paranoid, Reed." Miller was now stuffing dark oily shreds of tobacco into the bowl of the meerschaum. "Mr. Reedman is a stockbroker," he explained to Randollph. "He handles the investments of our cash endowment. On his advice we have gone into common stocks. Our account hasn't been doing too well."

"You bastard," Reedman hissed, "you know the market's been doing badly."

"But you haven't been doing badly, have you, Ward? At least, if the size of the commissions you charge us are any indication. You see"—he turned to Randollph—"Mr. Reedman's firm is on the smallish size. I expect Good Shepherd's by far his largest account. Must be about ten million by now, isn't it, Ward? Some of it is in good safe triple A bonds, but there's enough in stocks to give our broker plenty of action. They call that churning, don't they, Ward?"

"You—"

"Save it, Ward," Miller snapped. "You just want to swear at me, and your invectives aren't very imaginative. I have always objected to investing any of our money in common stocks, but my colleagues always outvote me five to one." His pipe packed to what must have

41

been exacting standards, the professor pulled a lighter out of a worn tweedy jacket and shot a finger of blue flame into the bowl.

Well, Randollph thought, now I know who voted against Smelser.

"You're in the market yourself, Don. You've told me so," said McNutt, a middle-aged man running to fat. "I don't see why you're so hoity-toity righteous about the church doing it."

"Of course I'm in the market, Jamie," the professor replied. "But then, I'm rich and can afford the losses. It amuses me more than playing the ponies, and it's nearly as safe. But I've been doing better than Ward—a lot better. That's why I don't accept his complaint that our account's been doing badly because the market's been doing badly. He's supposed to be a professional, and I'm only an amateur."

"Ha, hum, well, I think we'd better be moving on to the business of the evening," Little Bobbie said.

"And another thing," Miller went on, ignoring the interruption, "while Mr. Reedman submits us a list, from time to time, of all our holdings—both bonds and stocks—they are never inventoried except by Mr. Reedman."

"Miller," Reedman snarled, "I'll sue you for slander."

"For what?" Miller asked innocently. "How did I slander you? Is it not true that in all the years you have had custody of our securities there has never been an independent inventory? I did not say that the securities were not there. I only said that the sole information we have is what you furnish us."

Randollph thought Reedman looked ill.

Professor Miller, who apparently had exhausted his subject coincidentally with his pipe, began the reaming process. There was a thick, sullen silence. The air was heavy with hostility. And fear.

Randollph pushed back his chair and got up. "I think, gentlemen, that I'll change my mind and defer my questions to another time and leave you to the remainder of the evening's business. However, so that Mr. Reedman may be relieved of any suspicions, I shall have an auditor of my choice inventory our securities, in the next few days if possible. And, Mr. Smelser, I'll ask you to provide me with copies of all our contracts for services immediately so that I may have them reviewed by qualified advisers. Are there any objections?"

There were no objections.

6

MISS WINDFALL, having seen how the land lay, had switched her loyalty from the beloved but deposed Dr. Hartshorne to Randollph with the smoothness of a well-adjusted transmission. She now badgered Randollph, benevolently but firmly, as she had badgered Hartshorne, into performing the trivial duties pastors are wont to shirk.

Randollph had hoped for a long, uninterrupted morning in which to activate auditors, investigators, and anyone else essential to fishing facts out of the slough of Good Shepherd's financial operations. He had visions of summoning crisp, efficient men and dispatching them to sleuthlike tasks and had dressed himself in his most conservative suit, a subdued plaid, so as to look like an executive. He had to settle for a blue shirt because he didn't own a white one, but the tie—blue silk with a small red design—was not startling. He thought he detected approval in Miss Windfall's appraising glance. "After I've seen Mr. Gantry," Randollph told her, heading for his own office, "we'll tackle the day's chores."

Dan, by prearrangement, was Randollph's first appointment. He was waiting, exuding triumphant righteousness and an eagerness to smite Philistines.

"Boss, last night was the greatest night of my life—well, of my professional life anyway," he amended. "One word from you and bang! Zowie! Little Bobbie bites the dust. Never happened before. Beautiful, beautiful! Let's kill the bastards off before they have a chance to regroup."

Randollph gazed absently at a blank patch of wall lighter than the wall itself and realized that Miss Windfall had, however reluctantly,

43

removed the marcelled head of Christ which reportedly had been such an inspiration to Dr. Hartshorne. He'd have to look for something to replace it, he supposed. A good reproduction of "A View of Toledo," perhaps, with its craggy angularities and phalliclike perpendiculars under a dark and menacing sky.

"All we did last night was to stir up some possibly muddy water," he told Dan. "Putative misdeeds don't equal established malfeasance. Maybe the trustees aren't guilty of anything but bungled management."

"Ha!" Dan replied, the euphoria of last night's rout of Little Bobbie and company vanquishing latent doubts. "I think they are guilty as hell, and I think we have them by the balls."

"Not yet. Maybe never. All last night told us was that Freddie's—how did he put it—'dark conviction that even the best of men become ethically confused when exposed continually to very large and accessible sums of money' might possibly have some basis in fact."

"They aren't the best of men," Dan said. "Except Don Miller."

"No? Well, let's leave the moral judgments to God, as the Scriptures, I believe, instruct us to do, and assess the situation objectively."

As Dan glumly composed his vision of a world in which greedy businessmen are brought to swift and awful retribution with the real world where the avaricious all to often bank their stealings and accept trusteeships from the admiring public, Randollph meditated on how to proceed.

"How would you like to become a detective?" he asked Dan.

Dan brightened perceptibly. "I'd like that," he said, conjuring up an image of himself as a relentless pursuer of evildoers. "I'd like that a lot."

"You'd better make some notes," Randollph instructed him. "First, do you know a reputable auditor who has no possible connection with the church or any of the trustees?"

"I don't, but I know people who do."

"Good. Find one. I want an immediate inventory of our investments. I want to know that the stocks and bonds this Reedman says we own actually exist. Get a list of them from Smelser. And I want an analysis of why our investment income is shrinking. Got it?"

"Got it."

"Second, find someone—it'll probably take a lawyer—to find out who owns every company we do business with. Insurance, janitorial service, leasing arrangements, everything. I want to know if any of the trustees have an interest in any of these companies or a possible financial arrangement with them. That'll take some digging."

"I'll dig, I'll dig."

"Would it be a good idea to have a talk with this Professor Miller? He seems to have detected the stench of skulduggery some time ago. Can you trust him? Who is he, anyway?"

Dan ticked off the relevant items in Miller's dossier like a CIA bureaucrat briefing an agent.

"You can trust him. Don's old family—old Chicago and old Church of the Good Shepherd—like Ward Reedman. Only, Miller's older family and richer family. He could probably buy and sell all the other trustees with plenty left over. Bachelor. Teaches something or other at Chicago University. Plays the violin. Skis in Switzerland. Devils the other trustees. Says he stays on because it's a family tradition, but mostly because he likes to watch clowns. Projects a disillusioned man-of-the-world image, but underneath he's mad as hell at the way those old bastards run the church."

"A disillusioned pose is often a mark of moral outrage," Randollph observed.

"Well, he enjoyed putting it to those old poops last night." Dan glowed with approbation.

A firm knock on the door was followed immediately by Miss Windfall's purposeful bulk. Behind every executive, Randollph supposed, there is a secretary who chivies him into performing tasks he would otherwise neglect. The file under her arm told Randollph that this morning, when he was eager to slay dragons, Miss Windfall would insist that he sign pieces of paper.

"Morning, Addie," Dan greeted her, not rising, "what bad news you got there under your arm?"

"I'm sorry to interrupt your conference," Miss Windfall began, managing to imply that whatever they were talking about was of little consequence, "but these matters simply must be attended to."

"Well, then, let's attend to them," Randollph proposed, he hoped cheerfully, reflecting that in winning Miss Windfall's loyalty, he had acquired a slavemaster.

Miss Windfall snowed papers on his desk along with instructions for their disposition. Enough and to spare, Randollph thought, but Miss Windfall wasn't satisfied.

"Mr. Bailey failed to turn in the minutes of the trustees' meeting," she announced severely. "They are supposed to be sent out today. Mr. Torgeson is very insistent that they be in the mail the day after the meeting."

"If I were you, Addie, I'd forget about it," Dan reassured her. "I don't think there will be any minutes for last night's meeting. I think old Harold was too busy to take them. And you can bet that Little Bobbie won't mind if they aren't in the mail today."

"It is most unusual," Miss Windfall pronounced. Tampering with routine, she believed, was at least a venial sin. "Also, the printer must have the copy for the Sunday worship bulletin in an hour, and Mr. Agostino has failed to turn in the anthem again."

"Tony's probably out at the school. Why don't you call him there?" Dan instructed her.

"I have tried the school," Miss Windfall stated. "He has left and didn't tell them where he was going."

"Probably on the trail of some new chick," Gantry said, "in which case we'll not locate him for hours. All that wop thinks of is music and *l'amour*, or however you say skirt in Italian," he added.

Miss Windfall sniffed.

"Tell you what, Addie," Dan said, "why don't you trot down to the choir practice room? More than likely Tony left a copy of the anthem on the lectern. Since the choir practiced last night, it's probably still there. I'd go for you, but the boss and I are making big medicine."

Miss Windfall docilely made for the door. I must take a lesson from Dan in the cultivation of boyish charm, Randollph decided. It works beautifully.

"By the way, Miss Windfall," Randollph said, stopping her at the door, "before I forget it, will you prepare a memo for Mr. Smelser instructing him to double Mrs. Creedy's compensation. I'll sign it when it is ready."

46

"Mr. Smelser will just ask Mr. Torgeson about it, and Mr. Torgeson will say no," she told Randollph. Miss Windfall, without doubt, understood the channels of power at Good Shepherd.

"Why will Mr. Torgeson say no?" Randollph asked. He was curious.

"Because Mr. Torgeson says a hundred dollars a month and room and board is more than enough to pay a returned missionary, seeing that they are supposed to be dedicated and used to poverty. He says that in view of her tragedy, she is lucky to have a job at all. He says what Good Shepherd is doing for her is an act of Christian charity."

"Mr. Torgeson is not the first Christian businessman to practice exploitation and call it Christian charity," Randollph told her, wondering if he sounded like a Marxist rhetorician. "Prepare the memo. I doubt it will get any argument from Mr. Smelser or Mr. Torgeson."

Miss Windfall departed, jiggling like a huge mold of Jello.

"Well, well," Dan commented, "coming to the aid of the downtrodden masses, boss?"

"What in the world did she mean about Mrs. Creedy's 'tragedy'?" Randollph asked.

"Well, it seems that the Reverend and Mrs. Creedy were missionaries to some outlandish place," Dan replied, happy to drag a small skeleton out of Good Shepherd's closet. "Good Shepherd underwrote their financial support. Guys like old Torgeson just love to spout off about how the church nickels up to save the heathen in deepest Africa," Dan editorialized, "but they raise hell if I ask for money to help the niggers right around here. Niggers," he added, "is Old Torgeson's word, not mine."

"The tragedy." Randollph pulled Dan back to the subject.

"Oh, well, as I get it, while Mrs. Creedy was teaching the natives mournful Christian hymns and persuading them to wear petticoats, the Reverend Mr. Creedy took up with one of the local beauties.

"Uncle Harry's not a missionary now," Dan broke into the Coward tune. " 'He's really livin'. Uncle Harry's not a missionary now!' "

Randollph, who had had to endure Mrs. Creedy's stern Calvinistic demeanor as recently as breakfast, concluded that while the Reverend Mr. Creedy's conduct was deplorable, it was understandable.

"Go on," he told Dan.

47

"Well," Dan continued, pausing to light a cigarette, "one of the local beauty's other boyfriends knocked him off—Reverend Mr. Creedy, that is. Fed him to the sharks, I understand. Finis for the Creedy missionary project. The church kind of had Mrs. Creedy on its hands, so St. Torgie saw a chance to get some cheap help and hired her for pocket change, the crummiest room in the hotel, and board in the coffee shop. She works like a dog—you wouldn't believe the number of teas and wedding receptions and what not that go on here, and she has to manage all of them, plus inspect the building for cleanliness and keep the janitors on their toes and other odds and ends. She's good at it, I admit, old sourpuss that she is. But Little Bobbie's right about one thing, I give him that. Who else would hire her? Returned missionaries, especially as full of offensive piety as Mrs. Creedy, aren't very employable."

"All the same, the church shouldn't take advantage of her helplessness," Randolph said, making a note to move Mrs. Creedy to a better room in the hotel, charge it to the church, and Mr. Smelser and Little Bobbie could lump it. "Oh, come in, Miss Windfall, you found the anthem, I hope. Miss Windfall, what's wrong? Are you ill?"

Adelaide Windfall stood in the doorway, her meaty face gray. She struggled for breath. "Oh . . . choir room . . . awful . . . oh." She managed to push the words out, then slowly collapsed and slid down the door frame like a great accordion closing. Dan reached her in time to prevent her head from hitting the floor. Randollph sprang quickly to the grotesque tableau.

"Let's get her on the couch, gently now," he said, with the crisp, unsuperfluous words of a man accustomed to dealing with emergencies.

"Right," said Gantry. "God, she's heavy. Maybe we'd better slide her along."

"I say, what's going on?" This from a new voice, high-pitched and girlish.

"Oh, hello, Arnie," Dan answered. "Addie's fainted. Give us a hand, will you?"

"Oh, dear," Arnie chirped.

The three of them managed to lift Miss Windfall's tenth of a ton bulk onto the office's big leather sofa. Randollph was momentarily grateful that when the office was furnished, tastes ran to oversize furniture. Feeling Miss Windfall's lumpy wrist for a pulse, he announced, "She'll be all right. Cold cloths on her forehead, a drink of water, she'll come around. Arnie, ring a doctor, the hotel doctor if he's in. But first, tell one of the other secretaries, Evelyn if she's handy, she's a steady girl, to get in here with a cold cloth and some water."

"Right away, Dr. Randollph," Arnie fluttered, glad of an excuse to get out.

Very shortly, Evelyn hurried in and began to do womanly things competently. Miss Windfall emitted a reassuring sigh.

"Boss," Dan said, "something must have scared the"—he glanced at the busy Evelyn—"the hell out of Adelaide. She was mumbling about the choir room. We'd better check."

They crossed the large reception room where the spiritually troubled, miffed parishioners with complaints, and church goods salesmen waited audience with the pastor. In the hall outside was an elevator serving all the floors occupied by the church, but it was in use. Randollph and Dan took a stairway which brought them down to the rear of the nave, then through a door and another stairway descending to the underground level, where the choir practice room was located. Here a long hallway led past a series of what once were Sunday school classrooms, built at a time when the rapid decline of the Sunday school was unanticipated. These rooms, now housing broken blackboards, malfunctioning slide projectors, tattered hymnals, and all the detritus of a religious organization, were a symbol, Randollph thought, of the church's appealing conviction that things would always be as they are now. As a specialist in the history of the church, he knew that every Christian era believed this to be true and that they were always wrong.

Beyond the last of the classrooms, the hall finally led to the choir practice room. Dan Gantry, who knew the way best, tried the door, which, Randollph remembered, opened into the larger portion of the curtain-divided room. It was unlocked.

"That's funny. It ought to be locked," he said. They stepped in as he snapped on a light switch. "Well," he observed, "nothing here to scare Addie. Let's have a look at Tony's lounge. Light's on over there, so that's where Addie must have seen the bogeyman." Randollph followed as Dan pushed aside the curtain, looked around casually, then moved into the room. Randollph almost collided with him as he stopped abruptly, stiffened, and suddenly turned his head away. "Jesus," Dan spoke in a strangulated voice. "Oh, jumping Jesus!"

Randollph stepped around him to see for himself. On Mr. Agostino's commodious institutional plastic sofa lay a woman, entirely naked, sound asleep.

But she was not asleep. When Randollph got close enough, he could see that she had been strangled with a heavy purple brocade ribbon.

7

DETECTIVE LIEUTENANT Michael Casey, homicide, did not conform to Randollph's image of a policeman. He watched the cop shows on television and was thus led to expect a grizzled, bulky veteran who wore a battered hat and chewed on a dead cigar and told people menacingly that they'd better come clean or else. Lieutenant Casey, Randollph imagined, would not stand out in the crowd of eager young stockbrokers who swarmed out in the subway each morning or be distinguishable in the packs of editors and advertising men making their way to client luncheons at fashionable restaurants.

Lieutenant Casey was collecting facts. While the technical crew was about its grisly business below in the choir practice room, the lieutenant was comfortable in one of Randollph's oversized office chairs, questioning Randollph and Dan Gantry.

"Mr. Gantry has identified the deceased as Marianne Reedman—Mrs. Wardlow Reedman. I presume you can confirm that, Dr. Randollph."

"Not really," Randollph told him. "You see, I've only been here a few days. I've seen her only once. She doesn't look much like she did when I first saw her."

"It's Annie, no mistake about that," a shaken and subdued Dan Gantry said.

"Annie?"

"Everyone who knew her called her Annie."

"Why would she have been in that underground room last night?"

"Because that is the choir practice room, last night was choir practice, and she was a member of the choir." Randollph, sensing that succinct answers were in order, supplied the information.

51

"Was she a faithful member of the choir—I mean, would someone who wanted to kill her know for certain that she'd be there for practice?"

"All our choir members are faithful, because they are all exceedingly well paid to be faithful."

"Oh." The lieutenant, memories of the pickup choir at St. Aloysius Church screeching through venerable Latin hymns as fresh as last Sunday's ten o'clock mass, thought it must be nice to have real professionals to listen to. "That must cost a pretty penny."

"The Church of the Good Shepherd has a pretty penny," Randollph said. Lieutenant Casey made a note of it.

"Then Mrs. Reedman earned her living as a professional musician?"

"No," Dan Gantry replied, "she didn't need the money. She was loaded—she was a very wealthy woman."

Randollph could see the flicker of interest in Casey's eyes. Money, he supposed, mixed well with murder in a detective's world.

"Perhaps," he said, "it would help if we made it clear to you Mrs. Reedman's entire connection with the church. Briefly, her husband is a trustee of the church—there has been a Reedman on the board of trustees ever since the church was founded. Mrs. Reedman, while a member, was also a highly trained musician or she wouldn't have been in the choir."

"If she was wealthy, why did she take money for singing?" Casey asked. "Was she greedy?"

Dan jumped to the dead woman's defense. "No, she wasn't greedy. She was a pro, and being paid is the mark of a pro. I happen to know that she gave it all back, and more, to the music program of the church."

"You say she was wealthy. Do you mean by that that she was married to a wealthy man?" This to Dan.

"I don't know," Dan answered. "The Reedmans are what you could call, I guess, socially prominent. I've heard gossip that Ward Reedman was on his uppers until he married Annie and that she is the one who has the dough. But then," he added, "I couldn't swear to it. You hear all kinds of gossip."

The lieutenant's nostrils were positively twitching, Randollph could see, scenting an early and easy solution to the crime.

"And Mr. Reedman, what does he do?" Casey asked.

"He is a stockbroker. He has his own firm." Randollph supplied the information that he had gleaned from last night's meeting.

Casey crossed one well-pressed olive hopsack leg over the other, looked thoughtful, and abruptly switched subjects.

"Tell me about Mrs. Reedman. What was she like as a person?"

"She was a honey, a sweetheart, a dish." Dan appeared to be about to cry. "Must have been about thirty-one or two—"

"She was thirty-eight, according to her driver's license," Casey interjected.

"Didn't look it," Dan said.

"Anyway," Dan went on, "she had lots of class. Plenty of sparkle. Vivacious is a good word for her. If she was an heiress and all that high-toned stuff, you'd never know it."

Casey smiled, the kind of smile that crinkles the skin around the eyes.

"Reverend Gantry," he asked, "do people ever call you Elmer?"

"Hah!" Dan said, relieved to change what was obviously to him a very painful subject. "Ever since seminary they've called me that. Every day nearly some joker pulls it and thinks he's being original."

"No offense," the lieutenant said pleasantly. "I just wondered. Tell me about Mr. Reedman. What kind of person is he?"

"Well, I only met him last night—" Randollph began.

"Oh," Casey interrupted, alert as a bird dog sighting quarry, "where?"

"Here at the church. There was a meeting of the trustees—"

"Oh, then Reedman was here in the building last night. Interesting. Interesting."

"He is a bastard," Dan said flatly. "Ward Reedman is one of the world's great bastards."

Though Lieutenant Casey kept an impassive countenance, Randollph had no difficulty sensing what was going on in the lieutenant's policeman mind. He was certain that the lieutenant was thinking, Aha! We have a murdered woman, whose husband was a bastard and who was here in the building where she was killed, and it will probably

53

turn out that he was here, or could have been here, at the time she was killed. We ought to be able to wrap this one up pretty fast.

A sharp rap on the door announced a visitor who did not wait for an invitation. He was a big man with an ex-athlete's frame now accumulating fatty deposits, especially in the belly.

"Yes, Pete?" Lieutenant Casey looked up, then remembered the amenities. "Dr. Randollph, Mr. Gantry, this is Sergeant Garbaski." Sergeant Garbaski grunted and turned to Casey.

"Need to see ya a minute, Lieutenant."

Casey followed him to the door, and Randollph could hear the sergeant muttering something about an APB. Casey nodded, and the sergeant disappeared. The sergeant did look like a policeman. He wore a sweat-stained old felt hat and chewed on a dead cigar. Randollph felt better.

The lieutenant resumed his seat and glanced briefly at his notebook.

"Mr. Gantry, could you elaborate on your statement about Mr. Reedman's, er, character?"

Dan could. "He's selfish, he's mean, and I think he's a crook."

Casey looked up from his notebook. "You think he's a crook? You must have reasons."

Randollph decided it was time to take a hand. He would have preferred to say nothing about the nature of last night's meeting with the trustees, but he suspected that he was no match for the lieutenant.

"Lieutenant," he said, choosing his words carefully, "I'm afraid we're going to have to let you inspect a little of Good Shepherd's dirty linen." He then rendered a condensed and edited account of the trustees' meeting.

"However," he concluded, "on the basis of our present information Dan has overstated the case against Mr. Reedman. Reedman no doubt has earned generous, perhaps excessive fees through his handling of Good Shepherd's securities. But we have no evidence at present that he has done anything illegal."

"You can be legal and still be a crook," Dan interjected truculently.

Randollph let that pass. "Mr. Reedman does not have a winsome personality. On the basis of a very superficial acquaintance with him, I would have to say that he has what my father called a 'shifty look.'

He is rude. He is also too much the dandy—a little too sharp, a little too neat, certainly out of character for a stockbroker. What an earlier generation referred to as 'spiffy.' His appearance would not inspire me to entrust large sums of money to his care. A man's taste in haberdashery should not be held against him"—Randollph thought of Miss Windfall's clear distaste for his own jackets and ties—"but perhaps you understand what I mean."

The lieutenant understood.

"Also," Randollph added, "none of this indicates that he is a crook or that he murdered his wife—which, I gather, you regard as a strong possibility."

Lieutenant Casey laid his notebook aside and shifted position in the deep leather chair.

"Dr. Randollph, I am a policeman. Policemen, good ones anyway, do not jump to conclusions. They collect facts. When you collect enough facts, then a theory emerges." He smiled. "In theology it is no doubt quite sound to begin with an intuition or a hypothesis. My own official religious faith rests on deductions by St. Thomas Aquinas, deductions based on undemonstrated and undemonstrable premises. Your Luther and Calvin and Wesley did much the same sort of thing."

Randollph was startled. A dapper young cop explaining theology to a theologian did not fit into a well-ordered world.

"However," Casey went on, "when it comes to murder, the only theory worth anything is one built on facts. And speaking of facts, the lab boys have the cord or ribbon with which Mrs. Reedman was strangled. You both saw it. Did either of you recognize it?"

Randollph swiveled around in his desk chair and stretched out his legs which were cramped and aching from the tension of the morning's horror. Casey's question recalled the gruesome scene in the choir room. He had nearly managed to quell the nausea he had been fighting but now felt queasy again. A strangled corpse, a routine for a homicide detective perhaps, is not a pretty sight.

"Yes," he answered, "it is a Bible marker, a bit of antependia which Mr. Agostino, our choirmaster, always used to mark the place in his anthem volume. It was always on his lectern in the practice room. That is," he amplified, "it wasn't always the same marker. Mr.

Agostino had a set and changed them with the seasons of the church calendar."

"Tony's the arty type," Dan explained.

"Then the purple one would be the one he was using currently, I presume, this being Lent," Casey said.

"That's right."

"And it would have been in plain sight, even to someone who would not have known that it was there or where to look for it?"

"You mean if some stranger wandered in and took a sudden notion to strangle someone, would the marker have been handy?"

"Yes."

"He couldn't have missed it," Randollph said, "if he glanced around for something, ah, appropriate to his purpose."

Casey snapped his notebook shut. "You've been very helpful. I'll need to talk to you later, of course. May I have your permission to question your staff now?"

"Do you need permission?" Randollph asked.

Casey smiled. "No. Just my Catholic reflexes when dealing with the clergy. We are not allowed to forget that awe and deference are the correct attitudes when associating with the cloth. And, I might add, you represent a prominent institution. I wouldn't push you around."

"You wouldn't," Randollph said, "but I'll wager Sergeant Garbaski would."

Casey's smile widened to a grin. "The department is not unaware of public relations. That's why they put me in charge of this case instead of Sergeant Garbaski. Now, could you give me a list of your staff? It would be helpful if you could round them up for me. You'll be having a busy day, you know," Casey told Randollph as he stood up and moved toward the door. "There were a number of murders committed in Chicago yesterday, but this one has everything the press loves—prominent family, money, religion, maybe sex, unusual weapon, spooky site, well-known church. If I were you, I'd count on spending a lot of time talking to reporters."

"I will," Randollph answered ruefully.

"And," the lieutenant said, pausing at the door, "you were right.

56

I do regard Mr. Reedman as a strong possibility as the murderer of his wife."

"Then you have jumped to a conclusion," Randollph accused.

"Not at all," Casey replied pleasantly. "In a murder case the surviving mate always comes in for special attention. This is not an ill-founded hypothesis; it is merely routine."

"Routine? How so?"

"Police routine," Casey explained patiently, "is simply condensed experience. Experience has taught us that husbands often murder their wives. And vice versa, of course. An unpleasant commentary on the institution of marriage, I'm afraid. But I'm not a moralist, I'm a cop."

"I suppose you'll be questioning Reedman shortly then," Randollph said.

"I would if I could," Casey answered, "but he is not at his home, he hasn't been to his office today, and he has left no word of his whereabouts. Mr. Wardlow Reedman seems to have decamped."

8

RANDOLLPH SUPPOSED that as he declined into senescence, he would look back on this day as one of the most exciting of his life. Right now, though, shock, a state of emergency in the church, and the demands of unfamiliar responsibilities made it seem grim indeed.

Lieutenant Casey had no sooner departed to round up the staff, with Dan to help him, than the press began pestering for interviews, for permission to bring in television cameras for shots of the murder room, and even for confirmation that the victim's husband had skipped town. He instructed Miss Windfall to tell all reporters that he was too busy coping with the crisis to give interviews today, that any pictures taken would have to be cleared with Detective Lieutenant Michael Casey, and that he would have a statement available to the press in an hour. He called Freddie for instruction and advice but was told that the bishop was on an episcopal jaunt to some solemn conclave of clerics and wouldn't be back until tomorrow.

As he tried to compose a statement for the press, he chewed his pencil and felt a sympathy for politicians, whose ambiguities and circumlocutions he normally despised and condemned. How to say the right thing without saying too much or too little wasn't as easy as it looked. He finally turned out a hundred words to the effect that the church was shocked by the tragedy, had no idea why it had taken place in the building, and was confident the police would soon clear it up. Meanwhile, the church would carry on with its normal schedule. He gave it to Miss Windfall to Xerox and have available to the press. By the time he had finished Dan had returned.

"We've rounded up everybody but Tony," Dan reported, "and he's on his way. The Loot asks if you'd mind sitting in on the questioning. Says it's a little irregular, but he thinks you there might help keep things calm. I think he must be afraid of hysterical females or something."

No such thing, Randollph thought. He doesn't want anyone connected with a prominent church yelling that the police were rough or rude, and he wants me there as a witness that they weren't. Astute chap, Casey.

Miss Windfall, apparently recovered from the shock of finding Marianne Reedman's strangled corpse, sailed in imperious as ever, trailing Evelyn like an acolyte. Asked to recall the details of her discovery of the body, Miss Windfall turned out to have been surprisingly observant. Yes, the light had been on in the room, a fact she noted as irregular. She had ascribed it to carelessness on the part of Mr. Agostino. A man who consistently forgot to turn in the anthem for Sunday's worship bulletin could be expected to neglect trifles such as turning off the lights. Yes, she had noticed that Marianne Reedman's clothes were neatly folded on a chair near the sofa on which she reclined in death. No, she had no idea what that signified.

"Where were you between nine and eleven last night?" Sergeant Garbaski barked. From the way Lieutenant Casey winced, Randollph guessed that this was the sergeant's normal speaking manner. Garbaski probably didn't think of it as barking.

Miss Windfall did think of it as barking. She withered Garbaski with a look of infinite contempt.

"Lieutenant," she said, "if you feel it necessary, I will account for my whereabouts last night. Meanwhile, I suggest you teach your man some manners." And she swept out.

Casey, suppressing a grin with only mild success, said, "Who's next, Mr. Gantry?"

O. B. Smelser was next.

He came in, his pale-blue eyes behind the granny glasses darting around the room, then dropping to study some pattern in the patternless carpet.

"You knew Mrs. Reedman, of course," Casey said, trying to put the little man at ease.

59

"Fairly well. I am better acquainted with her husband."

"You attended the meeting of the trustees last night, at which he was present?"

"Yes."

"Was there, to your notice, anything unusual about his behavior at the meeting?"

Smelser looked quickly at Randollph, then quickly away. "Just how do you mean Mr.—Lieutenant Casey?"

"Did he seem perturbed, upset?"

Smelser thought about it.

"He was late," he finally answered.

Randollph watched Casey carefully. The lieutenant tugged thoughtfully at the button-down collar of his blue oxford cloth shirt but showed no inclination to pounce on this revelation.

"Oh?" he commented almost negligently. "Was he often late for the meeting?"

"No. Not that I recall. Any of us are occasionally a little late."

"But he wasn't particularly upset or agitated during the meeting?"

Smelser took off his glasses and began polishing them vigorously.

"I didn't say he wasn't."

"Then he was?"

"Yes. Yes. During the meeting he became quite angry. He objected strenuously to some things one of the trustees was saying and, well, to some of the policies Dr. Randollph was proposing." Smelser looked at Randollph unhappily.

"That's all right, Mr. Smelser." Randollph comforted him. "Lieutenant Casey knows all about that."

Lieutenant Casey consulted a piece of paper he had before him. "According to this preliminary report from the coroner," he said, "Mrs. Reedman could have died as early as eight o'clock and as late as eleven o'clock. We know she was alive as late as eight thirty because that's when the choir practice broke up. Then we can assume, I think, that about a quarter of nine would be the earliest she could have been killed. Probably it was somewhat later. When did the other members of the trustees arrive, Mr. Smelser. Do you recall?"

"I was the first to arrive in the boardroom," he said, putting his glasses back on. "That is, except for Mrs. Creedy—our housekeeper.

She always tidies up and makes coffee for the meeting. I doubt if we could hold a meeting without coffee." He smiled weakly.

"And the others."

"Let's see. I arrived about ten after nine. Mr. Torgeson came in shortly after that, say a quarter after. Mr. Bailey, Mr. McNutt, and Mr. Craft arrived together about five minutes later. I gather they had dined together. Professor Miller came in almost the same time, say, a minute later."

"And Mr. Reedman?"

"He arrived at nine forty-two. I glanced at my watch. It's quite accurate. It's electric." He glanced, Randollph thought, with something akin to affection, at the chronometer on his wrist.

"Yes, they're very good, the electrics," Casey said. "Wear one myself."

"Lieutenant, ah, that is—" Smelser was hesitant.

"Yes, Mr. Smelser."

"Well, uh, I'm sure you're not asking these questions out of curiosity. Do you, would it be out of order for me to ask if you suspect someone—some member of the trustees?"

"As I told Dr. Randollph earlier," Casey answered, "I'm only collecting facts at this stage. We have to know not only who could have done it, but who had a powerful motive to do it."

"If she was killed by a quarter to nine," Smelser said, shifting nervously in his chair, "then anyone at the trustees' meeting could have done it. Even I could have." He shuddered. "I don't know about motives."

"You have just answered the question I was about to ask you," Casey told him. "Thanks so much for your cooperation."

When Dan brought in Tony Agostino, Casey said, "You may as well stay if you like, Mr. Gantry."

Tony, Randollph saw, was not the same ebullient young man he had met on Sunday. Perhaps the Italians moved from gaiety to grief more rapidly than Anglo-Saxons. His blue and red striped blazer over a red shirt open at the throat and blue figured neckerchief proclaimed him a man interested in the world and interested in the impression he made on the world. His anguished face said that at the moment he found the world a distasteful place.

61

"Mr. Agostino," Casey began, "you knew Mrs. Reedman quite well?"

Tony looked as if he was blinking back tears. "Yeah, yeah, I knew Annie well. I know all my choir people well. But Annie was special. She was the best."

"So everyone says," Casey said. "Can you think of any reason why she would have been in the choir room after the others had gone?"

"Oh, sure. She was choir librarian. Volunteered for the job. Annie was rich, you probably found that out already. But you'd never know it, the way she acted. Worked harder than anybody for the choir. Like I told Dr. Randollph, she was our den mother. Everyone in the choir loved her."

"Explain to me why the choir librarian stays after everyone else has gone."

"Well, see, every choir member has to have a copy of the anthem, usually a copy of two different anthems because we practice ahead. Sheet music's expensive, you leave it around anywhere, and it disappears. You got to keep it in order, too, in the place where it's supposed to be or you'd never find it. That's what Annie did. After practice she'd collect all the stuff and put it back. Took time."

"And she stayed last night as usual?"

"Yeah. We talked awhile."

"What about?"

"Well, something was bothering her. We were pretty good friends, and she talked to me sometimes when things got her beat."

"What was troubling her last night?"

Tony wrinkled his brow. "I don't know for sure. She didn't spell it out. Had something to do with her husband, something financial. She said she thought she was going to have to blow the whistle on him and was trying to figure out some way to do it without too much scandal. I didn't press her for details. What do I want to know for anyway? I mostly just listened. That's what she needed. Somebody to listen."

Casey showed no emotion, but Randollph suspected the lieutenant's nostrils were quivering.

"Was there any other conversation, Mr. Agostino? Remember everything you can."

"Well, I told her just before I left to be sure and turn off the light or Addie Windfall or Mrs. Creedy'll hear about it being on all night and give me hell for it. That's the last thing I said to her, maybe the last thing anybody said to her except whoever killed her." Tony tried to stifle a sob that had been hovering in his throat but couldn't. Detective Sergeant Garbaski, looking up from his notebook, did not conceal the contempt the tough-fibered feel for men who can't control their emotions.

Detective Lieutenant Casey, Randollph observed, was regarding Tony with renewed interest. Randollph couldn't be sure what the lieutenant was thinking, but he supposed Casey was feeling reassured about the importance of routine. A simple question had given him a fact—to wit, why Mrs. Reedman had been in the choir room after everyone else had left. She was only doing her regular duty of putting away the choir music. Randollph could see the possibilities this opened up. Ward Reedman must have known that this was her habit. Also, if Marianne Reedman was thinking of exposing her husband for some financial malpractice, he had a reason to silence her. But then, many others knew that she would have been alone in the choir room. If her murderer had known, which he surely must have, that she would be alone, say, from about eight thirty on, it would have been a simple matter to slip down there unobserved, throttle her, and get out quickly. Ten minutes, fifteen at the outside, would have been sufficient for the whole operation. This fact by no means eliminated Reedman. It might be one more confirmation of his guilt in Lieutenant Casey's eyes. But the lieutenant was certainly intelligent enough to know that it opened up the possibility of any number of other people being guilty. It was a matter of matching opportunity with motive.

Randollph also thought he detected Casey looking at Tony speculatively. If Tony had been the last person to see Marianne Reedman alive except for some unknown murderer, maybe Casey was wondering if he had done her in. Motive? Randollph unleashed his imagination. Could it have been that Marianne, married to something of a stinker, was being comforted by Tony Agostino? It was not illogical. Tony was handsome, virile, and charming. Younger than Marianne, but not that much younger. Randollph had known much stranger sexual liaisons. But why would Tony have killed her? Maybe

Marianne had had enough and had given him the gate. In a sudden fit of frustrated rage he had grabbed the first thing handy—the Bible marker—and strangled her. Preposterous on the face of it, Randollph thought as he looked at the blubbering Tony Agostino, but possible. Randollph didn't know, but he suspected that a good many of Lieutenant Casey's investigations had to do with sobbing and whimpering murderers who had yielded to a sudden impulse to kill. A surge of temper, a flashing anger over some fancied wrong, a jealousy-crazed mate, a rejected lover's mangled ego and bang! or stab! or choke! and it was done. The murderers often blubbered and whined when they realized what they had done.

Randollph noticed Lieutenant Casey making a note in his book. Randollph bet that it read "Check out Agostino."

Tony, full of snuffles and assurances of full cooperation, was excused.

When Dan brought Arnie Uhlinger in, it was obvious that he had been crying.

"I'm all broken up," he announced, "I'm devastated. Completely." His voice was so high it almost squeaked, Randollph thought. "I loved her very much, you know. Everyone who knew her very well did." Sergeant Garbaski looked disgusted.

"We're asking everyone on the staff to tell us anything they might know which will help us," Casey said. His tone was very gentle, Randollph noticed, admiring him for it. "How did you happen to know Mrs. Reedman? In the course of your pastoral duties?"

Arnie looked surprised. "No. I sing in the choir. That is, when I can. Sometimes I have to help in the service and sometimes I preach at the mission. But when I can, I like to be in the choir. Didn't anyone tell you?"

Casey looked at Randollph, then at Dan.

"I didn't know," Randollph said.

"I didn't think to mention it," Dan said. "Not much time today to think of stuff like that. Arnie's got a fine tenor voice."

"That's why we go through this routine," Casey commented, "so that we can find out what people don't think to tell us. It can be dull, but if we didn't do it, we'd miss things we ought to know. Mr. Uhlinger, I suppose then that you were aware that Mrs. Reedman was responsible for putting away the choir's music after practice and was usually the last to leave the choir room?"

"Of course. Everyone knew that. Everyone in the choir anyway." Arnie's prominent Adam's apple bobbed like a fisherman's cork with a big bluegill on the hook. "I often helped her when I didn't have to get back to school to study."

There was a sudden silence.

Arnie looked around in puzzlement, then in consternation. "Ooh, I see, did I help her last night, that's what you're wondering?" he piped.

"That's what we're wondering," Casey answered in a flat, matter-of-fact voice.

"No, no, no." Arnie hastily removed himself from the scene of the murder. "No, I wasn't even at choir last night. It was the night of the honors banquet at the seminary, and I had to be there. I was being honored, I mean, it wasn't a banquet for me, they have it every year, and I was just one of many—"

"I know what an honors banquet is," Casey interrupted. "Is there anything else you can tell us about Mrs. Reedman that might be helpful?"

"She was the loveliest person I have ever known," answered Arnie, a raptured expression transforming his long face. "Except my mother, of course," he added hastily, like a man who had suddenly remembered a clear duty. "I can't imagine—can't even dream of why"—his voice broke—"why anyone would want to destroy anything so beautiful—"

"None of us can," Casey said sympathetically. "But someone did. If you think of anything else that might be useful to us, please let us know."

Arnie was replaced by Mrs. Creedy, who furnished a list of anyone who had an occasion to be in the choir room and an aura of stern righteousness.

"I inspect the room once a week, usually on Fridays. Choir's messy, and the janitors, well—" Mrs. Creedy's thin lips did not need to add that she considered janitors, in addition to committing the deadly sin of sloth, guilty of neglecting the puritan virtue of cleanliness. "Besides the choir and the custodians, there's the outside cleaners. Once a month. They do a thorough job." Randollph was glad that someone, if only a professional cleaning company, was able to meet Mrs. Creedy's standards.

"Must cost a lot to run a place like this," Casey said. "Who else has occasion to visit the choir room, Mrs. Creedy?"

"The trustees. They inspect the whole building, the church part, four times a year. Supposed to. They neglect it sometimes. More like every six months they inspect it, if that." Trustees who dogged their prescribed duties Mrs. Creedy did not expect to meet in heaven.

Casey sighed. Evidently nearly everyone around Good Shepherd had reason to visit the choir room, which meant that quite a few people were familiar with it and its uses. This investigation could turn into a wearisome job.

"Did you know Mrs. Reedman, the deceased?" he asked the housekeeper.

"Never spoke to her in my life."

"Where were you around nine thirty last night?" Sergeant Garbaski asked. Randollph supposed it was the sergeant's normal interrogatory manner, but it came out as an accusatory growl. Mrs. Creedy fixed him with a look austere enough to cow emperors and kings.

"I was in my room saying my evening prayers," she said. "And by the look of you, you could benefit from doing the same."

Randollph tried to intercept a chuckle, half-succeeding. Dan guffawed. "Attaway to go, Clarabelle," he said. Lieutenant Casey said, "Thank you, Mrs. Creedy. That will be all for the present." His face was impassive, but Randollph could see a twinkle in his eyes.

"Who's next?" Casey asked.

Sergeant Garbaski consulted his notebook. "Janitor that was on duty last night. Name of Renfro Verban. I already talked to him some. He's uppity."

Randollph saw Casey stiffen. "That isn't necessary, Pete," Casey said. Although he didn't raise his voice, there was a hard quality in it that Randollph hadn't heard from Casey before. Garbaski bit hard on his cigar as if it helped him choke off the retort he'd like to make. Randollph guessed that Casey and Garbaski must have had a number of conversations on the subject of a policeman's keeping his gratuitous opinions to himself and that none of these conversations had been pleasant for Garbaski.

Renfro Verban, in clean chinos, desert boots, and a dark-green pullover sweater, looked like a white man with a heavy suntan.

"This the janitor workin' last night," Garbaski said to Casey.

"I'm not a janitor," Renfro said coldly. "I am a law school student who works evenings here as supervisor of the building."

"Of course," Casey said soothingly. "I'm sure the sergeant meant no harm." He looked hard at Garbaski. "I'll handle this, Pete. Now, Mr. Verban, just what are your duties?"

"I'm available to anyone using the building," Renfro answered. "You see, Lieutenant, there are groups meet here every night. I see they have enough chairs or blackboards, whatever they need. Sometimes lights burn out. People need all sorts of things you wouldn't think of unless you were around here of an evening."

"Was last evening especially busy?"

"Thursday nights are always worst. Busiest evening of the week. Boy Scouts, AA, Employed Women's Guild, choir, always six or seven other things. Trustees once a month. Thursdays I keep hopping."

"Sounds very much like the program at St. Aloysius," Casey commented. "Only at St. Al's it's Wednesdays. Do you suppose," he asked Randollph, "that the main difference between Protestants and Catholics is that one meets on Wednesdays and the other on Thursdays?"

"Probably as significant as most of our differences," Randollph said.

Casey turned back to Renfro Verban.

"Did you have any occasion to be in the choir room at any time last night?"

"No, Lieutenant, I didn't." Verban had obviously been expecting the question. "Tony, Mr. Agostino, hardly ever needed me. Sometimes a light would burn out during practice, he'd call me to change it. The regular groups, like the choir, they're not much trouble. It's the ones don't meet here often need the looking after."

"Yes, well, let's see if you can help us on this. You know the building well?"

67

"Backwards and forwards—or better, up and down." Renfro smiled at his little joke.

"Let's say someone, whoever it was, wanted to murder Mrs. Reedman. He'd want to get in and get out unnoticed. Would that be feasible?"

"Easiest thing in the world," Renfro replied. " 'Specially on Thursdays. Must be two, three hundred people in and out of here every Thursday night. Lobby's like Forty-second and Broadway. People coming and going all the time. Simplest way would be to duck through the door in the lobby that leads to downstairs. Do it when nobody's looking. Do the job, come back up, and go out the same way. Even if there's a crowd in the lobby, who'd notice? People popping out of elevators, other doors, they don't pay any attention to each other. These are city people. They don't know each other. They don't care what you're doing."

"Could, say, a wino off the street just wander in, find his way downstairs without anyone intercepting him?"

"Been known to happen," Verban said. "In cold weather. They come in to panhandle. Churches and church folks supposed to be easy marks for panhandlers. I shoo one or two out 'most every night. Sometimes they find their way downstairs. Find it's empty and say, 'Hey, I got me a free hotel for tonight.' "

Casey had been afraid the answer would be something like this. It meant he could not ignore the possibility that Marianne Reedman's assassin was one of the large and floating derelict population of Chicago.

"Now if this whoever wanted to be real secretive," Renfro continued, "he could go in the hotel, take an elevator to the fourth floor, get out, and go across the hall. Then he'd catch the church elevator, ride it to the basement level. He's got a good bet that no one's going to stop the elevator at the lobby level to go on down. With luck, no one sees him at all. Then he gets it over with and gets out the same way. People mostly trying to catch the elevator down to the lobby after nine o'clock. With luck again, he gets on the elevator in the basement, rides up to the fourth without being stopped. He gets out, maybe meets someone waiting at the fourth to go down. But so what?

They just think he's some guy thirsty after his meeting ducking over to the hotel to grab a quick one for the road."

Sergeant Garbaski took the cigar out of his mouth and spat a sodden fragment of tobacco at an ashtray, missing.

"Here we got a dead dame that'd been screwed," he said disgustedly, "and from what this—from what *Mr.* Verban says, anybody in Chicago or the whole U.S.A. could have done it, it was so easy."

There was a shocked silence. Dan broke it. "You said Marianne had been screwed." It was a stricken plea for someone to deny it. Garbaski started to speak, but Casey's look warned him off.

Casey cleared his throat and pulled a piece of paper out of his pocket.

"I was going to tell you," he said, looking at the paper. "According to the coroner's preliminary report, Mrs. Reedman had sexual intercourse, forcibly or with her cooperation—there's no way to tell which—not too long before she died."

There was another silence, and again Dan broke it.

"Oh, Jesus," he said, "now we've got a sex murder."

9

C. P. RANDOLLPH had looked forward to his appearance on *Sam Stack's Chicago,* whether for the ego-gratifying exposure television afforded or for an opportunity of further association with the impertinent Ms. Stack, he wasn't certain. Probably, he decided, for both reasons. But now he wished his appearance had been scheduled for a different day, any other day. A day that had begun with the discovery of a particularly gruesome murder, and during which he had endured Lieutenant Casey's polite grilling, plus the harrassments of reporters, photographers, and television news crews, was not a day to conclude with a lighthearted TV talk show. He had even suffered through a growling, sputtering phone call from the recently cowed Little Bobbie Torgeson. Little Bobbie hadn't actually accused Randollph of the murder. He had implied that it was somehow the result of Randollph's incompetence, or interference into areas which were none of his business, or perhaps neglect of building security. The Little Bobbies of this world, Randollph reflected bitterly, were far more resilient than the children of light.

He had, in fact, considered canceling or at least rescheduling his appearance. But that not only would have been unfair to Samantha Stack, who would have had to scrounge up a last-minute replacement, but would have violated his own self-image as a responsible man. So after a hasty sandwich in the hotel coffee shop (and even there besieged by lurking reporters), he was walking the few blocks to the studio. The mucky slush of a week ago had disappeared, but the wind from the lake knifed around corners and whipped down the canyons created by the walls of high-rise buildings. Sparse crowds trickled joylessly toward the havens of movie houses or convenient bars, hardly glancing at the elaborate windows of Marshall Field, which displayed fetching mannikins disporting themselves on simulated palm beaches. Randollph, accustomed to benign Pacific breezes, wondered if the hard-nosed deity preferred by Midwestern Christians was somehow connected with the foul and capricious climate of the region. A God of wrath with a beady eye out for deviant behavior, large or small, seemed more credible here than in the milder airs of California's oceanfront. Do harsh climates breed harsh gods? He supposed someone had written a doctoral dissertation on the subject.

The lobby of the building which somewhere in its capacious bosom housed the studio was monitored by a uniformed guard with a very obvious gun on his hip. He checked Randolph's name off a list on a clipboard, indicated a bank of elevators, and said, "Seventh."

On the seventh floor a pretty little girl who, Randollph guessed, carried the title of assistant producer or talent coordinator was sorting over arrivals for talent destined for the Sam Stack show.

"Dr. Randollph, I recognize you from your picture in the evening paper," she chirped with the aggressive friendliness he had come to associate with television studios. "We're so sorry," she said, shifting to a somber tone, "for the sad incident at your church today." The amenities observed, she shifted back. "Sam asked me to bring you directly to her office."

Sam's office was not a showplace. The television industry lavished slabs of expensive floorspace and corner views on its executives, but cubicles and windowless closets were deemed adequate for the working staff.

Sam Stack didn't mince around the subject. "Thanks awfully for coming under the circumstances," she said. "I hope you won't mind a question or two about this murder. Personally, I'd rather not get into it at all, but everybody knows about it by now, and we can't very well play like it never happened, can we?"

"No, we can't."

"How would it be, then, if I asked a couple of questions right at the end of the show? Nothing to give you any trouble."

"That would be the best way, I think."

Samantha Stack, that problem efficiently disposed of, moved on.

"This is a live program—live with quotes. That means we tape it and it is shown later this evening. We don't edit, and since it is a late show we don't bleep mild swear words—not that I expect any swearing tonight. We have three guests tonight—you, a nice little lady from Wheaton who has written a book on crocheting, and the Reverend Jeff Davis Troutman. Have you ever heard of Jeff Davis Troutman?"

Randollph replied that it was difficult to live in the United States and not have heard of Jeff Davis Troutman.

"Well," Samantha told him, "Jeff Davis, whom I have had on the program several times, is beginning a campaign here in Chicago to bring us the word of the Lord on the subject of pornography."

"I thought anticommunism was his line of goods," Randollph said.

"Oh, it is. He still operates his Christ Against Communism Foundation, all nice and tax-exempt. But I think the cream has been skimmed off that act. Anyway, the competition is pretty stiff. Jeff Davis is a shrewd businessman. He smells a large market for fearless opposition to four-letter words and girlie magazines. He is launching his new line here because *Playboy* is published here, and he'd like to get them into a big controversy. It would be worth a fortune to him if *Playboy* would take him on."

"And just what is the word of the Lord on four-letter words and girlie magazines?" Randollph asked her.

"The Lord says no," Samantha said. "According to Jeff Davis the Lord says no to most everything."

"He must be a grim sort of chap," Randollph observed.

"Not at all. He's friendly and full of Dixie charm. He always pats my fanny."

Randollph didn't like the thought of Jeff Davis Troutman patting Sammy's fanny but decided against asking himself why he didn't like it.

Sammy continued her briefing. "What we do is to focus on each guest in turn. I elicit the main facts about them."

I'll bet you do, Randollph thought.

"Then," she continued, "we all sit around a big table and drink coffee and talk. Some guests manage to smuggle hooch into their cups and top it up during the breaks. Now and then one of them is a mess

72

by the end of the program." She wrinkled her nose. "You can get pretty squished swilling straight gin or vodka for an hour or so."

"I promise to imbibe only coffee—without cream or sugar," Randollph assured her.

"One thing more—I'm a blunt interrogator," she informed him. "I hate sweet-type talk show hosts. That's dullsville. I don't mean that I'm nasty. I hate that kind of host, too. I'll be nice, but I'll be to the point. You mustn't take it personally." She measured him with a searching look. "I like you. I like you a lot." This with a smile Randollph thought absolutely radiant. "But I can't go easy on you just because I like you, can I?"

Randollph admitted that she couldn't.

"Also," she added, "you'd better be prepared for the fact that I do my homework. I know who you are, Con Randollph."

Randollph, with a sinking feeling that this was going to be a long evening, said, "You do do your homework, don't you?"

He was whisked away to a makeup room where a glum woman in a white smock surveyed him without interest, patted his face with a dusting of beige powder, and said, "You'll do." Retrieved by the girl who had deposited him in Sammy's office, he was led over snaky cables and past cardboard commercials urging the purchase of depilatories, laxatives, deodorants, and dog foods to the set of the Sam Stack show. Jeff Davis Troutman was explaining the horrors of sexually explicit novels to a sweet-looking little lady of about seventy, who, Randollph guessed, was Miss Lillit, the authority on crocheting.

"Sam will be here in a minute," the girl guide announced, and fled. Abandoned, there was nothing for Randollph to do but introduce himself.

"You pastor of a big fancy church, I unnerstand," Jeff Davis made it sound like an accusation. "Yore church backin' our Chicago crusade against filth and smut?"

"I'm an interim pastor," Randollph informed him, "and I have barely arrived on the scene. I'm afraid I am uninformed about your crusade. I heard of it only this evening." He hoped he had sidetracked Jeff Davis but felt certain the evangelist wasn't that easily put off. Jeff Davis was plying him four-color promotional folders and explaining

73

how a financial contribution from each church in the city was earnestly desired ("After all, we doin' yo' work for ya," he pronounced), when Sammy arrived and hustled them into place.

"This is *Sam Stack's Chicago*," Sammy, perched on a high stool, informed the glass eye of the camera staring at her. "I'm Sam. Tonight our first guest is Miss Aretta Lillit—"

"Arbetha," Miss Lillit corrected her.

"Oh, damn," Sam said. "Sorry, reverend gentlemen," nodding to Randollph and Troutman. "Start it over, Frankie. This time, Sammy," she addressed herself severely, "get it right."

She got it right. Miss Lillit, perched uncertainly on a twin stool, said yes, she was the author of *Crochet Your Way to a Happy Day*, and enlarged on the psychological and spiritual benefits of a passionate devotion to the art of crocheting. Miss Lillit mentioned the title of her book fourteen times. Randollph counted them. Sammy shot no blunt questions at Miss Lillit, but then, Randollph supposed, a maiden lady who was an authority on crochet and who lived in Wheaton was likely to have led a somewhat uneventful life.

When Sam got Jeff Davis Troutman on the stool, though, Randollph got a preview of the sort of thing he was in for. Sam sweetly brought out the facts that he was a widely known Christian crusader against communism and now was taking on the menace of pornography. Jeff Davis began an arm-waving peroration against *Playboy* magazine when Sam cut him off abruptly.

"Reverend Troutman, what was your income last year?"

Jeff Davis, derailed, gaped and stuttered.

"Who, why. . . ."

"How much?" Sam insisted.

Recovered, Jeff Davis launched into a speech which told Randollph that the evangelist was dealing with a familiar question.

"Well, now, Miz Stack, I don't rightly know the answer to that question. I don't worry 'bout money. The Lord provides."

"The Lord is a good provider," Sam said, referring to a sheaf of notes. "He has provided you with two Cadillacs and a Lincoln Continental Mark IV—all brand-new."

"And all white," Jeff Davis told her proudly, "white for purity." He was at ease now. "Y'all don't understand. People what support me

74

don't want a Christian crusader ridin' to battle in no raggedy lil Chevy. No, sir. They want the Lord's servant to ride in style."

After that, Sam couldn't shake him. Randollph thought she had thrown him out when she said, "Reverend Troutman, you are crusading against *Playboy* magazine and its pictures of unrobed girls?"

"That's right. It's a downright sinful corrupter of innocent young minds—"

"And you are against lewd and lascivious thoughts?"

"You betcha I am! Why—"

Randollph tuned him out.

Having witnessed Jeff Davis Troutman under the gun, Randollph was wary when it came his turn to perch on the stool. Besides, Sammy had warned him that she had done her homework. She identified him, welcomed him pleasantly, then asked, "You are a professional clergyman?"

"Not really. I'm a professional teacher. I am, however, an ordained clergyman."

"Are you a religious man?"

Randollph hadn't expected that. He tried to answer thoughtfully.

"If you mean by that do I spend long hours in devotional activities or do I hold conventional pious attitudes, then no, I'm not a religious man."

"Were you ever that kind of religious man?" Sammy pressed him.

"Yes." Randollph did not amplify the answer. He knew what she was getting at, but let her dig it out, he thought.

"At what period of your life were you a religious man?"

"During my college years. I went to a small denominational school where religious fervor was encouraged," Randollph explained.

Sammy shuffled through a folder of notes. "Ah, here it is," she said, fishing out a paper. "I have here some excerpts from a cover story in *Sports Illustrated* a few years back. It says, 'Los Angeles Rams' Quarterback C. P. Randolph—Randolph spelled with one *l* instead of two *l*'s as you spell it," Sammy interpolated, looking up at her guest, " 'doesn't have a great arm. He is not a devastating runner. He is an outstanding ball handler, but that isn't enough to get by in the pros. Yet Sunday after Sunday, he beats you. He beats you this way one week, and that way another week. One NFL coach says,

"Randolph shouldn't even be able to move a team in this league, no more than he's got going for him. But the blank-blank is a blank mind reader. He has an uncanny knowledge of the defense's state of mind at any given moment. You expect him to do the unexpected, so he sets you up for it, and then he does the expected. Or the other way around. And he does have fast hands, like a shell game operator at a carnival. But basically Randolph has the psychology and the soul of a confidence man. He sells us the Brooklyn Bridge Sunday after Sunday, and we keep buying it. No wonder they nicknamed him Con. It's the only appropriate name for him."'"

Sammy looked up again.

"Are you Con Randolph?"

"Yes," he said.

"Were you," Sammy asked, glancing briefly at her notes, "a member of the Association of Athletes for Christ, and were you on its staff of evangelists?"

"Yes," he answered.

"You quit professional football at the height of your career," she said, "and you dropped out of the Association of Athletes for Christ at about the same time. Why?"

"Because they both seemed unreal."

"You ought to explain that, Dr. Randollph," she instructed him.

Randollph thought a moment before replying. "I became convinced that playing a boy's game was no way for a grown man to spend his best years," he said. "And, concomitantly, I became convinced that, however sincere, the Association of Athletes for Christ portrayed a view of reality to which I could not subscribe."

"So you put it all behind you?"

"Yes."

"Is that why you changed the spelling of your name, adding an extra *l*? Something like Jacob who changed his name when he changed his nature? You see," she said pertly, "I went to Sunday school, too."

"Something like that," he said. "Also, to be honest, it's an affectation. Randolph with one *l* is very common. Randollph with two *l*'s is unusual. I am not exempt from the compulsions of the ego. Besides"—he smiled—"it puts me first among Randolph's in the phone book."

76

Sammy Stack, who, Randollph had been thinking, was Lieutenant Casey's equal at interrogation, abandoned her aggressive questioning.

"I think you have a perfectly fascinating personal history, Con Randolph, and I'd like to have you back on the show to explore it in depth. But now, we'd better ask the question all our viewers will be wondering about. Most of us have heard by now that Mrs. Wardlow Reedman, a well-known name in Chicago society, was murdered in the choir room of the Church of the Good Shepherd last night. Do you want to say anything about it? Does anyone know why she was murdered? I won't insist if you'd rather not talk about it."

Randollph had given a lot of thought to what he was going to say on the subject of the murder. He had decided that the less said the better.

"I can add very little to what the newspaper stories have already reported," he said, picking his verbal trail carefully. "Mrs. Reedman was a popular and valued member of our choir. None of her many friends at Good Shepherd can imagine anyone having a motive for killing her. Of course," he added, "someone did. I'm sure that Lieutenant Michael Casey, who is heading the investigation, will soon get to the bottom of it. Lieutenant Casey," he tacked on, remembering that a bit of public praise might do the lieutenant's career no harm, "impresses me as being an unusually competent investigator."

"Well, it's too bad it had to happen, and especially at the beginning of your stint—is stint the right word for a clergyman's job?—at Good Shepherd. We all hope it will soon be cleared up. And now," Sammy said brightly, a change of tone and mood putting strangled corpses and nude victims out of mind, "why don't we join our other guests—right after this commercial message, of course for the next portion of *Sam Stack's Chicago?*"

The sitting-around-drinking-coffee-and-chatting-with-the-guests portion of Sam Stack's show got going on the subject of professional football because Jeff David Toutman was entranced by the revelation that the Reverend Dr. C. P. Randollph was in fact Con Randolph, widely known, wily professional quarterback.

"You ol' Con Randolph for a fack?" he asked. "Why, boy, I was one of your big fans! I recollect once when y'all was playin' the Saints —that's a professional football team," he explained to the ladies, then

77

regaled them with a tale of Con Randolph's extrication of the Rams from certain defeat and leading them to ultimate victory.

"It seems strange," Sammy interrupted Jeff Davis before he could run off with the ball, "that you would quit your career to go to a seminary. It's a little like entering a monastery, isn't it?"

Randollph chuckled. "I never thought of it that way, but the analogy isn't too inexact." He thought of the honey-haired starlet who had given him an impersonal but remarkably athletic night not long before he traded football for the seminary. He wondered if the starlet, whose name he could not now remember, had been the agent of his renunciation.

"Why?" Sammy was asking him.

"Why what?"

"Why did you go back to school?"

"Because I had collected quite a number of questions to which I did not have the answers. I went back looking for answers."

"Did you find them?"

"To some, yes. Mostly no. Some questions don't have any answers."

"Then your search was a failure?"

"Not at all. You've learned something important when you learn to live with mystery."

"Now there I gotta disagree with you." Jeff Davis Troutman apparently couldn't be kept offstage long. "No question humans can think up, there isn't an answer for it in the Good Book. Yessir. Why'd you quit preachin' for AAC? Lotta good ol' Christian boys in that group. Why'd you quit?"

"Because," Randollph said, "I decided I didn't know what I was talking about."

Not knowing what one was talking about did not appeal to Jeff Davis as a cogent reason to quit talking.

"All you gotta do," he explained, "is tell the kids to make that touchdown for Jesus, kick that field goal for Christ." He illustrated with a swipe at an imaginary ball with the toe of a hand-tooled cowboy boot. "That's money in the bank for the Lord. Man, I'd like to have ol' Con Randolph on my team. How about sharin' the platform with me at the kickoff for the crusade against filth and smut?"

78

"No," Randollph said.

Jeff Davis was shocked. "Whatsammatter, you favor dirty words and lewd pictures?"

"Oh, dear," said Miss Lillit.

"No," Randollph answered. "I favor any man's freedom to read or see whatever he likes. And I do not wish to be identified with your commercial exploitation of some people's desire to be their brother's censor. Particularly since you are on the wrong side of the issue."

"Dr. Randollph," Sammy said, firmly cutting off Jeff Davis Troutman, "what does the C. P. stand for?"

Randollph hesitated. "Cesare Paul," he told her with a weak grin. "Don't laugh."

"Cesare," Miss Lillit bubbled, "why, I have a cat named Cesare."

"Cesare!" Sammy exclaimed. "Good Lord."

"It does have a dubious sound to it, doesn't it? Cesare, I mean. Like decadent Mediterranean courts and sins too repugnant to mention. I expect my mother, an inveterate reader of novels, had been reading bad Italian romances about the time I was born. But the Paul part balances it. That's a good New Testament ascetic-type name."

Sammy shook her head in amazement. "I never met a man named Cesare," she said.

Jeff Davis Troutman was squirming with impatience. "About my crusade to eliminate filth an' smut, we gonna enlist every purity-lovin' citizen in Chicago to drive the devil off the newsstands and bookstores, an' theaters—"

"That'll be a big drive, Reverend Troutman," Sammy said. "Dr. Randollph, you quit professional football because, if I heard you right, you thought it not worthy of a serious commitment. Do you, then, dislike professional football?"

"No. I love it. Go to games whenever possible. Watch it on TV."

"Then aren't you being hypocritical?"

"It isn't easy," Randollph answered, "to make our behavior conform to our convictions."

"About my crusade against filth an'—"

"We pause here for a message," Sammy spoke crisply, reading from a cue card off camera. "Have you treated your beloved pet to Doggie Dinner? Watch this demonstration of. . . ."

10

"WELL, I'LL be damned! Hey, Liz, come in here," Michael Casey shouted.

Elizabeth Casey finished folding the shirt she had been ironing, unplugged the iron, and went into the living room of the modest flat.

"What's all the excitement?" she asked. Michael had to keep his cool all day, she knew, so when he was home, he often blew off steam by getting excited over trifles like a big inning by the Cubs or some such foolishness.

"Look, that's the fellow I was telling you about, Randollph, the priest at Good Shepherd Church where the woman was murdered last night."

Elizabeth studied the picture tube for a moment. "He doesn't look like a priest," she said, "but, then, how can you tell these days?"

"He isn't a priest, I guess. Protestants don't call their pastors priests. . . ."

"Episcopalians do," she said.

"Well, anyway, he isn't even a pastor—"

"Then what is he doing running a big important church like Good Shepherd?"

"Well, he is a pastor—"

"Make up your mind," Liz told him.

"Oh, hell, I'll explain it later, just watch."

After a few minutes Elizabeth Casey turned to her husband and asked, "Is he married?"

"Is who married?" Michael Casey was absorbed in watching Sam Stack grill Randollph. She'd make a great policewoman, he thought.

"That Randollph, who else?"

"How would I know?"

"You're a detective, aren't you?" she asked logically.

"Jesus, Liz," Michael exploded, "you don't go around asking personal questions of a big shot like Randollph. He isn't suspect."

Silence. Then Liz said, "I'll bet he has trouble with women."

"Now what do you mean by that?" her husband demanded.

She studied Randollph's image on the tube. "He's good-looking. Polished. Speaks well. Women like men who speak well. Dresses neatly, which shows he respects himself, but also with a little flair, which shows he has imagination. He has dignity, but it just covers a passionate nature, like Lance. . . ."

"Who's Lance?"

"He's Robin's lover in *Matilda Moore's Secret Sorrow,* it's on every day at one thirty—don't interrupt." She continued to study Randollph. "He's got a sense of humor—that's important to women. He's a challenge. Any red-blooded American girl would want to break through that polite shell and release the tiger underneath. Run their fingers through that hair; those little flecks of gray are a sign of maturity. I think that girl that's interviewing him is planning to have a go at it."

Lieutenant Casey stared at his wife in openmouthed amazement.

"Maybe," he said sarcastically, "I ought to stay home and cook and keep house, and you could do my job, you can tell so much just looking at a person on TV."

"I probably could solve your old case just as quick as you can, maybe quicker," she said confidently. "You just hunt for facts, facts, facts. You never look at people as they really are. I could look at your suspects and tell right away which one did it."

"Oh, shit," Casey said.

"Don't be crude, Michael," Liz admonished him. "Now you tell me you're practically certain the husband did it, but you haven't even seen him, so how can you tell if he is the murderer type or not?"

"How can I see him if he's taken it on the lam, maybe somewhere out of the country, maybe Argentina or somewhere, and he's snatched about ten million of the church's money? I don't know whether Randollph even knows yet the money's gone, probably does, though. I got it out of his special auditors. . . ."

Liz interrupted him. "What has stealing ten million dollars got to do with murdering his wife?"

"How the hell should I know?" Casey growled. "Not yet, anyway. I'll find out, though."

"Maybe you will, and maybe you won't," she said. "The important thing is to find out if he is the kind of person who would murder his wife. Maybe she was having a mad affair with this Randollph and her husband found out and strangled her in blind fury."

Liz, Casey decided, was watching altogether too many soap operas.

"No good," he corrected her. "First, Randollph just came here, didn't even know the woman. . . ."

"How do you know? He might have known her before—"

"And anyway," the lieutenant cut her off, "so far as we've been able to check up on her, she was a very straight type, raised conservatively, devoted to the church, popular, apparently happy. Not the type to have a mad affair as you call it. Not the type at all."

"Oh, pish! Any girl's the type to have an affair if the right guy comes along. For a detective who's supposed to have no illusions left you can be awfully naïve, Mike."

Casey eyed his wife speculatively. "What makes you such an expert on affairs?"

"I know." She gave him an impish smile. "I just know. Now tell me what you have found out about the husband. You must have found out something by now."

Casey recited a profile of Ward Reedman.

"He's forty-seven. They'd been married fifteen years. Reedman is an old Chicago family, very social. Meat-packing money originally. His branch of the family was more social than rich, though. His parents both dead. Left him a modest inheritance, which he ran through pretty fast. He was on his uppers until he married. Mrs. Reedman is an heiress. Had a very large trust fund from her maternal grandfather. I gather they lived on her money. She also stands to inherit from her father who is a wealthy Wall Street broker. He set his new son-in-law up in the brokerage business here in Chicago. The business never prospered. The only big piece of business Reedman had was the church's endowment funds. He got that because he's a trustee of the church—there's always a Reedman who is a trustee, Randollph tells me."

"Well, that's all very interesting," Liz said, "but what kind of person is he?"

"Mr. Gantry—the Reverend Mr. Gantry—who is one of the pastors at Good Shepherd, says Reedman is a bastard. One of the world's great bastards is how he put it, if I remember correctly."

"My, my, they must have an unusual type of pastor at Good Shepherd," Liz remarked.

"Well, it turns out Gantry's description is pretty accurate," Casey continued. "Reedman is a gambler, a woman chaser, has a mean streak in him. We couldn't find a person who really liked him."

"Did his wife like him?"

"Oh, we've looked into that," Casey answered. "There is every indication that they pretty much went their separate ways."

"Then he didn't kill her," Liz pronounced.

"What? How could you know that?"

"Because," she explained patiently, "a man like that, he's utterly selfish. He doesn't care enough about anyone to kill them. Maybe for money, if he thought he could get away with it. But he's already got ten million dollars. I mean, how many millions do you need?"

Casey pondered that, turning his attention back to the program. Suddenly he sat up. "Hey, Liz, did you hear that? He's Con Randollph! How about that! I wouldn't have guessed, seen him play many a time, but I wouldn't have guessed. Boy, is that impressive!"

"I'm not impressed," Liz stated.

"Why not, for heaven's sake?"

"What's so impressive about men putting on knickers and funny helmets and banging each other around?" she asked. "Now, he had the good sense to quit; that impresses me."

Casey decided he'd never understand his wife's reasoning processes. "Here comes a commercial. Get me a beer, will you, hon?" he asked.

"Yes, master," she said, and went to the kitchen.

While Sammy Stack devoted her charm to selling a brand of corned beef hash, Casey considered what Liz had said. He wasn't going to give up on Ward Reedman as the best bet for the murderer. You had to follow out your most likely line of investigation first, confirm it or eliminate it. The motive was elusive, but you could count on spouses having motives, and who else, for heaven's sake, would have wanted this attractive young matron dead? His money was on Ward Reedman, ten to one at least.

"And another thing," Liz said, putting a sweaty can of beer on the table beside her husband's chair, "she was having an affair."

"Oh, Christ, Liz, now how could you know a thing like that? You have second sight or something?"

"It's easy," Liz replied, unperturbed. "She was married to a creep like Reedman, but all her friends say she was a very happy person. Now Reedman wasn't making her happy, so someone else was. See?"

Casey wasn't sure that he saw.

"Listen," Liz told him, "Randollph's talking about you." Her husband, she observed fondly, gulping cold beer and hearing himself praised on television, looked like a very happy man.

"Say," he said at the next commercial break, "I hope some of the department brass are watching. It won't hurt me a bit if they hear that."

"I hope they do, Mike," she said tenderly. "I just want them to hear what they probably know and what I know, that you're very good at your job."

He reached over and pulled her onto his lap, cupping a hand over her breast. "Lady," he said, "I feel good! I feel great! I feel like demanding my connubial rights. As a good Catholic girl, you can't deny me."

"As a good Catholic girl who practices birth control and believes women are more than objects, I can and I would deny you," she said, kissing him on the top of his head. "But I don't want to deny you. Let's go to bed—copper."

11

RANDOLLPH HAD left word with the bishop's secretary to have Freddie call him as soon as possible after returning from his clerical powwow. The phone rang at 7 A.M. Saturday, rousing Randollph from a restless sleep.

"C.P.? What an awful thing to have happen!"

"What? Who?" Randollph's sleep-insulated mind slowly began to function. "Oh, Freddie." He flung back the gold silk coverlet that made him think of a bed in a harem and swung his feet to the floor. "We need to talk, soon as possible. I'm so glad to hear your voice I won't complain about you calling me in the middle of the night. Where are you? At home?"

"No, in the office. When I go away for a day or two, I have to make up for it, you know. I'm up here talking to my dictating machine."

"Well, come up here and talk to me instead. Mrs. Creedy'll be here in half an hour to fix breakfast. Have breakfast with me. I need your episcopal guidance."

"Fine," the bishop said. "I've breakfasted, but a cup of coffee is always welcome."

So, under the unmotherly eye of Mrs. Creedy, Randollph plowed through a plate of ham and fried eggs while the bishop sipped coffee.

"Glad to see all this trouble hasn't ruined your appetite," the bishop said.

"Hardly anything does, not for breakfast anyway. I can be temperate at lunch or dinner, but not for breakfast. Mrs. Creedy's cooking slowed me down until I discovered that while she can't scramble or poach eggs fit to eat, she does fry them passably. And she does make an excellent oatmeal."

"Most Calvinists can," the bishop said. "It apparently fits their idea of food tasteless enough to be no great sensate pleasure, but wholesome enough to sustain life. I believe, if you don't mind, I'll have a wee piece of toast with some of that luscious-looking gooseberry jam. One hardly ever sees gooseberry jam anymore."

"It's a minor passion of mine," Randollph said. "Be my guest. But we'd better get down to business. What do I do next?"

"According to what I read in the morning paper, no one has any idea who killed that poor girl."

"It's sin," Mrs. Creedy announced. She had come into the breakfast room silently, whisking away Randollph's plate before he'd had a chance to sop up the last bit of egg with his toast. Mrs. Creedy, as she frequently proclaimed, couldn't stand anything messy.

"Sin, Mrs. Creedy?" the bishop asked.

"That dead woman in the basement," Mrs. Creedy snapped. "Sin did it."

"Well, of course, murder is always a sin," the bishop said.

"That's not what I mean, you ought to know that." Mrs. Creedy was not awed by bishops. "You mark my word, the strong right arm of the Lord reached out and smote a sinner."

"You mean," Randollph asked her, "that you have evidence Mrs. Reedman was a sinner? Above and beyond," he hastily added, "the original sin we all inherit."

"Don't need evidence," Mrs. Creedy answered with the certainty of the righteous. "Something like this happens, it's the work of the Lord. Every time." She left abruptly. Mrs. Creedy did not believe in unprofitable conversations.

"Ah, well." The bishop sighed. "It may have been the strong arm of the Lord that struck down that girl, but I expect the police will be wanting something more specific before they make an arrest. Is there anything the police think that isn't in the papers? They must have some suspicions."

"Lieutenant Casey, who's in charge, leans toward the husband."

"Ward Reedman? An unprepossessing man, to be sure, but a murderer? I find that hard to imagine. Why does the lieutenant suspect him?"

"Because he claims that the surviving spouse is always the most likely suspect in a murder case. Also, I expect that the fact Ward Reedman seems to have disappeared tends to confirm his theory."

"Good heavens! Reedman's not to be found?"

"No."

"Now that will be lovely. A trustee of Good Shepherd murders his wife. How are we to explain that to the public? He could have at least had the grace to do it somewhere other than on church property."

"Ever the administrator, eh, Freddie?" Randolph needled him.

The bishop reached for another piece of toast and smeared it liberally with gooseberry jam. "I can't bring that poor girl back to life, C.P. That's beyond the powers vouchsafed even to a bishop. The police are far more able to track down the murderer than I, even if I fancied myself a detective. What I can do, and what I am charged with doing, is to minimize the shock to the public and especially to our constituents."

"And just how do you propose to do that?"

The bishop patted his belly. "My, that was good! I don't know how I'm to do it, C.P. Murder in a soundproofed choir practice room in the very depths of a large city church does have a spooky quality. Very stimulating to the public imagination, I'm afraid. Also stimulating to the press."

"A quiet place for dying, that choir room," Randolph said, "but it's causing a lot of noise. And, Freddie, you haven't heard all the bad news yet."

"Oh, dear." The bishop winced. "I was hoping I had."

"Telephone for you, Dr. Randolph," Mrs. Creedy announced sourly, placing a phone on the table but leaving Randolph to plug it into the jack. "The man says it's important."

The caller identified himself as one of the Mr. Burns of Burns, Burns and Murphy, auditors. "Mr. Gantry employed us to audit Mr. Wardlow Reedman's accounts relating to endowment investments for the Church of the Good Shepherd," he explained, "and to inventory securities held by the church. He asked us to do it as rapidly as possible and report to you."

"Yes, I know."

"You are aware that Mr. Reedman is, er, temporarily absent?"

87

"Yes."

"That made our job quite difficult, or perhaps easy. We couldn't do an audit because we were unable to locate the records for Good Shepherd."

"I see," said Randollph, seeing all too well.

"Also," Mr. Burns continued, "we were unable to locate any securities belonging to Good Shepherd. We searched very thoroughly. There is nothing in the lockbox at Reedman's office in which, according to his secretary, he ordinarily kept the church's stocks and bonds. Inquiries among sources of information we have in the business community—most discreet inquiries, I assure you—have turned up the information that Mr. Reedman has been selling heavily for the past several months. Nothing to indicate he was selling stocks and bonds belonging to the church. This is a preliminary report, of course, and we'll continue our investigation if you wish."

"Please do."

"But, Dr. Randollph, I think it only fair to tell you that our considerable experience in this area leads us to believe that there are no securities in the name of the Church of the Good Shepherd to be found at Wardlow Reedman and Company, Stockbrokers."

Randollph hung up and looked very, very thoughtful.

"I must say, C.P.," the bishop said, gazing out toward the lake, "that though I have misgivings about very rich churches—leads to all sorts of unchristian attitudes in my experience—it does sometimes have advantages. This magnificent view! A poor church couldn't afford such a penthouse parsonage as this."

"Perhaps then, Freddie, you will be relieved to know that, as of now, you have one less rich church."

"What do you mean?" The bishop paused as he was about to dig into the jam again.

Randollph told him.

Randollph had never seen the bishop look so stricken. "Ten million dollars," he said, tapping a knife against his plate as if counting it. "That rascal absconded with the church's ten million dollars. And murdered his wife for good measure. Ten million dollars. And I could have prevented it."

"How so, Freddie?"

"By following my instincts, my intuition earlier. I could have instigated a formal investigation immediately when I felt that something was wrong, somehow, at Good Shepherd. I suppose there is no doubt that it is gone?"

"That was our special auditor I just talked to," Randollph said. "He will keep looking for our securities, but he has no real doubts they are gone. Money missing, along with the man who had charge of it, is a pattern with which I expect he is all too familiar."

"How could he have managed it?" the bishop asked. "How does one suddenly cart away ten million dollars in securities?"

"Bearer bonds. Swiss or Panamanian numbered bank accounts," Randollph answered. "But one doesn't do it suddenly. He must have been converting the church's securities into transportable funds for some time. Remember, no one ever questioned the reports he submitted to the trustees—not even the auditors."

"Smelser should have questioned it." The bishop sighed. "But then, we know why he didn't. Awful thing, rampant ambition. Ten million dollars! No man should be exposed to that much temptation. It would strain even the sturdiest sense of ethical responsibility. And to a man a little short in moral character—a man like Reedman—it would be irresistible. Do you suppose Mrs. Creedy would fix me another slice of toast? When I'm agitated, I find solace in food."

"I'll ring her," Randollph said. "I'll ask for two slices, because you're going to need it after I tell you that the coroner says Marianne Reedman had sexual intercourse shortly before her death."

The bishop looked stricken again. "Why? Why?"

"Because some man wanted to copulate with her and either forced her or enlisted her cooperation."

"I don't mean that." The bishop looked exasperated. "I know why. And how. I was asking why the Lord has sent us this extra burden. Not having ever served as a parish pastor, C.P., I wouldn't expect you to know this. But ask any pastor. Sex is the worst thing to have coupled with a church—no, I'll rephrase that, it sounds like a bad pun. The wise pastor avoids preaching about, teaching, discussing sex. It is one of our middle-class Christian taboos. But to have it going on in the choir room and mixed up with murder—well, this is just too much!"

"Wringing our hands won't do any good, Freddie."

"No, of course not." The bishop straightened up. "There isn't much we can do, but there is something."

"Enlighten me," Randollph said.

"For the good of the church, we've got to suppress the news of Mr. Reedman's defalcation. If it gets out that our financial procedures are so careless as to permit a church official to lift ten million dollars, it would endanger contributions not only to Good Shepherd, but to all our churches. Financial mismanagement in one place casts suspicion on the whole institution. We'd be years recovering."

Randollph hadn't thought of that.

"You'll be dealing with this policeman who is in charge of the investigation, what's his name?"

"Lieutenant Michael Casey," Randollph supplied.

"Would it be possible to withhold the information about Mr. Reedman's purloining the church's securities from him?"

"Now who's getting ethically confused?" Randollph rebuked him. "No, it wouldn't be possible. First, because it is evidence which may be relevant to a murder. And second, if you had met Lieutenant Casey, you would realize that he doesn't miss much. He certainly would ferret out this kind of information—maybe already has. He knows we were planning an inventory of the church's securities."

"You're right, of course," the bishop said. "I find it easier to make moral choices for others than for myself. Still and all, I've got to do what I can to protect the institution. That's a moral responsibility too."

"What can you do?"

"I can call the police commissioner and see to it that Mr. Reedman's fiscal shenanigans are treated as evidence for police use only and not to be divulged to the public. I am morally opposed to people in high places using their influence to withhold information from the public," the bishop said, "except, of course, when it is information that might damage me."

Randollph pondered that for a moment. "Well, Freddie, you could rationalize it on the grounds that you expect the money to be recovered shortly and that no good purpose can be served by advertising the unsavory details of its temporary loss."

"It's a lame rationalization," the bishop replied. "But then, when you've already made up your mind what you are going to do, a lame rationalization is better than none." He picked up the phone.

12

"I HAVEN'T made up my mind," Samantha Stack said, solemnly as a diplomat pondering a subclause in a treaty.

"Oh?" Randollph responded, slivering a forkful of rosy flesh from the salmon mayonnaise on his plate. "You haven't made up your mind about what?"

"Whether to seduce you or not."

Randollph choked.

"Don't sputter," she told him. "Now on the one hand, you're a very attractive man—"

"Thanks," Randollph managed to mutter through his napkin.

"Don't interrupt," Sam said. "But do I find you attractive mostly because you're so different from the creeps I work with, they all think I should be thrilled to roll over for them anytime, and you haven't even tried a teeny little pass—"

"One doesn't pass, as a rule, so early in the game." Randollph decided the best defense against this charmingly brash young lady was to match her patter.

Miss Windfall had buzzed him while he was in conference with a wretched and scared O. B. Smelser. "There is a Samantha Stack calling," she said. "I told her you were engaged, but she insists on speaking to you. Do you wish me to tell her you are unavailable?" Miss Windfall clearly believed that the pastor of the Church of the Good Shepherd should be unavailable to pert and demanding young ladies.

"No," Randollph said, "I'll talk to her."

"This is take-an-ex-jock-to-lunch week," Sammy, without preamble, announced, "and I have chosen you to be my guest. So meet me at the Ninety-fifth in Big John—that's the John Hancock Building. Twelve thirty OK?"

"Twelve thirty is OK, and I am very grateful for the invitation." Randollph spoke gravely into the phone.

"You'll be even more grateful when you see the prices in that joint," Sammy said. "See you," and hung up.

It was pleasanter, Randollph found, to think of lunch with Samantha than to come to grips with the grubby problem of O. B. Smelser. So he told Smelser that they would postpone their conference as he was unexpectedly called away. Smelser looked as relieved as Randollph felt.

If his job entailed enduring a smarmy O. B. Smelser, Randollph thought as he surveyed the high-ceilinged opulence of the 95th, it also included listening to a fetching redhead debate the pros and cons of seducing him.

"There's this against it, though," Sammy was saying, ignoring Randollph's riposte. "I'd be getting involved with a preacher. No girl in her right mind would do that."

"Oh? And why not?" Randollph sounded defensive and wished that he didn't.

"Because she might actually fall in love with him, and marry him, and then have to live in some crummy old parsonage in some God-forsaken place, and have to wear mended pantyhose, and be sweet to nasty old ladies, and never be able to swear. Did anyone ever tell you you look like a sensual John Calvin?"

Flabbergasted, Randollph managed to reply that a sensual John Calvin was a contradiction in terms.

"I know that, silly," Sammy said. "I was raised a Presbyterian. We had pictures of John Calvin all over the church, we called him old J.C. Isn't that funny, he has the same initials as Jesus Christ. Some of our pastors confused the two, I'm sure. No one could imagine a sensual John Calvin, the old bugger. But I still say that's what you look like."

Randollph was helpless in the face of this logic.

"And speaking of sensual, I see by the papers that the late Mrs. Reedman—let me think of some prissy way to say it fit for delicate clerical ears—had carnal connection shortly before she died. Imagine poking around in a dead body to find that out. Ugh! What do you suppose happened—by the way, what the hell do I call you?"

"You might call me the Reverend Dr. Randollph." That ought to slow her down, he thought.

"Don't be a dope," Sammy said. "What do your good friends call you?"

"Most of them call me by my initials, C.P."

"That won't do. I don't care for it. How do you pronounce that goofy first name of yours?"

"Che-sah-ray." Randollph sounded it out for her. "Go a little soft on the *ray*."

"How weird," she said. "It has an evil sound. I'll call you Chess or maybe just Randollph—Randollph sounds like a first name—whichever suits me at the moment. Now tell me if Marianne Reedman had a last passionate rendezvous with her lover there in the choir room, and they made mad love, and then he killed her. I know you don't know, but guess."

"That little fact that she had, as you put it, carnal connection shortly before she died has everyone guessing," Randollph told her, "including Lieutenant Casey. It just doesn't fit into the picture."

"I don't see why not," Sammy said.

"It doesn't fit into the picture we are able to put together of Marianne Reedman. Oh, I know," Randollph forestalled Sammy's interruption. "You are going to say that just because she didn't seem like the kind of girl who had a lover doesn't mean that she didn't have one. It only means that she was very discreet about it."

"So?" Sammy said.

"Well," Randollph went on, between bites of a very tasty wilted lettuce salad he wished he could persuade Mrs. Creedy to duplicate but knew he probably couldn't, "try to imagine the scene. Marianne Reedman, using her convenient duty as choir librarian to linger after everyone has left, waits for her lover to appear. How is she feeling?"

"Horny," Sam Stack said.

Randollph choked on a bit of crisp bacon. "Er, yes. So when this nameless chap shows up, she—"

"She cries, 'Darling,' throws wide her arms." Sammy animatedly enacted the part and knocked a menu from the hand of a hovering waiter. "Oh, sorry." She gave him a dazzling smile. "We're rehearsing a play."

"Quite so, madam." The waiter, accustomed to the foibles of the kind of people who could afford to dine in this restaurant, was imperturbable. "Would madam care for a sweet?"

"Madam would, but madam has to watch her figure or other people won't watch it. That's a joke," she explained to the waiter.

"Quite so, madam," the waiter replied gravely. "You, sir?"

"Just coffee," Randollph said. "Anyway, she rushes into his arms, passion rising, insistent—"

"My, my, how poetic."

"As I was saying before I was so rudely interrupted"—Randollph grinned at her—"does she then carefully remove her clothes and fold them neatly on a chair? No. My impression is that a lady in the grip of, ah, the mating urge, disrobes hastily—and remember, this is probably taking place in a darkened room—and scatters her garments where they chance to fall."

Sammy gave him an impish smile. "Dear the Reverend Dr. Cesare Paul Randollph, how would you know about that?"

"I read racy novels," Randollph answered. "Doesn't the heroine always breathlessly urge the hero to 'Oh, hurry, hurry'?"

"I think the clergy is getting altogether too worldly," Sam said. "But, yes, I admit that's the way I would act under the circumstances you describe. I'd shuck out of my dress and scatter bra and panties and that stuff wherever it fell." Randollph hoped she wouldn't actually act out this scene, although he was sure it would be interesting.

The waiter brought coffee, serving it with a wary eye on Sammy.

"So Lieutenant Casey feels he doesn't have enough facts, and he can't arrange the ones he does have into a pattern," Randollph explained to her. "A murder without apparent motive, connected with sex but the connection unclear, nothing about this business falls into place. It's a picture out of focus. No wonder Casey's frustrated. So am I. I'd like to get on with learning what it's like to be pastor of a church, but mostly I'm wrapped up in a particularly unpleasant murder which happened on our premises and involves members of the church."

"You're a picture out of focus," Sammy said.

Randollph was surprised. "I'm afraid I don't understand that remark," he said.

"Preachers should be sweet old duffers in frowsy black suits that take tea with the ladies and say uplifting things in an unctuous voice," Sammy said. "Big-name football players do not turn into preachers—"

"It is not unprecedented," Randollph protested.

"—and when clergymen dress like, well, smart, and talk like David Brinkley and . . . and know how ladies in the grip of the mating urge behave—well, it just confuses people. I just can't figure you out, Reverend Dr. Cesare Paul Randollph."

Randollph erupted in laughter so uproarious it drew the attention of several adjacent tables. "Perhaps," he told Sammy, "at the end of my year at Good Shepherd I'll have acquired the manners and the unction necessary to fit your stereotype of the clergy."

"God forbid!" Sammy snapped back at him.

"Let me tell you how happy I am that this was take-an-ex-jock-to-lunch week and that I was the recipient of your beneficence," Randollph said as Sammy signed the check. "I understand that take-a-beautiful-lady-television-star-to-dinner week is coming up, and I wonder if you would care to be my guest?"

"See," Sammy said.

Randollph didn't see.

"I mean, see, you don't talk like a preacher at all." She regarded him thoughtfully, then said, "As to that decision about whether I'm going to—"

"Yes, ah, um." Randollph thought it best to divert the trend of the conversation.

"I'll let you know." Sammy beamed on him. "I'll let you know."

13

RANDOLLPH COULDN'T remember exactly when it was that he decided to become a detective. Perhaps it was when Lieutenant Casey said, "This murder just doesn't make sense." Again, maybe he made up his mind when the bishop replied to Casey, rather petulantly, Randollph thought, "Well, I wish something could be done to clear it up quickly. It isn't doing the church any good having this lurid crime hovering over it like a dark Satan's presence." He made a mental note to speak to Freddie about curbing this predilection for purple theological prose.

Returning, euphoric, from his lunch with Samantha Stack, Randollph stopped by Miss Windfall's office to ascertain what, if anything, had transpired in his absence.

"The bishop asked you to call him," Miss Windfall told Randollph with the solemn grandeur of a cardinal archbishop sanctioning a dogma. Randollph was aware that Miss Windfall considered mayors, senators, bank presidents, or for that matter ex-football heroes as mere spear carriers on life's stage when a bishop was one of the players. She might not like the bishop personally. She might just barely know him. No matter. His slightest request had the force of a royal summons. Randollph determined never to refer to the bishop as Freddie in Miss Windfall's presence.

What the bishop wanted, it turned out, was a talk with the policeman in charge of investigating the murder and finding Wardlow Reedman. Could Randollph arrange it? And bring Dan Gantry along. This concerned the church. Might as well make it a council of war.

The Chicago police department, Randollph discovered, rated

bishops at approximately the lofty level Miss Windfall reserved for them. Even Protestant bishops. Informed that the bishop desired a conference with Lieutenant Casey, the police department hurriedly located Lieutenant Casey and sped him to the Shep Building.

So Casey, Randollph, and Dan Gantry paraded into the bishop's office, interrupting a surprised Keith Farmer, the bishop's fat little assistant, in the midst of a chat with the secretary-receptionist.

"Hello, monsignor," Dan Gantry jocularly addressed the bishop's assistant. "What's cooking up here in the chancery these days? Issued any bulls recently? Excommunicated any heretics?"

"Hello, Dan," Farmer said without enthusiasm. "I'll tell the bishop you're here."

"No need for that," the bishop said from the doorway of his office. "Anyone with average hearing can tell when Dan is here. Come in, gentlemen."

"Sorry to interrupt your important conference, Keith," Dan said as he stepped into the bishop's office. Farmer glared helplessly at his tormentor.

Randollph presented Casey to the bishop, who said, "You're young for a detective lieutenant."

"I've been fortunate, your"—Casey fumbled for a proper title for a prince of the church clad in a white shirt and foulard tie—"your grace."

"I'm afraid that appellation doesn't apply," the bishop informed him with a smile. "You see, we—I suppose you'd call us separated brethren—have pretty much secularized the hierarchy. Since you must call me something, 'bishop' will do very nicely. And as to your good fortune in achieving the grade of detective lieutenant so early, it is my observation that fortune tends to smile on those who deserve it. Now," he said, in a now-that-the-amenities-have-been-taken-care-of-let's-get-down-to-business tone, "could we talk about where we stand as to the resolution of this unfortunate affair which so perturbs us all? Have you made any progress in locating Mr. Reedman?"

Ah, Freddie, you do have a keen sense of priorities, Randollph thought. The girl's dead and can't be resurrected until the last trump blows, which may be sometime yet. But Ward Reedman is presumably alive and well and spending our ten million dollars God knows how rapidly, so each day he is unapprehended is another day of nail-biting anxiety for us administrators.

"Nothing definite yet, but we're working every angle." Casey smoothed the lapels of his faultless blue double-breasted blazer. A good Catholic lad, no matter how sophisticated, was apt to be nervous in the presence of a bishop, Randollph supposed. Even a bishop in mufti.

"What are the assumptions you are using as the basis of your investigation?" the bishop queried.

Casey quickly became the professional policeman. "We assume, first, that he'd been planning this for some time. No one can convert ten million dollars of securities into portable form on a day's notice. Nor is it easy to vanish into thin air at a moment's whim."

"I can see that," said the bishop. "But why the particular moment he chose? Coincidence?"

"We think he had to speed up his timetable because of the trustees' meeting," Casey replied. "Dr. Randollph has related the substance of the meeting. Apparently he was firm in his insistence on an inventory of the church's securities, and that it be done immediately. Reedman would have known that the game was up; it was now or never. But he couldn't have managed it unless he'd planned it well ahead."

"So he planned it well ahead," Dan commented, "but where's the jerk now?"

Casey was patient, but not apologetic. "You have to remember, Dan, that we've only had a day or two to look for him. He's left traces, and we'll find them. My guess is he got out of the country carrying a false passport. But I have no basis for that except a hunch, and I don't trust hunches."

"Meanwhile," the bishop said mournfully, "he's got the church's ten million. Is it your theory that he stopped by the choir room and killed his wife on the way out of town?"

"It's the best theory we've got at the moment," Casey answered not very confidently.

"Any suppositions as to why?"

"About what you would expect. There are indications that Reedman and his wife were not entirely compatible. Went their separate ways. And you are aware, Bishop, of the evidence that Mrs. Reedman had a, well, a lover?" Casey was embarrassed to call a bishop's attention to the messy details of sin in the choir room.

"I am aware of it," the bishop said, "but surely, Lieutenant, you are not suggesting that her husband found her in the choir room and made love to her as a prelude to strangling her?"

"I admit it doesn't seem very likely, but—"

"Then who did make love to her? And where was he when, as you think, her husband strangled her?"

That was when Casey said this murder didn't make sense. And after the bishop said he wished it would be cleared up rapidly, Randollph said, "This murder made sense to whoever did it."

"Oh, yes, I understand that," Casey said. "We'll turn up a motive, all right. We need time, time to assemble more facts."

"I yield to no man, not even you, Lieutenant, in reverence for facts," Randollph assured him. "After all, I'm a historian, and facts are my stock-in-trade. But suppose that the relevant fact escapes you, you can't turn it up."

"We always do, sooner or later," Casey insisted.

"But suppose that Marianne Reedman was done in by someone with an unconventional motive, nothing to do with the common reasons why people kill people—money, or lust, or revenge, or to remove an impediment to some scheme of theirs. What do you do then?"

"We just keep digging. If we can't turn up a standard motive, then we look over our facts for indication of an unconventional motive, as you call it." Casey defended the police doctrine with all the doggedness of a theologian debating the inerrancy of Holy Writ.

Randollph was not convinced. "If you are as familiar with history as I am, and I'm certain you are—"

"I've been to college, Dr. Randollph," Casey interrupted with a grin. Don't look down on me as a dumb flatfoot, he was saying. Randollph guessed that Michael Casey might be suffering from a touch of intellectual pride, brought on, no doubt, from associating with too many Sergeant Garbaskis.

"So you know that people have always committed atrocities for reasons incredible to a normal, balanced mind. Tomás de Torquemada, for instance, slaughtered people wholesale and claimed he was doing them a favor. Very few of us, I suspect, would view being burned at the stake a favor, but Torquemada had no doubt that it was."

"You *would* pick a Roman Catholic example," Casey twitted.

"All right, let's be ecumenical about it. Take John Calvin burning Dr. Servetus. That's a skeleton rattling around in our Protestant closet. He executed Servetus, without qualm or conscience, because Servetus questioned the doctrine of the Trinity. We can't even imagine someone murdering somebody over so trivial an issue—"

"My pastor at St. Aloysius doesn't think the doctrine of the Holy Trinity is a trivial issue." Lieutenant Casey offered a slight rebuke to any cavalier dismissal of Father, Son, and Holy Ghost. "Still, I don't think he'd approve of murder to defend it. I must ask him."

"That's the trouble with theologians today," Dan Gantry said, "no guts."

"My point is," Randollph said, thoroughly warmed up to the subject now, "what would strike a professional policeman as an absurd reason for murdering someone could well appeal to the murderer as the only rational course of action. If history teaches us anything, it is that you can't count on the next fellow having the same perceptions of reality as you have. Unless somehow you know the state of mind of whoever throttled Marianne Reedman, you may be a long time clearing up this mess."

Lieutenant Casey shook his head. "I respect your credentials as a historian, Dr. Randollph, but I doubt that you'd be a very successful homicide detective with those methods. When we have enough facts about Mrs. Reedman—her habits, her associates, her true relationship with her husband, her lover or lovers, if any—then the facts will point to someone. It's our plodding, unimaginative, boring routine that will lead us to the answer. We aren't very romantic or glamorous, detective novels to the contrary, but we are thorough."

"I'm inclined to think you're right," the bishop chimed in. "When I first became a bishop, I was strongly prejudiced in favor of pastors who had a bit of dash and imagination. They create excitement and stir up the people and are, I'm sure, a blessed relief to a congregation which has been relentlessly bored for decades by good, colorless men. But the colorful pastors are fueled by inspiration and dreams, and they forget to call on old Mrs. Griper when her gallbladder is bothering her, and they neglect to raise the money for the church mortgage. I've come to value the pastor who follows a plodding, unimaginative, boring routine as you put it, Lieutenant. No great white light of revelation ever breaks over his congregation, I admit, but you can count on him to get the job done." The bishop looked as if he had just delivered himself of an undeniable but unhappy truth.

Freddie, Freddie, you've been a bishop too long, Randollph mused. I must undertake to rearrange your shockingly mundane priorities. But not here, not now. Instead, he said, "Well, Lieutenant, no one will be happier than I if your routine turns up the information you need. I'd like to get on with the real business of the Church of the Good Shepherd, whatever that is, but it won't be easy until we have the matter of the Reedmans taken care of."

"Has it occurred to you," a genial Casey said to them, "that this crime—assuming that the embezzlement is connected with the murder—has violated not only 'Thou shalt not kill' and 'Thou shalt not steal,' but also, perhaps, 'Thou shalt not commit adultery'? Three of the Ten Commandments shot down in one whack. It isn't every day you get a crime like that." Lieutenant Casey, Randollph thought, was not entirely devoid of imagination.

"I hadn't thought of it, but I don't feel any better now that you've pointed it out to me," the bishop said, rising. "May I count on you to keep us up to date on your progress?"

"Of course," Casey replied. "And please pass along any information you think might help us." This addressed to Dan and Randollph. Randollph considered telling Casey that he had decided to have a go at detecting but then thought better of it. Better see if he could detect something first.

102

14

AT LAST, he thought, at long last I am to discharge a purely pastoral task, do the kind of duty I came here to perform and learn about, feel the feelings a professional clergyman is supposed to feel as he ministers to those that mourn.

Only, Randollph remembered as he draped the black funeral stole over his shoulders and seesawed it until the fringed ends hung evenly, this is a funeral with no mourners. At least no bereaved members of the immediate family. Marianne Reedman's parents, hobbled by age as well as grief, remained in seclusion in Montclair, New Jersey, hoarding strength for the service there tomorrow. Wardlow Reedman, if Lieutenant Casey's hunch was accurate, was disporting himself in the fleshpots of some far country and—unless he had killed her himself—perhaps unaware of his wife's death. There were a few Reedmans from collateral branches of the family in attendance, but they were there more for reasons of social form than to shed tears. Only the choir was there because the deceased was one of them, comrade, meant something to them as a person.

She didn't mean anything to him as a person, Randollph realized, because he hadn't known her. How did a practiced professional pastor, who must have to preside at the obsequies of people little known to him scores of times each year, feel on such occasions? What thoughts coursed through his conscious mind as he read the rites? Randollph inspected his feelings carefully and concluded that he had a sense of loss at the death of Marianne Reedman. A young life wasted. At the least a trained musician capable of contributing her talent shut off forever. A human being for whom life offered years of

103

possibilities, ended, all possibilities nullified. Yes, not having known her, he still shed a tear for her. And add to the tear an imprecation on all those who saw the killing of other human beings, whether singly or in batches, as the solution to anything.

Randollph took a last look at the notes for conducting a funeral he had scribbled under the tutelage of the bishop. "Precede casket down the aisle saying the Scripture sentence indicated in ritual," he read. Whoever figured out this procedure at least had a sense of theater, he reflected.

"Hell of a lot of people in there for a private funeral," Dan Gantry commented, peering through the big double doors to the center aisle of the church. Randollph had asked Arnie Uhlinger to assist today. Arnie was an occasional member of the choir and a friend of Marianne Reedman's. Arnie was serving an intern year, and participating in a church funeral (which, the bishop had commented, you didn't have too often anymore since undertakers preferred the convenience of their own chapels) would be excellent training for him. And Arnie read Scripture beautifully, with the true actor's sure sense of underplaying. But Arnie had begged off. He had been nervous and upset at the suggestion that he should help with Marianne Reedman's funeral. Randollph had been afraid, at one point, that Arnie would break down and cry. So he had drafted Dan to help him.

"Ready when you are, Dr. Randollph," the frock-coated undertaker murmured, ostentatiously pushing back the cuff of his gray glove to stare at his wristwatch. Randollph ignored him, thinking that it would be good for the fellow's chilly commercial soul to take orders from the clergy instead of giving them. After an interval he deemed sufficient to establish in the undertaker's mind who was in charge here, he instructed the fellow to fold back the doors.

"Jesus said, 'I am the resurrection and the life, he who believes in me, though he die, yet shall he live, and whosoever lives and believes in me shall never die,'" Randollph intoned as, with Dan beside him, he led Marianne Reedman's coffin into the long aisle that bisected the nave from narthex to chancel. "The eternal God is your dwelling place, and underneath are the everlasting arms."

It occurred to Randollph that the stern Gothic façade of the Shep building certainly gave the casual passerby no clue to the elegance that lay within. The Church of the Good Shepherd, belying its medieval exterior, was a veritable cave of Byzantine splendor burrowed into a brick-and-concrete cliff. To be sure, its stained-glass windows were evenly flushed with concealed neon tubes instead of the whimsical variations of sunlight. True, no low dome perched on pendentives. The church nave was capped with a pitched roof which owed more to the Romans than to Carthage or Constantinople. But there were columns aplenty crusted in blue and gold mosaics. There was a triptych of gold-leafed saints peering down on the altar. There was a pulpit of blue tile aflame with gold symbols. The whole effect was of spirituality gone to seed, an ecclesiasticism in which money was an acceptable substitute for prayer. Randollph liked it. He supposed that this was because he liked color and didn't mind vulgarity.

He wondered a little that the same ethic which urged men to scar the landscape and insult the eye for a high net return on investment should also inspire them to lavish a portion of those profits on a church which cost a bundle and sat there empty most of the week. Expiation, perhaps? Well, no matter, man is not an entirely rational animal.

"The Lord is my light and my salvation; whom shall I fear? The Lord is the stronghold of my life, of whom shall I be afraid," he read, his tone a descant above a normal speaking voice.

Had Marianne Reedman feared her murderer?

If it had been some wino or prowling sex deviant, as Casey admitted it could have been but didn't think very credible as a theory, a stranger who had chanced on her alone in that remote dungeon of a choir room, she probably had known fear.

If, on the other hand, it had been someone from whom she was expecting no harm, a lover, say, with whom she had a tryst, then she had not been afraid.

"Hello," she had probably whispered, "I've been waiting for you." If, indeed, it had been a lover who for some perverse reason had made love to her and then throttled her. . . .

"Bless the Lord, for he has heard the voice of my supplications," Randollph read. Had Marianne uttered a supplication as the garrote bit into her lovely neck? What had it been? "Oh, no! Oh my God, don't! Why—" the rest of it strangled into silence?

105

They were almost at the chancel now. "For we know that if the earthly tent we live in is destroyed, we have a building of God, a house not made with hands, eternal in the heavens." The abundant mosaics glittered and winked in the half-light of hanging lanterns. This was the architecture which came to life in the time of the man who had written the words he had just read, Randollph recalled from some forgotten crevice of his memory.

The six pallbearers following the casket peeled off, three to the left and three to the right, into their appointed pews. The undertaker and his assistant in tailed coats and gray striped trousers swung the catafalque around with professional skill and softly nudged it into place as if they were docking a boat. They would like to have opened the casket, fussing around, patting a pillow here, smoothing a coverlet there, calling attention to their handiwork. In fact, the solemn mortician had suggested "a viewing after the service," coupled with a discreet bribe. As he had many funerals of people who had no pastor, he could throw four or five of these services a week Randollph's way, fifty dollars a service; it was included in the bill. Randollph coldly refused both the bribe and the request but felt guilty that he had spoken with an unearned moral superiority. It was easy for him to turn down these questionable honoraria. He didn't need the money. What if he had been the typical impecunious pastor with a wife and four children and burdened with debts? Would he have been coldly contemptuous of the offered bribe? At what price would he compromise his integrity? O. B. Smelser, who probably would have scorned the undertaker's offer as beneath him, had thought the pastorate of Good Shepherd worth a calculated and dishonest silence. Randollph wondered what it would take to buy him. Not a lousy undertaker's fee, but he supposed there was something. Temptation had to be commensurate with the needs of the tempted. This was, he concluded, a decidedly depressing line of thought.

He could also understand the mortician's desire for "a viewing." No painter hangs his pictures in a cave. No writer, if he can help it, hides his manuscripts in a file. The artist needs exposure, a public, praise for his efforts. And Randollph had no doubts that the undertaker thought of himself essentially as an artist.

But Randollph felt less guilty when, remembering the bishop's warning that "they're all ghouls," he had firmly vetoed a viewing. He'd be damned if there'd be an open casket in his church. For all he knew the mortician, given leave to display his skill, would whip out a sign and plant it in the opened casket reading "Doesn't she look natural? For similar high quality work in your time of sorrow just phone——" In the clash between theology and commerce, commerce usually had a ridiculous advantage. But not this time.

"For All the Saints Who from Their Labors Rest," the choir sang, robed, solemn. Because Marianne had been one of them the choir members had come from Elmhurst and Park Forest and Glen Ellyn and Skokie, scurrying around for baby-sitters, taking time off from work, disrupting the routine of their lives to help bury a fallen comrade.

"Oh, blest communion, fellowship divine! We feebly struggle, they in glory shine" the choir sang on. Randollph, seated behind the lectern, peeked again at his notes to see what he was supposed to do next.

Tony put the organ up several notches, and the choir crashed to an ending with a triumphant "Alleluia! Alleluia!"

"Read opening prayers," his notes directed, and Randollph went to the lectern. "Almighty God, Our Father, from whom we come and with whom our spirits return. . . ." He prayed into the spiky microphone clamped onto the lectern to assure that the congregation, as well as God, heard his words. The prayers finished, he gave way to Dan, who read the lessons from the Old Testament included in the order for the burial of the dead. Dan read adequately, but he would never be in a class with Arnie Uhlinger, Randollph judged. He wondered why an uneasy Arnie had dodged this assignment—Arnie, who for public occasions could discard his normal, piping voice and summon up from some recess in his long bony torso a much deeper timbre. Perhaps all candidates for the ministry should, like Arnie, have some training in the theater.

"Glory be to the Father," the choir boomed out, signaling the end of the Old Testament lessons, sliding swiftly to "world without end, Amen."

"New Testament lessons—Randollph," his notes instructed him, and he was back at the lectern.

107

"Let not your hearts be troubled; believe in God, believe also in me. . . ." Did Mr. Robert Torgeson, sitting there in his triple role as president of the church's trustees, pallbearer, and friend of the Reedman family, believe in God? If he did, it was a conventional Protestant God, Randollph imagined. A no-nonsense God who assigned men their proper places in the scheme of things. A God who rewarded industrious insurance salesmen who had the wit and drive to organize their own agency and make the right political connections so as to do a lot of business at rates well above competitive pricing. A God who looked with disfavor on the shiftless mass of mankind and let them languish in the poverty and wretchedness they deserved. When Little Bobbie thought of God—if he ever did—Randollph suspected that he envisioned the Almighty as thin-faced with a narrow little wisp of mustache that twitched in perpetual irritation. God with a countenance very much like that of Little Bobbie Torgeson.

And Lieutenant Michael Casey, barely noticeable in a shadowed corner, here not as a mourner but as an observant bloodhound, did he believe in God? Was it a conventional Catholic God who granted special favors to Catholics, especially Catholics who were faithful at mass and confession and refrained from practicing artificial birth control? No. Casey would be more likely to reflect Teilhard de Chardin or Maritain or Hans Kung or even Paul Tillich on God, Randollph guessed. Casey was a college man, as he had so carefully informed Randollph. He might go through the prescribed Catholic motions out of habit or to please aged and devout Irish parents or prompted by his knowledge of Chicago police politics (a good word from his pastor dropped in the right place could make all the difference in a policeman's career). But Casey wouldn't be taken in by the hocus-pocus. Casey would know that you can't tickle God's fancy by devout posturing or wheedle His cooperation with candles and novenas. Casey was sharp.

"So it is with the resurrection of the dead," Randollph read. "It is sown in dishonor, it is raised in glory. It is sown in weakness, it is raised in power." What glorious sounding, sublimely phrased nonsense! Was Paul trying to make a hit with all those Greeks in the church at Corinth when he wrote this lilting dualistic goop? Since it had found its way into the Scriptures, were all Christians obligated to believe that procreation could only be accomplished in dishonor and weakness? Randolph hoped that the congregation wouldn't pay too much attention to these words. What possible comfort was there in the information that you were begot in sin? However, this was ritual, and people seldom reflected on the words of ritual. Ritual was beyond the clutching fingers of rational examination. In the blessed mutter of the mass it was the mutter and not the words which comforted the spirit and reassured the soul, he supposed, but—

It was, he saw by his notes, time for the eulogy.

Randollph had thought out the eulogy very carefully because he knew it would be reported in the press. Talk theology rather than the history of the deceased, Freddie had said. So, after alluding to Marianne Reedman's faithfulness and contributions to the choir, Randollph headed for safe theological territory. Her death was a tragedy, and tragedies are never the will of God, he said. (He wished Mrs. Creedy, who had insisted that the strong right arm of God had smote Marianne Reedman in her wickedness, was present, but she had no reason to be and was probably tidying up things somewhere, her puritan soul soothed by her brisk eradication of dirt and mess.)

Mrs. Reedman's death had cast a shadow on all their lives (he tactfully omitted any reference to the absent Mr. Reedman) and the life of the church, he continued. No one as yet knew why she had died, but in good time they would. Whoever was responsible would be apprehended, and he hoped soon—not to slake a thirst for punishment (he noticed Little Bobbie Torgeson's mustache twitched in double time at this), but to prevent any further tragedies from the same hand.

Like any death, he went on, here was a mystery that man could not entirely penetrate. Comfort was hard to come by in the midst of tragedy, and the mind hungered for explanations when explanations were not apparent. He would call their attention to the explanation that Jesus gave his Disciples, sorrowing that he soon would be with them no more—the explanation that they could trust in the goodness of God. . . .

Maybe this was too vague, a cop-out, he thought. But he wasn't going to offer any cheap assurance of a better beyond where Marianne

109

was now dwelling in a happiness unknowable to mortals. Marianne Reedman hadn't wanted to die. Someone, for motives that were horribly compelling, had wanted her to die and had seen to it that she did die. It was a corrupted, evil act, and evil would spread from it. And no one but God knew how many were still to be touched and stained by the released evil.

"Eternal God," he prayed, done now with his brief theologizing, "who commitest to us the swift and solemn trust of life . . . lift us above unrighteous anger and mistrust . . . draw us to the mind of Christ, that thy lost image may be traced again. . . ."

"A mighty fortress is our God," the choir chanted, "a bulwark never failing." Then Randollph, standing by the altar that had once graced a sixteenth-century church, raised his arm over the congregation of odd lots of the Reedman family, representatives of various groups to whose interest it was to be represented on this occasion, acquaintances, and, he hoped, some genuine mourners and said, "The peace of God, which passeth all understanding, keep your hearts and minds in the knowledge and love of God. . . ."

Then, as the choir chanted an amen, he and Dan Gantry walked down from the chancel to lead the body of Marianne Reedman on its last journey in this world.

15

THE 727 ROCKETED near-vertically according to Randollph's queasy prebreakfast stomach as if anxious to be out of the chilly drizzle which wet but did not wash Chicago's air. Playing detective, he had concluded while fumbling in the predawn darkness to stifle the insistent alarm, entailed an unavoidable measure of discomfort—a judgment reinforced by the soggy character of the day and the morose taxi driver who reluctantly hauled him to the airport.

After Marianne Reedman's funeral Randollph had come to the same appraisal of her character as, unbeknown to him, Lieutenant Casey had arrived at earlier. Casey, basing his estimate on considerable police experience, knew that nobody was ever as good as all her friends claimed Marianne Reedman was. Randollph, more theological in approach, relied on the doctrine of original sin to inform him that true saints are in extremely short supply and that they rarely are involved in lurid sex murders.

It was apparent, then, that more information about Marianne Reedman was required. But where to begin? Randollph was acquiring a belated appreciation for Michael Casey's dogma that good policemen collect facts.

What he was disposed to regard as divine inspiration had come upon him when, after the funeral, Dan Gantry had asked, "Boss, is anyone representing Good Shepherd at the memorial in Montclair tomorrow?"

"Not that I know of," Randollph had told him, "why?"

"Well," Dan said, "it would be good form, don't you think? After all, these are important people. . . ."

111

Randollph seized his opportunity. "You, Dan, the ultimate democrat, talking about important people?"

"Marianne Reedman was an important person, and I'm not talking about money or position."

"Do you want to go?"

"No," Dan replied, "I think you ought to go. Marianne's parents would think of me as hired help. They'd figure we didn't consider their daughter important enough for the head man to show." Randollph thought that there were nuances to the pastoral profession they didn't teach you in seminary and that you didn't learn while spouting off about Héloïse and Abelard in the classroom. "You could fly out tomorrow morning and back the same day," Dan added helpfully.

"You know, I think I'll do it," Randollph said, feeling like an executive capable of swift, sure decisions. "And who knows, her parents, her pastor, her background might provide some hint. . . ."

"You won't find anything bad about Annie." Dan stoutly defended his dead friend. Dan, Randollph thought, lacked the experience and the theological sophistication to realize, as Willie Stark had said, "There is always something."

And so Randollph found himself sleepily requesting the ticket clerk to change the tourist-class ticket Dan had reserved for him to first-class. It was a sinful self-indulgence, he supposed, but the thought of being squeezed in with two strangers, both likely to be salesmen and thus garrulous, was more than he could face at that hour. Odds were that first-class would be blessedly empty, and anyway first-class passengers were apt to tend to their own business and let you tend to yours. He was making a mental note to administer himself penance for incipient patrician tendencies when he heard a voice behind him say to the clerk, "Will you change mine to first-class also, please?"

"Hello, there." Samantha Stack greeted him, looking as if she had just come from ten hours' sleep and a brisk dip in the lake. "Surprise."

"Oh, hello," Randollph said stupidly, rummaging through his sleep-deprived brain for an explanation. "You flying East today?"

"Obviously," Sam told him. "I'm going with you. Why else do you think I changed to first-class? It's murder on a working girl's salary,

112

but it wouldn't do for you to travel in lonely splendor up front and me back with the peasants, would it?"

Randollph was too befuddled to understand. Sammy cleared it up for him.

"Dan told me you were going. He said he thought you intended to sniff around into Marianne Reedman's early life for clues. Well, when it comes to sniffing around into people's early lives, a good-looking girl is lots better than a dignified cleric. You need my help."

"Do I come off as a dignified cleric?" Randollph asked her, horrified.

Sammy Stack surveyed him like an auctioneer estimating the probable worth of a prize bull. "No, not really," she announced. "A touch reserved, perhaps. It's part of your charm, probably. Compared to most of the specimens from your profession which I have met, you are admirably human."

"Thanks." Randollph did not sound grateful.

"Don't pout, Chess." She patted his cheek. "I meant it as a compliment."

Mollified, Randollph noticed that she looked stunning in ice-blue slacks under a white belted raincoat. He was sure that the slacks fit snugly on her hips.

"You weren't, er, planning. . . ."

"To go to the funeral?" She had read his mind. "No. Relax. As you have been observing, I am not wearing weeds. What would I find out at a funeral?"

It was a pleasant flight. The 727 broke through the capsule of gray mist into a world of sunshine and a sea of cottony clouds. Sunshine, a ham omelet and a pretty companion to share it colored life considerably brighter, Randollph ruminated. And coffee. And an attentive stewardess in an extremely brief skirt.

"Men!" Sammy snapped.

"Yes, what about them?" Randollph attentively awaited a revelation.

"Here you are with me, a gorgeous girl, and you are staring at the legs of that little—"

"Well, you can't very well miss them." Randollph chuckled. He

113

was pleased to hear the pique in Sammy's voice. "But she's just a child, whereas you are a mature, fascinating woman—"

"Hell," Sammy interrupted, "you think that makes me feel better? You don't know much about women."

Randollph admitted that he didn't, but not to Sammy. He thought he knew enough about women to tell when a discreet silence was in order.

The 727, which had been cruising like a lazy well-fed shark, now put its nose down and plunged into the murk. Soon it was coasting over railroads and oil storage tanks and marshland. Thruways and toll roads laced together the ugly urban sprawl of industrial North Jersey. A tugboat wearily pushed a barge through the septic waters of a nameless river.

"Chess," a small voice said, "I'm sorry."

"For what?"

"For being bitchy. Forgive me?"

"Nothing to forgive," Randollph pontificated. "I hadn't given it a thought."

"Liar!" Sammy bathed him in a sparkling smile.

Tires screaming in agony, the 727 made solid contact with the earth. A sudden brief yowl from the reversed engines, and it was ambling toward the docking area.

"Welcome to Newark International Airport," the professionally friendly voice of a stewardess crackled over the public address system. "The time is now. . . ."

Randollph leaned back and smiled. He was immensely pleased with himself.

If the industrial sprawl was unprepossessing seen from above, it was downright frightening at ground level. Obtaining an anonymous Plymouth and a map of the area from a cheerful little blonde at the Avis booth, they began a halting, tedious creep toward Montclair.

"The scenery isn't improving much," Sammy remarked after two or three miles. "Marianne Reedman surely didn't live in a horrible area like this. Maybe," she suggested brightly, "Montclair is a walled city with guards at the gates to keep the rabble out."

"Very likely," Randollph agreed. "Only I expect the walls are in the form of high real estate values. They are just as effective, and the upkeep is much less than for real walls."

As he congratulated himself on a truth neatly put, Randollph noticed that the scenery had changed. Dingy clusters of sandwich joints, hole-in-the-wall insurance agencies, and filling stations gave way, gradually, to respectable-looking business enterprises. Down side streets neat lawns and disciplined hedges could be glimpsed.

"I think," Sammy said, consulting the map spread out on her lap, "we are about to enter Montclair. What, dear Doctor, is your program for the day?"

"I'll go directly to the church and have a chat with the pastor if he's available. Then the service—it's at one—and a visit with the bereaved parents. What about you?"

"I think you turn left here for the church," Sammy pointed. "And don't worry about me. I will, as they say, employ the time to advantage."

"I'm sure you will. Do you want the car?"

"No. Everything I have in mind can be done on foot. Wow! Some church!"

They had come in front of what Randollph would have called a mini-cathedral. Its nave, an imposing hulk of gray stone, was a magnified copy of an English country Gothic parish church. The history of the congregation's growth and prosperity could be traced in the jumble of additions to the main structure. The nave sprouted tendrils of offices, classrooms, gymnasium, and social halls, all in the same gray stone but in shades successively lighter because of fewer years to absorb the corrosive airs of the region. The structure and parking area occupied an entire city block. Its just off-downtown location proclaimed, Randollph guessed, that it had been there since the city was young and that the present edifice was successor to a more modest building which had either been destroyed by fire or was deemed insufficiently impressive to represent the impressive people who prayed there.

"See you back here, say, three o'clock," Sammy said. "Well, *avanti*." She slid out of the car and swung off toward the business district.

Randollph drove around the corner and found a driveway into the church's beautifully kept parklike grounds. It led to a paved area fringed with white lines giving precise permission to park. He noticed that the slot labeled "Dr. Turley" was filled with a fat Buick Electra. Surrounding it, like piglets nestling up to a sow, were a Volkswagen, two Toyotas, and a Pinto. These occupied slots marked "Reserved for Staff." There was no doubt about the pecking order at St. James Church.

Entering a door bearing the legend "Church Offices Upstairs," Randollph passed through a dining room heavy with the miasmas of a thousand church suppers, up a narrow and ill-lit stairway, which led to a gloomy hall. Guided by the rackety-rackety-rack of an unevenly struck typewriter he found a door marked "Church Offices." Inside, an old-young woman identified by a desk plaque as Miss Vinson abandoned her battle with the typewriter and said impersonally, "Yes?"

Randollph identified himself and asked to see the pastor. Miss Vinson, whose practiced eye could detect promoters of penny stocks and space salesmen for dubious advertising enterprises at forty paces, gave Randollph a passing mark. "He's engaged at the moment, I'll let him know you're here, just wait in there." Miss Vinson delivered her rote speech, pointed to a small waiting room, and punched the button on her intercom simultaneously.

Randollph did not have long to wait. The door of the pastor's study cracked open on a mink-coated back. "And remember, Mrs. Ballantyne," a rich voice rumbled, "God has provided prayer as the answer to our loneliness." Randollph could see a manicured hand pat Mrs. Ballantyne's arm and at the same time gently propel her out the door. Mrs. Ballantyne reluctantly withdrew, a hungry-looking, overly made-up woman in her fifties, giving Randollph an interested sidelong appraisal as she went out.

Cognizant of the Mrs. Ballantyne type's propensity to linger, given a half chance, Dr. Turley timed his entrance into the anteroom with her exit into Miss Vinson's outer office. Already apprised of Randollph's identity, he measured out just the right amount of cordiality due a visiting peer of some importance. "Come in, come into my sanctum," he urged. "So good of you to come." The sanctum was banked with quarto volumes of long-dead theologians, tooled leather editions of Gibbon, and yards more of expensively bound books which suggested scholarly labors but which, Randollph suspected, were uncut.

Dr. Turley murmured appropriate formulas deprecating the tragedy of Marianne Reedman, conveying the impression that such atrocities, while likely to occur in frontier towns such as Chicago, never happened among the better families along the civilized eastern seaboard.

Turley gave Randollph his opening by asking if there was any progress toward a solution of the crime.

"No, not much," Randollph replied. "The police are unable to find a motive—that is, unless you assume the husband had a motive. Did you know him?"

"Slightly. I married them, of course." Dr. Turley pushed a lock of expertly barbered gray hair from his forehead—the gesture, Randollph guessed, of a man who has been at it too long: too many hours spent listening to Mrs. Ballantynes; too many fancy weddings performed; too many remains of the rich and the prominent consigned to expensive burial plots. It was Dr. Turley's fortune, good or bad, to have possessed the appearance, manners, and education the privileged classes demanded (and paid for handsomely) in their chaplains. Dr. Turley looked weary of dealing with nice people and counting the months to retirement. Randollph did not envy him those introspective moments when he added up the sums of his lifework.

"Marianne Reedman was the first baby I baptized here," Turley was reminiscing. "Of course, I was just an assistant then—" He grimaced, perhaps pondering a comfortable misspent life. "Old Dr. McIntyre—bless his beautiful Scotch burr—was ill, his deathbed actually, although we didn't know it then, or he would have baptized her. The Sellersmans," he added, "are not the kind of people to ask an assistant pastor to christen a child, but they had no choice. So, after Dr. McIntyre's passing, I was chosen to succeed him, and that is why" —he sighed—"I baptized Marianne. I married her, and now I'm to bury her."

"I'm sorry that I never knew her," Randollph hastily interjected, lest Turley extend his reverie. "What was she like?"

"Ah." Turley's eyes lit up. "A jewel, a lovely person. She's an only

117

child, you know and should have been spoiled rotten. The Sellers-mans," he explained, "are people of means, and they lavished every material token of love on her that money could buy. But for some reason she remained unspoiled. Interesting, don't you think Doctor, how some children spoil easily and others don't? I could tell you some hair-raising stories—"

Randollph was sure that he could, but the eccentricities of the juvenile rich were not what he had come here to discuss. Hastily seeking to divert the conversation into more profitable channels, he asked, "Was Marianne active in the church?"

"Oh, yes," Turley assured him. "Beautiful voice. Always in the choir. A leader in our Christian Youth Club." As Turley spelled out Marianne Sellersman's youthful virtues, Randollph thought darkly that all this goodness was inimical to his hopes for some hitherto-unrevealed evil in the deceased's character.

"Didn't she ever even rebel against her parents?" he queried, a desperate stab, he knew. "Most kids do, you know."

Turley gazed dreamily at a beautifully framed reproduction of "The Last Supper" on the opposite wall. "No, nothing you could call rebellion. I recall that she had a schoolgirl crush on a handsome lad from our extensive Greek population here. Her parents were quite worried about it. They were afraid she was going to marry him. Not that he wasn't a fine boy, good, hardworking family"—Dr. Turley hastily absolved himself from race or class snobbery—"but, well, quite unsuitable as a prospective spouse for Marianne Sellersman. It is my experience that when someone marries beneath, ah, far outside their social and economic station, they are adding unnecessarily to the risks of what is always a hazardous enterprise." Randollph was wondering what sort of woman Mrs. Turley might be when the pastor dropped the footnotes to his story. "In any event, the Sellersmans were able to persuade her to see the light and break off with the boy. That, so far as I know," he concluded, "is the only time she showed signs of rebelling."

Randollph was disillusioned with himself as a detective. He was sure that Lieutenant Casey would have asked several incisive questions, probed beneath Dr. Turley's urbane surface, prodded the old pastor's memory and extracted some vital piece of information which, eventually, would lay bare the whole truth. But when Turley, with the practiced resignation of a man pressed by many concerns, looked regretfully at his watch, Randollph couldn't think of an incisive question to save his life.

"Would you care to take part in the service, Doctor?" Turley asked, rising and slapping away an imagined wrinkle in his trousers, which had never hung on a plain pipe rack. Randollph, translating this lukewarm invitation to read "Courtesy compels me to ask you, but this is my show today," declined and departed.

16

WHEN SAMANTHA STACK, leaving Randollph, loped purpose-
fully toward the Montclair business district, it was for Randollph's
benefit. When she estimated that Randollph was safely chewing the
clerical fat with whatever old duffer ran St. James Church, she circled
back to the church. Samantha had not been reared a Presbyterian for
nothing. She knew that where there was an old established church of
whatever brand, there was usually an old established church secretary
who was privy to all the parish dirt.

Confronting Miss Vinson, Samantha was gratified to see that she
had not been wrong. While Miss Vinson's dowdy clothes and
blemished complexion made her look fifty, Sammy accurately pegged
her for forty. Moreover, Sammy guessed, she had begun her employment at St. James after high school (business course). Also, that
there was probably in the background a querulous widowed mother
who had discouraged serious romances (if any) in order to hang onto
her meal ticket. Miss Vinson, then, would have to taste life vicari-
ously, if at all, and was thus bound to be an inveterate gossip.

"Hello." Sammy beamed a shy smile Miss Vinson's way. "I'm wondering if you can help me?"

Miss Vinson waited further light.

"You see," Sammy forged ahead, "I've flown out from Chicago for
the Reedman service—I was one of Marianne's dearest friends"—
here Sammy improvised a snuffle—"and I'm afraid I failed to find out
the exact time and where—"

"One o'clock, here," Miss Vinson stated, looking critically at
Sammy's blue slacks.

"Oh, I've brought appropriate clothes." Sammy, knowing that one lie often begot another, reassured Miss Vinson. Uninvited, she dropped into a chair by Miss Vinson's desk and passed a tired hand over her eyes. "Flying tires one so."

"It's very tiring," Miss Vinson, who had never been on a plane in her life, agreed. "Better rest a minute."

"Thank you. Did you know Marianne well?"

"I was in high school with her. Of course," Miss Vinson said with the inverted snobbery the poor exhibit toward the rich, "we didn't run in the same crowd."

"Oh?" Sammy said. Then, pulling the stopper a little more: "She was such a lovely person."

"Some thought so; some didn't," Miss Vinson said significantly.

"Some didn't?"

Miss Vinson, who clearly numbered herself among the some who didn't, had been in as much need of an audience as a junkie needs his three o'clock fix. Now she had one.

"She was a beauty, I'll give her that." Miss Vinson, obligations to Christian charity satisfied, got down to business. "She had everybody thinking she was Miss Goody Two-Shoes." Sammy translated this to mean "Marianne Reedman was rich, popular and attracted boys, while I, Martha Vinson, was poor and plain and didn't get many dates."

"The boys called her the Virgin Mary." Miss Vinson pursued her subject with vicious abandon. "Some of the boys, that is," she added significantly.

Sammy, hoping that she had struck pay dirt, mined a little deeper. "And some of the boys didn't?"

"Phil Kasko didn't," Miss Vinson stated obscurely.

"Oh, that must be the Phil she was always talking about," Sammy improvised. "Was he as great as she made out that he was?"

"He was marvy! All the girls were ga-ga about him!" Miss Vinson employed the idiom of her high school days to convey the virtues of the redoubtable Mr. Kasko. "He was the big football hero, always had the lead in the class play. And handsome!" Miss Vinson retreated momentarily into starry-eyed reverie. "He looked like Tony Curtis."

Sammy asked the operative question. "If they had such a thing for each other, what happened? Marianne never told me," she added hastily. That was the trouble with lying, Sammy thought. You always had to remember to cover.

"Oh, Miss Goody Two-Shoes was too good for him," Miss Vinson said contemptuously. "She was society, and he was just second-generation Greek immigrant. His parents ran a restaurant." Miss Vinson's social consciousness held that the upper classes were contemptible for looking down on the Miss Vinsons. However, a Martha Vinson, daughter of a seedy line of German artisans which had arrived (via steerage) in the mid-nineteenth century, had a logical right to think herself superior to Greek immigrants who delayed their crossing until after 1900.

"And Phil didn't call her the Virgin Mary?" Sammy hoped that sex would divert Miss Vinson from further examination of Montclair's social striations.

"Phil had all the girls he wanted who would do anything for him, if you know what I mean," Miss Vinson said ominously.

Sammy knew what she meant.

"So why would Phil take up with her if she didn't do everything for him?"

Sammy thought there might be a flaw in Miss Vinson's logic but did not care to explore it.

"What," she asked, "ever happened to Phil Kasko?"

"Oh, he still lives in Montclair. He runs the family restaurant. I don't mean the same restaurant; he's built a new one, it's in Caldwell, actually. He's done very well. Calls the place Kasko's Athens. I don't go there; the prices are too high. But they say it's always crowded. The heavy drinkers hang out there. I hear Phil's on his way to being a rich man."

Samantha Stack gauged that she had garnered the relevant information Miss Vinson had to offer. As soon as she could block, momentarily, Miss Vinson's Ancient Mariner compulsion to tell all, she murmured thanks and fled. Sammy figured she had fish to fry elsewhere.

17

MONTCLAIR, RANDOLLPH had discovered from the map Avis included with the clean ashtrays, was a cigar-shaped town laid out along the first ridge west of Manhattan. "It is most convenient for Wall Streeters to live here," Dr. Turley volunteered, "or was before they quit running the Hoboken ferry. They make good church people, Wall Streeters." Randollph wondered if qualifications for church membership and admission to the Yale Club were about the same thing in Dr. Turley's eyes.

"We also have a fair number of denominational bureaucrats living here," Turley further informed him. "That's because it's an easy commute to Riverside Drive, where so many of them have their offices. As a matter of fact, we have a dozen or so of them in our congregation." Dr. Turley was, Randollph sensed, much less enthusiastic about his denominational bureaucrats, preachers all, than he was about his Wall Streeters. Randollph could understand this and sympathize. It wasn't difficult to guess that ten or twelve professional saints in the congregation would constitute an extremely heavy cross for any pastor to bear.

Dr. Turley, apparently a font of local history, was transporting Randollph to a postburial luncheon at the home of Marianne Reedman's parents. While it wasn't necessarily customary, Turley explained, some of the older people felt obliged to feed their close relatives after a family funeral. The pastor was always invited, and, Turley assured him, the Sellersmans had insisted he bring Dr. Randollph along with him. Randollph had hoped for a time alone with the Sellersmans, a hope engendered by a vague notion that a detective worked best without a lot of people around. But he'd take what opportunity came his way and make the best of it.

"It's too bad this isn't a month or so from now," Dr. Turley chatted on as he chauffeured his fat Buick at a sedate pace. "When the flowers are out, our town is truely lovely. Gardening is a passion here, and many of our people keep a full-time gardener."

Randollph had had about enough of Dr. Turley and genteel Christianity. He had, in fact, had enough of him after their conversation in the study. But that had been followed by a half hour memorial service which consisted largely of Dr. Turley reading, with polished sonority, a lot of William Cullen Bryant and Khalil Gibran, sprinkling a little Scripture here and there. And now, it appeared, he was condemned to Dr. Turley's care for the duration of his visit.

"Ah, here we are," Turley, interrupting Randollph's meditation on the sacrificial life of an amateur detective, stopped in front of a vast Tudor mansion which would be completely hidden from street view once the now-barren trees surrounding it bore their leaves.

"Do you mean that two people live here alone?" Randollph asked.

"And the servants of course," Turley answered. "We run to large houses here in Montclair. Mind that snowdrift." Turley shepherded him toward a huge oak and leaded glass door, which was opened by an elderly black man in a shiny black suit who relieved them of their wraps. "He's an old family retainer," Turley explained, guiding Randollph up a stairs to the main floor level. "The Sellersmans do not keep a uniformed butler. They are not ostentatious people."

Entering a living room large enough to have served as refectory in a fair-sized monastery, Randollph observed that the Sellersmans' non ostentatious life-style did not prohibit the employment of a uniformed maid, who was engaged at the moment in offering drinks to fifteen or more guests. Turley took him immediately to Marianne's parents.

James Sellersman, Randollph would have surmised had he not known better, was a retired Army officer, probably at least a lieutenant general. Tall and spare, his impassive face held no hint of sorrow. Probably, Randollph judged, it was a face also incapable of reflecting joy. No one would ever know how James Sellersman felt by how he looked.

Mrs. Sellersman, standing beside her husband accepting condolences of the guests, was a plump little squab of a woman, obviously sagging under her burden of grief. Randollph, who estimated that talking to Marianne's father would be a chilly and unrewarding business, cast about for ways to isolate Mrs. Sellersman for a chat. He didn't have to. She isolated him. Dr. Turley, with hovering unction, spouted the correct formulas for comforting the bereaved ("Prayer is your shield and breastplate in time of sorrow"), then sidled away as soon as he thought seemly, gratefully snagging a bloody Mary from the passing maid.

"I'm exhausted. I must sit down. Come and talk to me a little, Dr. Randollph." Mrs. Sellersman led him to a small studylike room, an appendage to the living room. Randollph could see, beneath the ravages of time and grief, that Mrs. Sellersman had once been a beauty.

"We can't tell you, my husband and I, how touched we are that you took the time from your busy schedule to come today," she told him, an appreciation which he didn't merit, Randollph guiltily acknowledged to himself.

"Has anything been heard of Ward—Marianne's husband?" It was now apparent what Mrs. Sellersman really wanted to talk about.

"I'm afraid not."

"I can't understand it," she mused. "Ward is weak and, well, sensual. And I suppose you have discovered by now that he and Marianne weren't—how shall I say it?—highly compatible. But he would never have killed our daughter." Mrs. Sellersman, all tears shed, choked back a dry sob. Recovering, she asked, "Do the police believe he did it?"

"That is one possibility they are weighing."

"It does look suspicious, I know, his disappearing that way. And I'm sure I can't imagine why he did it—disappear that is. But he isn't a killer."

Randollph had to resist the temptation to tell her that her son-in-law had jumped ship with ten million good reasons for disappearing. But so far they had managed to keep the lid on that scandal, and Randollph didn't intend to be the one to lift it.

"She was such a good child." Mrs. Sellersman was assuaging grief by recalling happier days. A good pastor, Randollph felt, would encourage the catharsis of reminiscence. He was sure that a good detective, pawing through a haystack for needles of information, would encourage it.

Mrs. Sellersman needed no encouragement. "Being an only child made us an especially close-knit family." The maid appeared with a well-stocked tray. "Oh, my, I'm forgetting my duties as hostess. Will you have a drink, Dr. Randollph? Or. . . ." Randollph—who knew the "or . . ." meant "Do the clergy from the pietistic Western provinces frown on alcohol?"—took a thimble of dry sherry, although he disliked drinking in the middle of the day. Mrs. Sellersman helped herself to a substantial jolt of scotch on the rocks.

"Marianne was always, well, I wouldn't call her an obedient child," Mrs. Sellersman said between hearty sips, "because, well, actually there wasn't anything she disagreed with us over. Now I don't want to make her sound goody-goody, she had her little rebellions—she'd get crushes on the wrong kind of boys, and we'd have to discourage that sort of thing. Mostly, though, we didn't try to dominate her. Why, she kept a diary, wrote in it faithfully every night, and do you know, I never once pried into it? I could have, of course, but to this day I've never seen a word she wrote in it. Don't you think that shows we didn't try to run her life?"

Randollph agreed that it required a remarkable restraint for a mother to refrain from reading her daughter's diary. He wondered what guilt she was expunging by these intimate revelations.

"She kept on with her diary after her marriage." Mrs. Sellersman pursued the subject. "Kept it right up until her . . . her death, I suppose. I don't want to read it now. I didn't violate her privacy while she was alive, and I won't violate it now that she's dead." Beyond grief now, she paused, then went on. "Maybe I'm afraid I'd find that she . . . she resented us, and if she did, I don't want to know it. Sometimes I think we, well, urged too strongly that she marry Ward Reedman. It didn't turn out too well, as you know. He wasn't a very attractive boy—oh, he looked all right, I don't mean that. He was, I guess arrogant is the best word. But he came from such a fine family, and I think blood will tell, eventually, don't you?" It was not a question, and Randollph did not supply an answer. He was beginning to wish he had joined his hostess in a slug of scotch.

"Anyway, Ward had the background, and he was Groton and Princeton. Mr. Sellersman's Princeton, you know. He won't have anything but Princeton men in his business. He claims you can trust Princeton to turn out solid conservatives, but nobody can be sure of a Yale man anymore what with that awful Chaplain Coffin filling their heads with radical ideas and calling them Christian, the Yale graduates around here—and we have a lot of them in Montclair—are all upset—but to get back to Ward, he seemed so right for Marianne. Her father and I were so happy when he proposed, but Marianne—she could be stubborn—said she didn't love him and wasn't going to marry him. She was still mooning over a most unsuitable boy she had a crush on. We pressed very hard for accepting Ward Reedman, and now I feel that maybe we shouldn't have, the way it turned out. But he had a good family line and the right social background, and I've always believed that like should marry like. Anyway, it was Ward or that ignorant Greek boy who worked in a restaurant. Marianne wanted to marry him; can you imagine, he didn't even graduate from Montclair State, not that it means much to have a degree from there. So we convinced her and she accepted Ward. And," she said pensively, staring into the amber depths of her glass as if for solace, "it all went wrong. But we thought we were doing the best thing for her."

Not being, to his knowledge, a parent, Randollph could not share the apparently universal parental urge to determine what was best for their children, even when their children were well past voting age. Marianne Sellersman might have been as bad off had she stuck to her guns and married beneath her social class. But it would have been her bad choice. Dealing, as he did, with young adults, Randollph had no illusions about the superior wisdom of the young, but he stoutly defended their right to make their own stupid mistakes.

"Lunch, madam," the maid announced, and departed.

Mrs. Sellersman rose. "You don't know how much you've helped me," she told Randollph, "advising me and comforting me."

Randollph was astounded. Beyond a fragmentary sentence or two and an occasional grunt which could be taken for assent, he hadn't said a helpful thing. Dr. Turley, an old pro of the counseling chamber, could have told him that the art of pastoral counsel lies mostly in making the right sort of noises.

"Bring your drink with you," Mrs. Sellersman said, leading him to the dining room. Randollph was starving, but he would gladly have fasted a week in exchange for a look at Marianne Reedman's diary.

18

SAMANTHA STACK wished she had accepted Randollph's offer of the car, but now she would have to make do with a taxi. As she walked away from the church toward town, she was bucking a stream of mourners gathering for the Reedman service, some chatting in subdued tones, others looking stonily ahead. All, though, were turned out in somber costuming appropriate for an upper-middle-class funeral.

Two blocks away she found a taxi stand with a rust-pocked Ford labeled "Harold's Cab." Harold—she supposed it was Harold—sat slumped in the front passenger seat languidly reading the sports section of the New York *Daily News*. Her tap on the window brought him to life. Reaching back, he unlatched a rear door for her.

"Do you know the Athens Restaurant?" Sammy asked.

"Sure do, miss. Hop in." Harold's tone implied that everyone knew the Athens Restaurant. "That's Phil Kasko's place." Harold persuaded his worn-out engine to cough into noisy life. "You from out of town, aintcha?"

Sammy confessed that she was from out of town.

"Reason I could tell is that everyone around here knows where the Athens is. Local person would just a said, 'Take me to Athens.'"

"I was told it was the best place to eat around here." Sammy wondered how many lies she had told already today, and it wasn't even quite lunchtime.

"That's a fact." Harold agreed with Sammy's mythical informant. "Most expensive, too. Phil ain't givin' anything away."

"He's a good businessman, I gather." Sammy prodded the loquacious Harold for further revelations.

128

"He is that! Why, he took that crummy little Greek beanery his folks owned, built it up, sold it for a good price, and borrowed left and right to build the Athens. Worked out, though. He's coined it ever since. Owns a meat wholesale business, five other restaurants, God knows what else. I was in high school with Phil," Harold said pensively. "Played football with him. Phil's sure been lucky." Harold, Sammy could guess, felt that only the outrageous machinations of a hostile fortune had assigned him to driving a rickety old taxi instead of raking it in in the restaurant game.

Harold's Cab wheezed up a hill and nosed into a fenestration in a high hedge. "Well, here we are, miss," Harold said, as the rusty cab halted under a portico supported by Doric columns. "That'll be three fifty. Meter don't work, but I make this trip so often I know what it is to the penny." Sammy handed him a five, and while he fumbled aimlessly for change, she waved it away. "Thanks," Harold said cheerfully. "Can I pick you up after lunch?"

"I'm not sure how long I'll be here," Sammy told him. It was possible that Phil Kasko had gone to pay his last respects to Marianne Reedman. She intended to await his return, even if it required inebriation or gluttony to justify hanging around the restaurant.

"Just tell the desk to call Harold's Cab," Harold persisted. "I can be here in a jiffy. Have a good lunch."

Inside, the Doric columns gave way to the more flamboyant Ionic. The building, which externally had appeared modest in size, turned out to be immense. Phil Kasko had selected his site well, Sammy observed. Built into the side of a hill, one wall was three stories of plate glass, affording diners on two levels and drinkers in the ground-floor bar a magnificent view of a wooded valley. Waitresses, all nubile and fair, Sammy saw at a glance, were displayed in what a film costumer would design as slave girl dresses. Phil Kasko did not depend on the quality of his food alone to lure customers.

"Madame." A maître d' in an un-Greek dinner jacket greeted her. "Is madame perhaps joining a party already here?"

"No, madame isn't," Sammy retorted. "I'm here alone. I'm not a whore looking for business. I'm hungry as hell. And I wish to speak to Mr. Kasko. So if you can find me a table, bring me a martini—on the rocks please, they never stay cold enough up, and make it with

Bombay gin—then bring me a Greek salad and Mr. Kasko, and I'll be most grateful. Do you think you can manage all that?"

The thunderstruck maître d' mumbled something about Mr. Kasko perhaps being tied up.

"Yes, I expect he has a lot of pretty girls coming in asking for him," Sammy said calmly, "and some of them he probably doesn't want to see." The maître d's startled look told her that she had hit the nail on the head. "But I think he'll want to see me. Here, lend me your pad and pencil. I'll write him a note."

DEAR MR. KASKO [she wrote on the order pad plucked from the nerveless fingers of the maître d'],

I'm a feature writer doing a story on the late Marianne Reedman née Sellersman, and I'm out from Chicago to get the feel and atmosphere of her early environment. Her friends tell me that you knew her better than most, so I'd be most grateful if you would spare me a few minutes and tell me about her.

SAMANTHA STACK

P.S.   In case your maître d' was too shaken up to notice, I'm a very good-looking girl.

"Here." Sammy thrust the note into the maître d's hand. "Give that to Mr. Kasko, and I'll give you ten to one he'll see me. But first, the table and the martini please."

The intimidated maître d' led her to a banquette upholstered in deep red velvet. He evidently preferred to err in giving her too good a table for an unescorted woman rather than the poor one she would normally have drawn, just in case she was someone important. Rather quickly a slave girl with attention-riveting proportions made her way from the bar toward Sammy, bearing a tray with a pitcher and two large balloon glasses. The girl placed the tray in front of Sammy and, with an obsequious bow, withdrew.

"May I pour your drink, Samantha Stack?" She had not noticed his approach, but her quick glance told her he was a noticeable man. Large, six two, she estimated, maybe more, and well over two hundred pounds, he wasn't fat, but she'd bet he had to work at it to keep that belly flat. His black hair sprigged with gray, the expressive

Aegean eyes and sensually formed lips called for colorful dress—perhaps those long underwear and ballet skirt things Greek men liked to wear, Sammy thought. But he was dressed in black and white like a penguin—a well-to-do penguin. Poor boy raised among rich bankers and stockbrokers wants to look like a solid banker or stockbroker instead of a flighty ethnic, Sammy supposed.

"Sit down, please, Mr. Kasko, and do pour me a drink—and for yourself, of course."

"You did shake up Louis," Kasko said in a surprisingly soft voice. "What in the world did you say to him?"

"I told him that I wasn't a whore cruising for business," Sammy said. "Maître d's and waiters always look at unescorted ladies as if that's what they think we are."

Phil Kasko smiled. "I'll have to mention that in our staff meeting. I'm sure it isn't good for business in these days of equality of the sexes." He poured the martini into the two glasses, more in hers than in his, Sammy noticed, then quickly twisted lemon peel over each. "Perhaps," he said gravely, "we should drink to the memory of Marianne Sellersman."

"I wondered if you would be at the services for her today," Sammy said.

Phil Kasko swirled the liquid in his glass. "I thought about it but decided no. Anyway," he said with a tight smile, "old man Sellersman probably posted guards to see that I didn't get in."

"Why would he do that?"

"May I call you Samantha? Fine. Now, Samantha, Marianne's friends must have told you that she and I had a big high school and post high school romance going. Otherwise, you wouldn't be here."

"They dropped a few hints."

"Did they tell you that Marianne's parents finally broke up the romance?"

"No. How could they do that if you two were really in love?"

Kasko gave her a speculative look. "Samantha, you appear to be a girl who makes up her own mind. I'll bet that at an early age you decided that neither your parents nor anybody else would make your decisions for you. Right?"

"Right."

131

"So you wouldn't be able to understand a Marianne Sellersman. It wasn't that she was weak or indecisive. But upper-class-Eastern girls are brought up to believe in duty to family, social class, and God, pretty much in that order. To defy the first two anyway is a sort of treason they don't easily commit. The Sellersmans never let her forget that I was unsuitable. They didn't keep us apart. They were smarter than that. They invited me to all her parties. There I was among her slick prep school boys, a big dumb Greek kid in cheap clothes that didn't fit, and nothing in common with her crowd. She wasn't a snob, but the contrast must have affected her. Then, at the right moment, they brought this Reedman guy on the scene, and well, they just finally gunned me down. To you I know it sounds as if Marianne had no mind of her own, but if you understood how it is with people like the Sellersmans, you wouldn't blame her."

Sammy didn't look very understanding. "I'll try not to blame her," she told Kasko, "but I find it hard. For one thing, you don't look like a dumb Greek in funny clothes to me."

For the first time Phil Kasko laughed, a rich, chocolate sound. "Not now I don't. Now I'm rich and sophisticated and have the best New York tailors. And I owe it all to the Sellersmans—the old folks, not Marianne. When they rejected me, when Marianne finally told me she couldn't buck her parents any longer, I thought of killing myself or joining the foreign legion. What I did was to work about twenty hours a day to make something of myself and show these snotty SOB's that a Greek peasant was just as good as they are."

"Bully for you!" Sammy held out her glass for a refill. "I'm glad you showed them. I'm a peasant, too. I'm on your side. But now tell me something good about Marianne. So far, all I've got is that she finally caved in to her parents and her obligations to her class. That doesn't make for much of a story." Sammy had a mental picture of the recording angel in Presbyterian heaven shaking his head over all the lies she was telling today. "If you were so crazy about her, there must have been plenty of good things."

The big handsome Greek looked out over the defoliated valley, recalling personal history that was at once painful and glorious. After a ruminative pause, he said, "You know, Marianne and I used to park on this very spot. It was part of an old estate, and nobody much was around to bother us. We planned, when we were married, to buy this property and build our dream house on it. She thought it was the loveliest view in the world." He sighed and sipped his drink. "Well, I bought it all right. Maybe that's why I built the restaurant here." He shook his head as if to dispel a dream. "Yes, I'll tell you the good things. Marianne was beautiful, but there are many beautiful girls. Take Phoebe there." He nodded toward the slave girl who had supplied their martinis. "Have you ever seen a more stunning creature? She looks like a particularly sexy angel. But Phoebe is stupid and mean and greedy. Not a nice person at all. Marianne, on the other hand, was—well, she had a radiance of soul. She loved life. She loved her friends. She was one of the few, maybe the only truly good person I've ever known."

Sammy, who lived among the meaningless affections and sleazy relationships of show business, was overwhelmed by the intensity of Phil Kasko's testimony to the character of his early love.

"Did you keep in touch with her after, after you broke up?" she asked almost in a whisper.

"No. No, we had been as close as two human beings can ever be. When you break up something like that, you break it up. Neither of us could have borne a polite how-are-you-getting-along relationship." He signaled for Phoebe. "Miss Stack will have her Greek salad now," he told the girl. "I've taken the liberty of ordering your lunch," he told Sammy. "A filet with herb butter, potato poufs—a specialty of the house, light and fluffy—and strawberries in kirsch. You can always send it back if you don't like it." He smiled. "And, oh, yes, a very respectable claret. There may be other restaurants in northern New Jersey whose food is the equal of mine, but none can match my cellar."

"I hope you ordered double portions," Sammy said. "I hate to eat alone."

Phil Kasko, his mournful mood now passed, grinned. "Your note said you were a good-looking girl. Would I pass up an opportunity to lunch with a good-looking girl, a bachelor like me?"

"You must have had it bad to carry the torch all these years."

"It isn't like that," Phil protested. "At least, not exactly the way you mean it. I'm not a monk. I've had many lovely friendships with

133

many lovely ladies over the years, but I haven't felt like marrying any of them. Maybe I will one of these days. We old-world types are supposed to set great store by having sons, and as of now I don't have anyone to leave my business to." He gave Sammy an amused stare. "Would you be interested? You have a healthy appetite. I like girls that are good eaters."

"I have good teeth, too." Sammy bared them in a mock grin. "But no thanks, not right now. I'm a onetime loser, and I'm in no hurry to gamble again. But if I were, you'd be on my list." She considered him appraisingly. "Rich, handsome, suave, and I'll bet you're one heck of a good cook. What more could a girl ask?"

"Well, Samantha"—Phil laughed—"let me know when you're ready, and I'll put you on *my* list." He became sober again. "Do your Chicago police think Reedman murdered her?"

"They think it's a strong possibility. They'd like to ask him some pointed questions if they could only locate him. Meanwhile, they're asking everyone else pointed questions. They will no doubt get around to you in good time, put you under the hot lights, and say, 'Where were you on the night of the murder between nine and eleven o'clock?'"

Phil Kasko looked very serious. "No doubt they'll get around to me. It won't be pleasant for me, but that's their job of course." He stared out the glass side of his restaurant at the landscape waiting for spring to bring it alive. Sammy saw that he had almost forgotten her presence. "I can't help wondering if I'm not somehow responsible for her death."

"How could that be?" she asked.

"Perhaps if I'd tried a little harder to persuade her to marry me, I could have won her over. Then she'd still be alive."

Sammy felt like crying. "I think you are a very nice man, Phil Kasko." She rose to go. "I thank you for the lovely lunch and for the pleasure of your company."

"I hope you'll come again," he said.

19

RANDOLLPH WAS amazed at the things people who came in for pastoral counsel told him about themselves.

Zealous to play every role a good pastor presumably fills, he had announced in the *Spire* and in the Sunday bulletin that he would be available two afternoons per week by appointment to see anyone who felt the need of spiritual guidance and counsel. His appointment list, like that of a successful psychiatrist, promptly filled up for weeks ahead.

Dan Gantry told him this would happen.

"It's like this, boss," he said to Randollph, "there hasn't been any-one to listen to people here at Good Shepherd for a long time. Old Arty was hardly ever here, and when he was and someone cornered him with a personal problem, he just said, 'Let us pray, and God will make it right,' and then shuffled them out as fast as he could. Me, I try, but who's going to pay attention to a young squirt like me when they've got a serious problem? I get the kids and people in my age bracket, some at least, but people want a pastoral counselor, they look for a little gray in the hair. I've tried to tell the trustees that we ought to have a full counseling service here, with legal, medical, and psychological help available. People come in with the damnedest problems. You'll see. Some of them need a shrink, and plenty of them are in legal jams, and a lot of them probably just need a doctor to prescribe a better diet. There are some problems that need more than prayer."

"Leaving aside the faintly heretical tone of that last comment," Randollph said with a wry smile, "how did the trustees react to your plans for a full counseling service?"

"They said I was full of crap," Dan replied. "Oh, not in those words. What they really said, come to think of it, was that prayer *was* the answer. You'd be surprised at how pious those old crooks can get, especially when piety can save them money."

Randollph, who was familiar with the doings of pious old crooks throughout the history of the church, wasn't surprised. He was, however, alarmed at the demands his impending counseling would, according to Dan, place on him. So he sought out the bishop.

"Did you know, C.P.," the bishop said, swiveling his rickety old desk chair to afford himself a view of the Chicago skyline and the lake through the office window, "that I was a pastor before coming to the seminary?"

Randollph hadn't known.

"And of course I did a lot of counseling as dean. You might call it specialized, although the variety of problems young seminarians can acquire is startling. There was this one chap, quite religious too, who managed to marry three wives and keep them all happy. And on a student pastor's salary. Renews one's faith in miracles, don't you think? But then," the bishop continued with a sigh for happier days, "you didn't come here to listen to the senile prattle of an ex-dean."

"I came for counsel," Randollph said.

"Quite. And you shall have it, insofar as I am able to give it. Which is exactly the fix you'll find yourself in once you start meeting those appointments. On the whole, it might have been wiser to wait until this murder is cleared up to begin seeing people wholesale. I expect you'll get not a few macabre-minded strangers who'll just want to tell you how to solve the crime: people who have seen the murderer in a vision; people who are certain it is their ex-husband who is guilty; even perhaps people who wish to confess that they are guilty."

"I've thought of all that," Randollph said to the bishop. "I'll just have to get rid of the real nuts as rapidly as possible. Perhaps," he mused, "I'll just tell them that my housekeeper says it's the strong right arm of God punishing a sinner which is responsible and let it go at that. That ought to shut them off."

"You'd be surprised at how many would agree with her," the bishop informed him. "Mrs. Creedy, we are compelled to admit, is

136

a particularly unprepossessing example of the personality reeking of religion." He stopped, looking pleased with himself. "Reeking of religion—that's a splendid phrase! I wonder if I could work that into a sermon? No, I suppose not. Bound to be misunderstood. But anyway, it is my experience that people like Mrs. Creedy whose lives have been discommoded by tragedy and can't reconcile the tragedy with the goodness of God find solace in a God who clouts people around. And though the Book of Job examined and discarded the theory a long time ago, the Mrs. Creedys of this world are convinced that those whom the Almighty clouts are by definition sinners, if not open and obvious in their wickedness, then devious and secret in their transgressions."

"As I recall," Randollph said ruefully, "that is how she explained the murder to me. She was almost indignant that I had failed to grasp the answer."

"Indignation is the characteristic demeanor of the Calvinistically inclined," the bishop assured Randollph. "Not that there isn't more than enough in our world to arouse one's righteous anger. It's just that one can't go around with a moral chip on his shoulder all the time, can one?"

Randollph agreed that one couldn't. The bishop then gave him a short course in pastoral counseling. For practical purposes, the bishop told him, you may classify most people seeking your counsel as follows:

1. Harmless nuts

These are the people with a new theory on the identity of the lost tribes of Israel or who have discovered the date of Armageddon by arcane computation of selected numbers found in the Book of Revelation.

"How do you handle them?" Randollph asked.

"Hustle them out as rapidly as is consistent with Christian courtesy," the bishop answered. "Prearrange a signal with Miss Windfall, a buzzer or something, so that when she receives it, she can inform you of some emergency which requires your immediate attention."

"But, Freddie," Randollph expostulated, "isn't that dishonest?"

"Of course it is," the bishop replied, unperturbed. "But it is better to have a slight stain of dishonesty on your soul than a genuine harmless nut on your hands. The grace of God will take the stain off your soul, but nobody but you can get a harmless nut off your hands."

2. Dangerous nuts

You'll get an occasional psychotic who is dangerous to himself or others, the bishop instructed Randollph. Do your best to get him the kind of help he needs, but don't try to work with him. This is beyond the depth of the average pastor who has no clinical training.

3. Lonesome people

They will even cook up personal problems just to have someone to talk to, and a pastor, unlike a psychiatrist, doesn't charge to listen. Talking to lonesome people is part of a pastor's job, but he can't listen interminably. Try to get lonesome people connected with some group in church or community.

4. People with bona fide problems who need the ministrations of a wise pastoral counselor.

"But, Freddie," Randollph protested, "I have no training and no experience in pastoral counseling. How do I know what to tell people to do about their problems?"

The bishop put his hands behind his head and gazed at a freighter crawling along the horizon. "What you do, C.P., is mostly listen. In professional circles they call this nondirective counseling, and they adumbrate all sorts of sound psychological principles to support it. Actually, it is based on the knowledge that people are going to do what they are going to do, but that it helps them to know what they are going to do if they can talk about it. Is that too complicated?"

Randollph took a minute to digest the bishop's wisdom. "No, Freddie, I can grasp that. What you're saying is that common sense and the ability to keep my mouth shut should get me by."

"Exactly."

"And I suppose a certain sympathy for people with a malaise of the spirit. God knows I have that. But, Freddie, is it necessary to employ prayer and pious clichés?" Randollph recalled Dr. Turley's elegant unction and winced.

"I think prayer is optional, C.P. Much depends, I judge, on the character of the counselor. If he is one to whom the pieties come easily and naturally, then perhaps they are in order. On the whole,

138

though, the use of prayer and pious clichés, as you put it, to give your counseling a higher spiritual horsepower rating smacks of the shaman, the medicine man—or so it strikes me."

Randollph rose to go. "Thanks, Freddie," he said. "You've been a real help. I think I can manage now."

"I wish you could manage to clear up that awful murder and also locate the church's ten million dollars," the bishop said. "They both weigh heavily on me, I don't need to tell you."

"I can't do much about locating the money. We'll have to trust Lieutenant Casey and his connections for that. As for the murder, I'm giving it a lot of thought."

"I rather suspected that you were, C.P." The bishop turned regretfully from looking at the lake and ushered Randollph to the door. "You have the kind of mind that would naturally respond to such a challenge."

"You mean I have a criminal streak in me?"

"I believe some of the sportswriters have suggested that you think like a crook."

Randollph opened the office door. "They did at that, Freddie," he said with a grin. "They did at that."

It took only a day at the job for Randollph to discover that the bishop had been uncannily accurate in his analysis of the pastor's function as counselor and that a pastor as counselor hears a great deal more about marital discord than he cares to know.

Returning from lunch, he stopped by Miss Windfall's desk to look over his appointments for the afternoon.

"First we have a Mrs. Jones," Miss Windfall informed him. Miss Windfall had been using the plural pronoun for some days now.

"Mrs. What Jones?" Randollph inquired. "Do we know her?" He supposed it was good for Miss Windfall's morale to humor her with the "we."

"No, she made the appointment by phone. She said it was urgent. She sounded all right."

Randollph translated this to mean that Mrs. Whatever Jones had a cultured upper-class telephone voice and that she probably had had a fight with her husband.

"If she turns out to be a pest, you've just to buzz me, and I'll create

139

an emergency." Miss Windfall had fallen in with this deceptive practice with what Randollph considered almost shocking alacrity.

"Who else do we have?" he asked.

Miss Windfall read off three names he didn't recognize. "Then there's Don Miller," she added. "Professor Miller. I put him last because I thought he might take longer. After all, he's a trustee." Professor Miller's somewhat exuberant life-style and consistently dissenting voice on the board of trustees, normally qualities which would have earned Miss Windfall's instant disapproval, were wiped out by his formidable wealth and social standing.

Mrs. Jones was expensive and anxious. About fifty, Randollph estimated, minimized to forty-five for the superficial glance. She draped her dark silky mink coat on a chair and arranged herself expertly on Randollph's sofa. A simple red wool suit, which must have cost the equivalent of a month's salary for Miss Windfall, Randollph guessed, displayed a figure kept trim by rigid self-denial and plenty of exercise. Mrs. Jones knew all about casual elegance.

But Mrs. Jones had been doing some suffering, he saw by the look of her eyes and the lines around her mouth. Randollph, instead of remaining behind his desk, came around and sat on the sofa with her.

"May I smoke, Dr. Randollph?" she asked, extracting a gold cigarette case and matching lighter from her bag, laying them on the coffee table in the manner of people who know that one is not going to be enough.

"Of course. May I?" He flicked the lighter for her.

"Thank you." Mrs. Jones dragged hungrily on her cigarette. "And by the way, my name is not Jones."

"I thought perhaps it wasn't. So plebeian a name for so lovely a lady." Randollph sensed that his visitor needed reassurance.

She gave him a grateful smile. "That was nice of you. I decided last Sunday that you were a nice man—at least an understanding one. I attended your service, you see."

"Oh?"

"I wanted to size you up. I'm good at sizing people up. For example, you're very sure of yourself. Most men would have protected themselves behind the symbol of their position and authority—their desk. You came around and sat by me." Randollph, who was not at all sure of himself as a counselor, fielded the compliment as gracefully as he knew how. "Oh, I'm shrewd about people, all except husbands." She punctuated her speech with a short, bitter laugh.

Randollph, remembering the bishop's instructions, said nothing.

Mrs. Jones snuffed her half-smoked cigarette with an impatient stabbing motion and immediately lit another. "I gave a false name because I don't want you to know who I am. You might recognize it from the society pages. Although"—she surveyed him levelly—"you don't look like the kind of man who reads the society pages. That's a compliment."

Randollph thought the bishop would permit Mrs. Jones a "thank you" and gave it to her.

"You're welcome." She smiled. "But I'm dithering. I'm not even sure why I'm here. Partly from good motives and partly for selfish reasons, I suppose. That's probably the case with most people who come to confession, isn't it?"

Randollph agreed that people who acted from impulses pure and undefiled were rare.

"The good motive is this." Mrs. Jones mashed out another cigarette. "I thought it was my duty to inform you of what no one seems to have discovered—that your little Miss Goody-Goody Reedman was a whore!" She spat it out with the viciousness of a striking rattler.

Randollph speculated with interest on what would be her bad motive.

"How is it that you happen to be privy to this information?" he asked.

Mrs. Jones looked as if she were about to swallow a draft of extremely bitter medicine. "Because she seduced my husband and absolutely bewitched him."

Randollph noticed signs of an impending emotional eruption. Freddie had told him always to "have water and Kleenex handy." He went to his desk, took a box of tissues from a drawer and a silver carafe which Miss Windfall dutifully filled each morning. "Here," he said, returning to the sofa and pouring a glass of water for his visitor, "You'll feel better." He placed the tissues in front of her on the coffee table.

141

Mrs. Jones gratefully drank half the glass. "Thank you." She gave him a weak smile. "You're a real professional, aren't you? You must be quite accustomed to sniffling females. Don't worry, I won't break down. Now where was I?"

"Your husband—"

"Oh, yes. Well, you see, I bought my husband. Oh, don't look startled. I'm very wealthy, and he's ten years younger than I am. He is handsome, and he has lovely manners, and he is kind and loving. I know it's my money that keeps him with me. Like so many men who have the human qualities a woman admires, he is entirely unsuited to survive in the dog-eat-dog business world. He should have been born rich, but he wasn't. So the next best thing for a man like that is to marry rich. And so I bought him. I pretend that he is madly, passionately in love with me—or at least I did. . . ."

Randollph hastily poured more water and shoved the box of Kleenex toward her.

"Well, I found out he was seeing this Reedman woman," Mrs. Jones continued, pulling back from the brink of tears.

"How?"

"I hired detectives. I thought he was slacking off a little in the love department, so I guessed another woman. A rich middle-aged woman with a young husband is bound to be a snoop." Mrs. Jones laughed bitterly. "She has to protect her investment, you know."

"And?"

Mrs. Jones abandoned self-recrimination for narrative. "I went to see her. I thought I might buy her off, but it turned out she was richer than I was."

"So?"

"She just laughed at me. Said she was sorry, she didn't wish to hurt me. Said she had bought a husband, too, a fellow with excellent credentials, but that he had turned out to be a poor investment. Would you believe she was sympathetic? She volunteered to break off the affair. Said it was about time for her to change partners anyway."

"And did she?"

"She did. Immediately."

"With what effect on your husband?"

"He moped around for quite a while. He was just beginning to be his old self again when Marianne Reedman was murdered. Now it's like he's having a nervous breakdown. He pretends he's getting an ulcer to explain his behavior, but it's just emotional upset."

Randollph, fascinated by his anonymous visitor's story, remembered that he was trying to be a detective and that he should act like one. "Mrs. Jones," he shot at her severely, "do you think your husband murdered Marianne Reedman?"

"Good God, no!" Mrs. Jones exclaimed. "He couldn't harm a fly! Take my word for it, Dr. Randollph. Why, he's very religious—"

"Very religious people have been known to kill," Randollph pronounced, sounding more judgmental than he had intended.

Mrs. Jones brushed his protest aside. "Oh, Crusaders and the Inquisition and people like that. Fanatics. My husband isn't that kind of religious. He's deeply devout, an Anglo-Catholic, that's how we met. Anglo-Catholic is High Church Episcopal," she explained, "but then, you'd know that, wouldn't you?"

Randollph acknowledged that he knew that.

"Anyway," she swept on, "he's very concerned about human values and the sanctity of human life. He belongs to all kinds of liberal organizations. He also frets about his own soul." She paused, smiling slightly. "I'll bet he went to confession every time he screwed the Reedman woman—sorry, Dr. Randollph, I didn't mean to be crude—"

"I have heard the word before," Randollph assured her.

Mrs. Jones laughed. "I'm sorry, Dr. Randollph, I'm just thinking about our rector. He's a proper, prissy bachelor, like so many High Church clergymen, lives with his mother. I'll bet Theo—my husband's —confessions were a shock to his nervous system. It's not funny, I know. But if you knew our rector. . . ."

"You realize, Mrs. Jones, that this is information the police would dearly love to have."

Mrs. Jones was alarmed. "You wouldn't tell them, you couldn't! This is like a confessional, isn't it? You can't betray the sanctity of the confessional!"

"I'm not certain what the courts would hold, but I promise to treat this as privileged information," Randollph said.

Mrs. Jones sighed with relief. "Trust me. I know my husband. I might be capable of murdering Marianne Reedman, but not my husband."

"Did you kill her?" Randollph asked.

"No, I didn't." Mrs. Jones acted as if she were explaining basic psychology to a freshman class. "I'm worse off with her dead than with her alive. Anybody would know that. I think, though, that the police should look for some discarded lover of hers who isn't as sweet and kind and harmless as my husband. That was really my unselfish motive in coming. I can't go to the police because I don't propose to be dragged through all the nasty publicity that would involve. But I'm a citizen with some conscience. I want the police to have the knowledge I have of Marianne Reedman. You can tell them." She fumbled for another cigarette. "Tell them to forget about a rapist. Tell them to look for whoever was laying the woman at the time. What happened was that she gave him one last roll in the hay and then told him good-bye. Then he strangled her."

Randollph admitted to himself that Mrs. Jones' theory made sense.

"I'll report your information about Mrs. Reedman's sexual habits to the police," Randollph told her, "protecting you, of course. You said you also had a selfish motive for coming here?"

A suddenly nervous Mrs. Jones got up and paced to a window. "This place needs redecorating," she informed Randollph. "It's too drab. You need more color." Resuming her seat, she abruptly switched to Randollph's question. "Yes. I'm afraid. I'm afraid I'm under Divine judgment. I'm afraid God is punishing me for buying my husband, for holding him with money instead of love. And, oh, God," she cried, burying her face in her arms, "I'm afraid of getting old!"

Randollph decided it was time to abandon the monosyllabic approach to pastoral counseling.

"Mrs. Jones, do you love your husband?"

Mrs. Jones twitched a tissue from the box Randollph had provided, blew her nose, and said, "Very, very much."

"Does he know you know about Marianne Reedman?"

She looked at Randollph as if she suspected him of stupidity. "Don't be silly. Of course he doesn't. That would just precipitate a crisis, and he has enough on his mind or soul at the moment."

144

"But you think God is punishing you and will continue to punish you for what you believe to be your sins?"

"Yes. Isn't that how it works?"

Randollph assumed the most didactic tone he could muster. "Now listen to me, Mrs. Jones. You are wanting absolution, and while your rector has a formula for it, I don't. I can, however, assure you that, no, that isn't how it works. God isn't a judge or a policeman. It is true, of course, that when we act selfishly, or irresponsibly, or brutally, that we sometimes set in motion forces which, sooner or later, have an adverse reaction. Not always, but sometimes. This adverse reaction is not to be confused with the punishment of God." He paused to see if she was digesting all this. Satisfied that she was, he continued. "Your real problem, I suspect, is that because you have always been able to buy acceptance, you fear that is the only reason people accept you."

Mrs. Jones stoutly defended her unworthiness. "Why else would an attractive man ten years younger marry me except my money?" she asked. "The Reedman woman business proves that."

"Not at all." Randollph rebuked her. "You'd best regard that as an episode. Maybe Mrs. Reedman did bewitch him, as you yourself suggested. Some women seem to have that capability."

Mrs. Jones, he observed, looked a little more confident, but not much. Stronger medicine, he decided, was indicated.

"Mrs. Jones," he said severely, "you are underrating yourself. As a churchgoing woman, you must have heard Jesus' admonition that we are to love ourselves."

"Of course I have, but I don't understand it," his visitor said stubbornly. "Loving myself too much has always been my big problem."

"You are confusing excessive concern for yourself with a decent sense of your own worth, which is a pretty good definition of what Jesus meant by loving ourselves." Randollph wondered if he sounded like Dr. Turley.

"But what would my husband possibly see in me apart from my money?"

Mrs. Jones, Randollph could see, was a hard nut to crack. She apparently didn't have too much confidence in the precepts of her religion. Maybe, like most modern American women, what she really believed in was the power of sex.

"Mrs. Jones," he said, "I am probably about the same age as your husband. I hope I share at least some of the admirable qualities you attribute to him. So I ought to be able to think somewhat as he thinks. Do you agree?"

"Ye-es." Mrs. Jones couldn't see where this conversation was headed.

"Now, what do I see in you?" Randollph paused and surveyed his visitor with what he intended to be a lascivious gaze.

"What?" Mrs. Jones asked dully.

"I see a woman who—that is, with whom I'd—well, I'm uncertain just how to say this. . . ."

Mrs. Jones sat up with a start. "Dr. Randollph," she said with a slow smile, "are you trying to tell me that I look like I'd be a good lay?"

Randollph remembered a time when he fumbled the snap from center before fifty thousand people and decided he felt at the moment about as he had felt then. The best thing to do was to recover as quickly as possible.

"Mrs. Jones," he said firmly, "I am certainly not insensitive to your physical charms." Unorthodox counseling procedures, Randollph decided, had their limits.

Mrs. Jones was still smiling. "Dr. Randollph, if I didn't know better, I'd think you were propositioning me." She was looking much better, Randollph noted.

"No, Mrs. Jones, this is an appraisal, not a proposition. I'm trying to look at you objectively through the eyes of a man ten years or so your junior. But I mean what I say. What I'm saying is that you look good to me, and by extension you look good to any sensitive man who appreciates a beautiful, appealing woman."

Mrs. Jones smiled.

"Furthermore," Randollph went on, "I'd like to spend some time with you. You seem to have an interesting mind; you would be a charming companion. We might even debate the merits of Anglo-Catholicism, which you probably rate much higher than I would be inclined to. A woman with whom a man can carry on a sensible theological discussion is rather rare, you know. I'm a man with a few brains and a bit of experience. As, I gather, your husband is also, and

146

while I do not by any means underrate the joys of copulation, I know you can't spend all your time at it. What do you do between times? You talk. Thus my preference for a mature, intelligent woman over a twenty-five-year-old body out of *Playboy* who is too immature to have any real communication with me when we aren't in bed. I'll take you every time to the centerfold girl, Mrs. Jones, and so, I suspect, will your husband."

Mrs. Jones beamed.

"However, I wouldn't marry you. Now don't look so crestfallen," Randollph hastened to tell her, "until you hear me out. I wouldn't marry you until you got over the idea that you are only worth what your money is worth. I wouldn't want a wife with that low an opinion of herself." Randollph rose and retrieved Mrs. Jones' silky mink. "Now I suggest that you go home and get about the business of re-aligning your thinking about yourself."

Mrs. Jones let Randollph help her on with her coat. "I don't know what they taught you in seminary about counseling ladies in distress, Dr. Randollph," she said, "but I'll bet it wasn't anything like the way you just talked to me." Randollph, mentally reviewing the bishop's instructions, was certain that Freddie would have been as astounded at him as was Mrs. Jones.

"I'm not suddenly convinced of my own worth," Mrs. Jones said, pulling on her gloves. "I suppose that will take a lot of time, assuming I can ever manage it at all. Perhaps I ought to sell all and give it to the poor; then I'd find out. But I'm not that anxious to feel worthy." She smiled at him. She looked good when she smiled, Randollph thought. "But I do feel better, a lot better." Quickly she threw her mink-clad arms around him and gave him a very authoritative kiss. Randollph hoped Miss Windfall wouldn't pick this moment to interrupt.

"And so, Dr. Randollph," the little brown man with black plastered-down hair droned on, "if you will look at my chart, you will see how in one generation all Moslems in the world can be converted to Christianity. It is only a matter of each new convert winning two converts. If our Association for the Conversion of the Moslems can find enough money to send missionaries, we have many ready to serve and it costs so little. . . ."

Randollph, in desperation, surreptitiously pushed the buzzer summoning Miss Windfall and a manufactured emergency. The little brown man with his dubious enterprise for mission and preposterous chain-letter evangelical arithmetic had somehow slipped through Miss Windfall's protective netting. Randollph, from his days with the Association of Athletes for Christ, was familiar with religion of the unexamined premise. Would the Moslems of the world be better off as Christians? Would the world be better off? Was it spiritual arrogance to set out to wean people from one faith to another? These were questions for Randollph, but not, he knew, for the little brown man. Single-minded, fervent, the little missionary would slave for and sacrifice for his antic cause. Sublimely dedicated to the questionable, he would never question it.

Randollph had endured, subsequent to Mrs. Jones, two trivial and boring family problems—

". . . so I said, it doesn't make any difference if you are my brother-in-law, I'm holding you to the deal. Now what I want to know, Dr. Randollph, is there anything unchristian about. . . ."

". . . and my husband says no, sir, he isn't shelling out for any big wedding, but she's my only daughter, and I've always dreamed. . . ."

And then the little brown man who was determined to convert the Moslems. Randollph had listened to all of it with half an ear. Since none of his visitors required anything of him but an occasional mutter or grunt, he was able to mull over this new information about Marianne Reedman, push it here, shove it there to see where it fit in the puzzle. Actually, it was not a startling new fact, but more in the nature of confirmation of one theory that Lieutenant Casey was already working on. The most significant of Mrs. Jones' contributions, he thought, was her report of Marianne Reedman's remark that it was about time to change partners again. If Marianne Reedman was the kind of girl, as now seemed the case, who acquired and discarded lovers on a regular time schedule, then it was not unlikely that somewhere along the line she would miscalculate and jettison one who refused to obediently go over the side. It was not hard to imagine a certain type of man, unhinged by passion and infuriated by rejection, throttling his love. After all, it happened all the time.

But how far along did this get them toward clearing up the murder?

Not too far, Randollph had to admit. Mrs. Jones' information, after all, could be the product of, or at least the enlargement of, a jealousy-inflamed imagination. Randollph felt rather certain that Mrs. Jones had rendered a reasonably accurate report of Marianne Reedman's involvement with the anonymous Mr. Jones, but he wished he had some other source which would confirm the light Mrs. Jones had shed.

Miss Windfall whisked the missionary to the Moslems out and Professor Donald Miller in with ruthless efficiency. Miller, Randollph presumed, wanted to enlarge on his performance at the trustees' meeting or perhaps satisfy his curiosity on what all was happening.

"I'm genuinely glad to see you, Professor," Randollph said with warmth. "I'm anxious to talk about that, ah, rather unusual trustees' meeting."

"That was fun, wasn't it?" Miller pulled a chair to the corner of Randollph's desk and began unloading pipes, tobacco pouch, and all the paraphernalia required to keep a briar bowl of tobacco burning properly. "Been waiting for years for that moment. I've watched those buzzards flimflam the church for a long time, but whenever I protested, they just voted me down. Incidentally, let's be informal. Call me Don. What's your given name?"

"You wouldn't believe it," Randollph told him. "My friends call me C.P. I'd be glad if you'd call me C.P."

"Fine," Miller said. "That's settled." He was industriously packing an aluminum-stemmed model with a detachable bowl.

"Isn't that a lot of trouble?" Randollph asked.

"Yes," Miller said gravely, "but worth it. Well worth it." Pipe smokers, Randollph decided, must be a religious sect which, like Baptists and advocates of world government, see nothing funny about their faith.

"Now, C.P."—Miller's voice emerged from billows of smoke—"I think you ought to seize the opportunity and fire the whole board of trustees. Must be some legal way to do it. Better get rid of Smelser,

149

too. He wanted the head job, you know, so he went along with anything those barracudas did. Almost got it, too. I think if I hadn't voted no, the bishop—against his better judgment—might have consented. It's pretty hard to go against the unanimous request of the church's top officials. But that isn't what I came in to talk about. I have something in the nature of a confession to make, so I shall invoke the traditional privilege of the booth that my priest must hold it in silence. Do you agree?"

Now what? Randollph thought. Twice in one day to have the promise of secrecy extracted from him was something of a record, he imagined, for a pastor of a church which does not formally recognize confession as a part of the sacrament of penance.

"Yes," he said.

Professor Miller took this moment to relight his pipe. Finally leaning back in his chair, he said, "I don't know where to begin. I'll bet you hear that sentence with some frequency, eh, C.P.?"

Quite a few people, Randollph acknowledged, begin their talk that way. He thought it best not to add that this usually meant they knew exactly where they were going to begin.

"As you probably know," Miller said, "I teach at the university. But I don't work at it too hard. Oh, I like it, and I do it well enough, and I enjoy the frowsy intellectual atmosphere at the Faculty Club. But owing to prudent and avaricious ancestors who made vast sums of money, probably in ways I wouldn't care to scrutinize too carefully, I'm excused from the pestiferous necessity of earning a living."

"A very pleasant state of affairs, I would say," Randollph remarked.

"Yes, I find it so," Miller answered. "I justify my existence—that old devil the Protestant ethic, you know—and occupy my time with teaching. But mainly I have a good time. I travel, I patronize the arts —not for show but because I'm inclined that way, mind you. And though I'm a bachelor, I am not a celibate. Does this shock you, C.P.?"

"No," Randollph answered, slightly irritated that anyone would think he was that easily shocked. "I haven't thought about it, but now that you mention it, I wouldn't have supposed that you were celibate."

150

Miller, a little disappointed that racy personal confessions failed to dent his pastor, said, "Well, fine. I don't want to offend you."

"You won't," Randollph said shortly.

"I have some personal rules and codes about my association with ladies," Miller went on. "I won't involve myself with married ladies. I won't, ah, that is, make love to them until a firm personal relationship has been established."

Mrs. Jones, Randollph recalled, didn't mince words. She would have said screw instead of stuttering around with a euphemism. Was Professor Miller a puritan after all? Or were women just less romantic about sex than men?

"And when breakup time comes, I always take great care to manage it amicably. I want it to remain a beautiful memory, a lovely picture in the mind. Oh, yes, I have my own strict sexual morality."

Randollph, thinking that the professor with his beautiful memory morality sounded like a mortician's advertisement, said, "Whether it's a moral or an esthetic approach to the problem might be debated, but there's no denying it's most civilized and considerate."

"What?" Miller was thrown off stride. "Oh. Oh, yes, I suppose you're quite right. Well, anyway," he hastened on, "that is, I stuck to my code until rather recently."

Randollph could guess the rest of the story.

"What happened was that I . . . I had an affair with Marianne Reedman." Miller's pleasantly at ease manner had given way to a tense, strained air, almost mournful. He had also abandoned his pipe, for which Randollph was grateful. The air in the study was positively toxic.

"And so, for the first time, I committed adultery," Miller said, a little sadly, Randollph thought. He *was* something of a puritan.

"For what it's worth," Randollph said to him, "I think she was the one who committed adultery. You were guilty of fornication, if guilty is the word. At any rate, a moral technicality. Probably isn't relevant."

Miller brightened. "With Marianne Reedman I would have committed adultery, fornication, sodomy, incest, anything. There is no way to describe what she was like."

151

It was Randollph's turn to be surprised. Mrs. Jones had said Marianne Reedman had bewitched her husband, but he had put that down to the fevered ego of a jealous woman.

"For some reason," the professor gushed on, anxious now to get his tale told, "she picked me. She was the aggressor. You wouldn't guess where we, where she seduced me."

"The choir room," Randollph guessed.

"Yes, that was it." Miller looked disappointed. "We met there almost every choir practice night for half a year or so. We met many other places of course. She even spent a skiing weekend with me in Switzerland. But she had a thing about that room. Something about copulating in there got her excited. Of course, it was convenient, too. I'd go in the hotel lobby and call the choir room about nine o'clock every Thursday night. Did you know there's a phone down there on an outside line? Tony Agostino had it put in. Well, if the coast was clear, and it usually was, I'd just take the hotel elevator to the fourth floor, change over to the church elevator and ride directly to the basement. It's quite an easy and almost secret way to get down there, you know."

"Didn't anyone ever see you?" Randollph asked.

"Hardly ever. Of course, on trustee meeting nights once every month I had good reason to be there. On the other nights once in a while someone would stop the elevator at the main floor of the church building. When that happened I'd get out and mingle into the crowd —there's always a crowd around on Thursday nights—and slip on down the stairs when no one noticed. Of course, no one who knew me would be surprised to find me in the church on any night. After all, I'm a trustee. But I hardly ever saw anyone."

"I crave to know more about Marianne Reedman," Randollph said to the professor. "The picture you give me doesn't quite jibe with the picture I get from her friends and associates."

"I know," the professor responded. "That's really what I came in to tell you. You and the police have been getting a sort of Caesar's wife impression of Marianne, haven't you?"

"Something like that."

"And you haven't been able to fit it together with the evidence that Marianne had had, ah, sexual intercourse the night she died?"

"That's right. Lieutenant Casey has even speculated on the possibility of a rapist."

"Don't you believe it!" Miller was vehement. "It was my successor in her affections, whoever he was, or rather is."

Randollph pondered this for a moment, then asked, "Your affair had terminated when?"

"About three months ago."

"And it lasted how long?"

"About six months."

"And you don't know who your successor was?"

"No. I didn't even know for sure there was one, although I assumed there was."

"Didn't you ever think of sneaking down to the choir room on a Thursday night to find out who's kissing her now, so to speak?"

"Of course I thought of it," the professor said. "Who wouldn't? But I didn't."

"Why not?"

"Because I didn't really want to know. As long as I didn't know for sure, I could pretend to myself that there wasn't anyone new. Even though I was pretty sure there was someone, I could still pretend. It helped a little."

"Did you ever think of killing her?" Randollph shot at Miller in what he intended to be a brisk interrogative tone.

Miller looked mildly surprised.

"Did I kill her, you mean?"

"You must admit that it's a question that begs for asking," Randollph said. "The police, for example, would be asking it most imperatively if they knew about your relationship with Mrs. Reedman."

The professor, Randollph saw with annoyance, was about to start in on his pipes again. "C.P.," he said gravely, "I know it's kind of a dirty trick I'm playing on you, invoking the tradition of the confessional. I'm forcing you to be the judge and jury in my case. I have what the police would consider a strong motive. I was on the premises and had not only every opportunity but also the rather certain knowledge that Marianne would be in the choir room in the embrace of my successor. Don't you think that your policeman, what's his name—"

"Lieutenant Michael Casey," Randollph supplied.

"Don't you think he'd move me to the top of his suspect list?"

"Yes."

"Well, I'm telling you that I didn't do it. I'm not a violent man, and I'm not a vengeful man, and I'm not enough of an egotist that I can't sustain rejection. Oh, it hurt. It hurt like hell. Still does. I might have killed my successor, I suppose. I don't know. Maybe that's why I never wanted to know about him. But not Marianne. I was crazy, mad in love with her! She was the most powerful experience of my whole life. I would no more have thought of killing her than I would have thought of killing myself. Which," he added, "I'm not about to do. Although I mourn my love, and I hate the thought of a world without Marianne Reedman in it, I'm too much of a philosopher to give up. I know I'll recover. I know how much life has to offer. No, C.P., I'm not the killing type. I'm asking you to believe that."

"I believe you." Randollph was glumly aware that now two possible murderers, both with motive and opportunity, were counting on the privileged silence of the confessional to keep him from telling the police about them. Since he couldn't help himself, he'd better get back to his detecting, he supposed.

"You were about to reconcile Mrs. Reedman's public image with her energetic sexual conduct. What made her behave that way?"

"You know, I can't answer that," Miller answered, "because I don't really have the answer. You are thinking of her as two separate persons: the gracious, charming, vivacious public Mrs. Reedman and the libidinous private Mrs. Reedman. But she wasn't a dual personality or anything like that. No two faces of Eve here. The private Marianne Reedman was, in most ways, an extension of the public Mrs. Reedman. Can't you see that?"

Randollph confessed that he could not, and further light would be appreciated.

"Well," Miller said thoughtfully, "let me explain it this way. You know quite a few conventional, even dignified ladies, don't you?"

"Don't we all?" Randollph replied.

"And when you just know them casually it's hard to imagine them moaning in ecstasy, thrashing around in the throes of copulation. It doesn't fit with their cool, poised public personality. And yet you know that they are both poised in public and passionate in the bedroom. Some of them, anyway. Do you follow me?"

Randollph said he thought so but encouraged the professor to develop his thesis further.

"Well, that's the way it was with Marianne. Now you've met her husband. A brute. A no-good. They had little to do with each other. Marianne liked sex. Loved sex." Miller seemed almost to be talking to himself. "My God, did she love it! She was sweet and tender and wanton and violent all in one person. She would whisper endearments along with the crudest kind of vulgarities. She would be petting you and caressing you one moment, and clawing and straining the next. Why are some girls crazy about sex and others not? I don't know. Why do certain kinds of men appeal to one girl and not particularly to another? I don't know. Marianne didn't go for just any man. Only men who were very unlike her husband. Maybe that was why. Or maybe it had something to do with an earlier love. I don't know. And why did she get tired of one and discard him for another every few months? I don't know. I begged her to divorce Reedman and marry me. I pleaded with her to live with me without benefit of clergy if that's the way she wanted it. But no go. She said, 'It won't work, Don. I love you, but I'd get tired of you. I get tired of everybody sooner or later. Can you understand that?' I couldn't. She was everything a man dreams of in a woman. A saint and a wanton. A sophisticate in the drawing room and a primitive in the bedroom. A nun and a whore. Here"—he pulled a square manila envelope from some capacious inner pocket of his tweed jacket—"I'll show you." He selected a photograph from the envelope. "I'm a good amateur photographer, you know. This is Marianne the nun." He handed Randollph a photo of a brunette beauty. She was wearing a simple summer dress, and as she was gazing out at the sea, the wind blew her hair back from her face. The fine features, the chaste dress, the shining half-smile gave her an angelic look.

"She was a lovely-looking lady," Randollph commented.

"She was that," Miller said fervently. "Now look at this one."

The photograph Miller handed him showed a woman reclining on a richly pillowed couch. She was naked except for a garter belt which drew black stockings high up on her legs, legs spread in invitation.

155

It was, Randollph thought, like something out of one of the less inhibited magazines for men. The photography was of the highest order. The thick curly triangle of black pubic hair, the wanton smile, the spread legs proclaimed only one message: "Mount me! Hurry, hurry, mount me!"

"It's the same woman," Miller said.

"Tell me, Don," Randollph asked, pulling himself back to his detecting, "when Marianne Reedman was preparing to make love, did she fold her clothes and place them neatly in a pile? Would you remember that?"

"Oh, I remember," the professor said. "She certainly did no such thing. When Marianne was ready for love, she stripped with abandon. We used to laugh, afterward, how she had scattered her clothes all over the place."

20

RANDOLLPH THOUGHT it was just as well that Mrs. Sellersman had respected her daughter's privacy. He wished there had been no need to violate it now. But he had been longing to look at the diaries ever since Mrs. Sellersman had disclosed their existence. And now there was the necessity of telling the police that Marianne Reedman wasn't quite the chaste choir singer everyone thought her to be, but of telling them without betraying the confidences of his informants.

But how? Randollph pondered it. He could say, "Lieutenant Casey, it has come to my attention that Marianne Reedman regularly took lovers and just as regularly discarded them. It has also come to my attention that she has used, perhaps for several years, the choir practice room at Good Shepherd as a trysting place." Would Casey then say, "My, that's interesting. We must look into that."

He would not.

He would, Randollph imagined, badger Randollph for the sources of the information. Randollph could plead the sanctity of the confessional, but he doubted that this would satisfy Lieutenant Casey. No matter what the law said, Casey's vestigial Roman prejudices would question the non-Catholic clergy's right to silence. Especially when that silence thwarted a Casey investigation. Casey was ambitious. He didn't intend to be a lieutenant forever. Let him learn about Marianne Reedman himself. From her diaries. Randollph hoped the diaries would reveal enough to let him off the hook. If they didn't, then he'd have to think of something else. The diaries, though, were his best bet.

But where were the diaries?

When he had called Lieutenant Casey to inform him of the existence of these personal and intimate memoirs, there had been a pause at the other end of the conversation. Then Casey had said, "Why didn't you tell me this before? It has been several days since you returned from New Jersey."

"I've been awfully busy," Randollph said lamely. He was doubly glad that he had not given Casey any hint that he was really concealing information, however sacred his reasons. Lieutenant Casey would no doubt continue to be polite, but he probably wouldn't be very understanding.

"Well, I'd surely like a look at those diaries, but would you have any idea where they are?" He sounded almost petulant. Randollph supposed the frustration of a case that wasn't getting itself solved on schedule was a frustration and a nuisance to the lieutenant.

"In her home somewhere, I suppose," he said.

"No. We searched it naturally. We didn't find any diaries."

"Maybe you didn't look in the right place," Randollph suggested hopefully.

"Oh, we'd have found them, all right. They aren't there."

Randollph received an inspiration. "Did you direct the search, Lieutenant?"

"No, no, I didn't," Casey said. "I can't do everything myself."

"No one expects you to, I'm sure," Randollph said soothingly. "Do you recall who did?"

"Garbaski, I think. I can check."

"From what I know of the sergeant, I'd say that imagination isn't one of his hopefully numerous virtues, however obscure."

Casey chuckled. "I think that's a fair appraisal."

"What I'm getting at," Randollph said, "is that it would be easy for an unimaginative man to miss a diary unless he happened to be looking for a diary. Even then he might miss it."

"You want to go out to her house and look for it?"

"I want to go out to her house with you, and we'll both look for it," Randollph said.

Casey did not object when, wheeling an unmarked gray Pontiac sedan into a no parking zone in front of the Church of the Good Shepherd, he learned that another passenger had been added to the manifest. Randollph, enlarging on his original inspiration, thought that a woman might be more likely to guess where another woman had hidden an intimate diary and invited Samantha Stack.

Casey nosed the Pontiac up Michigan Avenue, past the Tribune Tower which looked as if it too housed a church somewhere in its Gothic entrails; past the big commercial hotels and chic shops spawned by Fifth Avenue; past the high-rise apartments where the annual rent was as much as a policeman's salary; past the old water tower, and Big John with its black snout stuck in a low drifting cloud; past the stately old Drake and out onto the lakeshore drive which rimmed most of downtown Chicago's eastern edge and reached toward the northern suburbs.

Casey, contrary to Randollph's fears, was in an expansive mood. "I've lived here all my life," he said, "and I still get a kick out of this drive. To tell the truth, I consider this trip a wild-goose chase, a waste of my professional time. But it's an excuse to get away, and mostly an excuse to make this drive. Would you look at that beautiful lake!"

Sammy Stack said, "You don't quite fit my image of a homicide detective, Lieutenant."

"We're people, too, you know," Casey said. He took her comment for a compliment.

"He's been to college," Randollph told her. "Maybe that confuses you."

"What I'm thinking is that you'd make a good guest on *Sam Stack's Chicago,* my justly celebrated television show. Would you be interested, Lieutenant?"

Lieutenant Casey was interested. He allowed a decent interval to pass, occupying the time by deftly jockeying the Pontiac into a speedier lane of traffic, then said gravely, "Perhaps that would be a help to the department's public relations. It needs all the help it can get, you know."

Randollph, remembering how he had told himself it would do the Church of the Good Shepherd much good to have its interim pastor appear on *Sam Stack's Chicago,* was comforted. Pious rationalizations of our ego drives were not confined to the clergy apparently, although that it should comfort a man to discover other people's mo-

159

tives were as mixed as his own was, he felt certain, a contemptible and ignoble reaction.

The Reedman house was in Wilmette, and they made rapid time because Lieutenant Casey, who was a proficient driver, did not have to worry about speed laws. The house, which was on the lakefront, looked as if the architect couldn't quite decide between ranch house and modernistic. It was, to Randollph's eye, a jumble of stone, glass, and redwood. But a big jumble.

"This is an unusual house," Casey said as he swung up a graveled drive and parked in front of a large ornamented metal door framed in slabs of plate glass. "Inside it's almost like two completely separate apartments. It looks as if Mr. and Mrs. Reedman kept their contacts at a minimum."

"Why in heaven's name did they stay together if they didn't want to live together?" Sammy asked. "If I couldn't stand the guy I was married to, I'd slice the knot but quick. As a matter of fact," she added, "that's exactly what I did."

Lieutenant Casey pondered her question as he riffled through a dozen keys on a large metal ring. "Ah, here it is. Well, Mrs. Stack, I can't answer that, of course. It would be helpful to know the answer. I'd guess, though, that it must have been mutually advantageous. I expect Mrs. Reedman actually owned the Reedman brokerage business, so from Mr. Reedman's point of view it was in his best interests not to be divorced from Mrs. Reedman. He'd be out of a job, and from what we know of him, he's not highly employable, at least not at a level his ego and his financial needs would demand."

"So it's a good deal for him," Sammy said, "but what about her? Why didn't she kick the crumb out? What did she need him for? Certainly not for companionship, the way I hear."

"No," Casey agreed. "But remember that she was a rich woman, and getting rid of an unwanted spouse could have cost a great deal. His price for a quiet divorce might have been exceedingly high. If she wanted to sue anyway, Reedman could have turned it into a very sensational event. I'm sure she didn't want that. Anyway, there were obvious advantages for her in staying married to him. She had a famous Chicago name, which gave her entrée to the best circles. She was having a good time. She didn't, so far as we know, have anyone

160

she wanted to marry, although we may find out differently when we locate the man who was with her in the choir room that night. Barring that, I should think Mrs. Reedman would have found it simpler all around to remain married."

Sammy shook her head. "It wouldn't be simpler for me," she said.

"The rich are perhaps different from the rest of us." Casey smiled. "Some of them seem to be in their house plans anyway." He led them across a huge flagstone paved entry hall. "This place is built like a large T. Now this parlor or whatever you call it—"

"Drawing room sounds classier," Sammy suggested. "It's big enough to call a gymnasium. Kind of standard elegant, isn't it?"

"I suppose so." Casey sounded as if he wouldn't mind living in standard elegance. "Anyway, the parlor and the formal dining room form the crossbar of the T. Then there's this hall and kitchen for the shaft. These are the common rooms. I expect they did quite a bit of entertaining. Now on each side of the shaft"—he indicated two matching doors—"are the two separate apartments." He opened the door to his right. "This is Mrs. Reedman's apartment." He stood aside to let them enter.

They were in a living room, maybe thirty-five feet long and half as wide, which culminated in a solid wall of glass looking out on the lake. The carpet, a deep-pile white, made a huge scarlet sofa almost startling. The bone-white walls displayed several paintings which Randollph couldn't identify because he didn't know much about paintings and almost nothing about abstracts, but they looked like originals, and they looked expensive. There were several occasional chairs in black and in gray. There was a grand piano near the glass wall.

"Through here there's a little hall." Casey conducted his guided tour across the living room to an arched doorless opening. "On this end is a den or library, then a Pullman kitchen and breakfast nook, then the bedroom-bath suite."

They all moved instinctively toward the bedroom.

Like the living room, it had a glass wall looking on the lake which made its generous dimensions seem huge. Here the carpet was the hue of rich coffee cream. The walls were apricot silk, and the oversized bed was dressed in a Prussian blue silk coverlet.

161

"A king-size bed for a queen," Sammy said. "Gee, I never realized till now that I live in a tenement. Well, fellas, let's quit envying how the other half lives and get to work."

"I thought you'd be impressed," Casey said to her. "I know I was. Now, Mrs. Stack, if you had a set of intimate diaries, where would you be inclined to hide them?"

Sammy, Randollph noted, was now all business. "In a wall safe or behind a secret panel would be best." She surveyed the silk walls. "Doesn't look like you could have a secret panel in here."

An examination of the other rooms turned up nothing. They ended up in the library-den, where, all agreed, a secret panel was most likely, but the walls of bookcases proved disturbingly solid.

It was Sammy, though, who found the diaries.

Randollph was absently looking over the titles of Marianne Reedman's library, which were mostly popular novels, when Sammy said, "Would you think a girl who subscribed to the Book-of-the-Month, the Literary Guild, and *Reader's Digest* books would have an interest in the complete works of the Nicene and post-Nicene Fathers?"

Randollph and Casey both admitted that this was unlikely.

"Some people have catholic tastes," Randollph said.

"You should be ashamed of yourself," Sammy said. She quickly pulled one of the large volumes from the case and flipped it open.

"Jackpot," she said.

21

THEY HAD quickly settled down to reading. Marianne Reedman had gone to no little expense to have some bookbinder excise the lofty spiritual meditations of assorted saints from the handsome covers and then binding in blank sheets of heavy imitation vellum on which she had inscribed, in amazingly frank detail, her life and loves. Randollph wondered if the anguished ghosts of Augustine and Chrysostom were hanging around, wringing their hands. If they had taken a glance at what had supplanted them, he was pretty sure they were. Although Augustine, though he would surely disapprove, ought to understand, he reflected. After all, the old boy had had an early history remarkably similar to Marianne's.

"Oh, wow!" Samantha Stack exclaimed in a voice in which Randollph could detect awe and reverence. "Listen to this!"

"Mrrumph," said Lieutenant Casey, and went on reading the volume he had selected.

Samantha looked at him disgustedly. "Here I'm about to read you one of the most beautiful personal accounts of a young girl giving up her virginity to her true love that I've ever read, and how do you react? With a 'mrrumph,' that's how."

"Excuse me, Mrs. Stack, I was absorbed in my own reading." Michael Casey looked up from his book. Casey, Randollph suspected was lying. He was accustomed to being alert to everything that was going on all about him. Lieutenant Casey, a modern man of the world, had not as yet expunged the guilt and shame about sex inculcated by a Catholic education. He was embarrassed to talk freely about it with a pretty girl of only casual acquaintance.

163

"Oh, boy!" Sammy had returned to her book. "She writes, 'I was afraid, because I didn't know what to expect. I had been led by what little I had read on the subject (how does a teen-age girl in my kind of home get her hands on any accurate information about sex?) to expect it to be painful and unpleasant. Mother has even hinted that it's a woman's burden, a price you have to pay for the privilege of having a home and children. But diary, it wasn't like that at all! It was beautiful, wonderful, just totally great! I love everything about it! I'm sure it helped that he was loving and tender, and that I love him so. I was afraid that when it was over I'd feel sinful and ashamed. Dr. Turley keeps lecturing us in Christian Youth Club about how awful it is to do it before we are married, and how if we do we'll be so ashamed and feel so awful we won't be able to face our parents and we won't be able to live with ourselves. Well, diary, Dr. Turley is an old poop. He isn't that old, really, but I think he was born old. Anyway, who'd want to do it with Mrs. Turley, the old prune? Well, when it was over, I didn't feel sinful. I felt marvelous! I thought nothing could ever be so good again. But do you know what, diary? After a few minutes of thinking how good it had been, I took the initiative and coaxed him to do it again (it didn't take much coaxing, ha!), and it was even better the second time.'"

"Now there," Samantha said with undisguised approval, "is a girl who got started on the right foot."

"Let me have a look at that, will you?" Randollph asked her.

"By all means have a look," Sammy said, passing over the book and selecting another from the case. "Can't help but do you good to read it."

Randollph leafed through the early schoolgirl prattle about the trivia that made up her small world.

The first love episode was fascinating. It was followed by many pages reflecting the glow of ecstasy. There was a week when she was worried that she was pregnant, then: "Hoorah! My period arrived. Better late than never!"

Quickly scanning, Randollph learned of the tension in the Sellersman family over "that nice Greek peasant boy" as, according to Marianne, her mother referred to her first love. She recorded, very honestly, her own doubts—planted ingeniously by her family—on the

164

suitability of the match. It was, Randollph perceived, a classic case of natural emotion in conflict with cultural and class values. There was a page on which she had written, "I give up! Maybe I'm a weak person, diary, but I simply can't go on like this. I love him, but I love my parents too! Do I love him enough to cut myself off from my family and friends and the kind of life I know and in turn enter a world of Greek immigrants (I can't stand his mother, a coarse and disgusting creature. His father is nice, though) and a drab little apartment and maybe have to help out in the restaurant (these Greeks are a tribe, everybody helps out in the family business)? I don't know how I'll live without him. But maybe my parents are right—I'm not cut out for that kind of life. Oh, diary, I'm so unhappy."

Randollph read of her agreement, laced with doubts about marrying Wardlow Reedman. "It's hard to explain what's wrong with him. He looks all right, and he has good manners. And as my parents keep telling me until I could scream, he comes from a fine old Chicago family. I don't even know if there is anything wrong with him. I just feel that he lacks something, but as I say, I don't know exactly what it is." Then, with the feminine optimism unquenched by the discouraging history of dubious liaisons, she wrote, "Anyway, I'm sure I can improve him."

She soon found out what was wrong with Wardlow Reedman.

"He's utterly, utterly selfish, diary. Take sex. He doesn't understand the meaning of tenderness. I'm just a convenience for his gratification. He just gets on me and rams it in me, and then he grunts like a pig for about thirty seconds; then he's done. Then he rolls off and goes to sleep. He doesn't care about me as a person at all."

Randollph read how she had fashioned a life for herself out of this sorry marriage. "Ward goes his way; I go mine. I have to keep him on what amounts to an allowance—his salary (very generous) at the brokerage. I pay all living expenses. He's always nagging me for more money. He's not worth anything as a businessman. In fact, the brokerage would do better without him. I get the Reedman name in exchange for keeping Ward. I suppose it's a fair bargain. . . . I began my first extramarital affair tonight. I selected him with care, of course. He was very sweet and—what is the word I want, diary? Virile? I had forgotten how wonderful and satisfying it could be. Am I oversexed?

If I am, I am." Randollph leafed through till he found the account of the end of the affair. "I told him it was over. He actually cried. That was touching, a strong man who wasn't ashamed to cry over me. But I have already selected lover number two."

By the time she had discarded lover number six, Randollph read, Marianne had got around to an attempt at self-analysis.

"Diary, I wonder why I get such a charge out of quitting one affair and starting another. Sometimes I think it is a kind of symbolic revenge against Daddy and Mother and Dr. Turley and the world in which I grew up, which decreed that Sellersman girls didn't marry nice Greek peasant boys. Daddy and Mother would be shocked and horrified at my behavior. I love them with my mind, of course, Mother and Daddy, that is. 'Honor thy father and mother.' But I do resent them with my heart. I shouldn't. They can't help what they are, I suppose. They had their outlook on life pounded into them just as they pounded it into me. But I do resent them. They could have looked at me as a young girl with her own special needs and uncertainties, groping for truth and values. Instead, they thought of me as a Sellersman, to be processed into the kind of person Sellersmans are supposed to become. I resent them, too, for picking Ward Reedman. They should have been mature enough, or at least been around enough, to see what kind of rotter he was. But they never saw past his excellent credentials. Sometimes, diary, when I spread my legs for a new lover, I have a vision of Dr. Turley watching and wringing his hands and saying, 'Marianne, Marianne, have you prayed about this? Marianne, have you asked yourself, "Will I be able to live with myself after this? Will I be able to look my parents in the face?"' And then, diary, I get terribly excited and have the most exquisite orgasm (what the dear empty-headed dames in my social set call the Big O and always complain they so seldom get it). What do you suppose all this means, diary? That I'm emotionally disturbed? That for me sex is a sickness? That I should see a psychiatrist? Well, I'm not going to. Anybody raised as I was is bound to be a little kinky about sex. I suppose if I ever find a man I want to marry, I'll divorce Ward. Until I do, though, I'm enjoying myself and, considering the unpleasant circumstances of my marriage, having a satisfactory life. There seems

166

to be an endless supply of attractive men anxious to get me in bed, so I can be very choosy. . . ."

"Well, how about that!" Sammy exclaimed, interrupting her reading.

"How about what?" Randollph asked absently.

"You rate a mention in Marianne's diary."

Surprised, Randollph could only think to say, "Oh?"

Sammy giggled. "You, dear Doctor, were being considered as a candidate for lover number twenty. Listen to this: 'Our new interim pastor was introduced to the choir this morning. He's very attractive. Judging from his sermon, he's intelligent. I understand he's not married, so he's probably vulnerable.'" Sammy stopped and gave Randollph a searching look. "Are you vulnerable, Chess?"

"Ahem," Randollph said. "Samantha, if that's the last volume, and you're finished with it, I'd very much like a look at it. I take it she mentions the last lover?"

"Number nineteen, but I think you just want to read about yourself. Here, I'll read you about number nineteen." Sammy flipped back a few pages. "Here it is. She says, 'Diary, I must tell you about number nineteen. He's different from the others. Oh, he's sweet and kind and considerate. You know, diary, I won't let anyone fuck me who isn't all these things.' My, my"—Sammy raised her eyes from the diary—"little miss piety-and-virtue can be crude, can't she?"

Lieutenant Casey abandoned his reading. "I'd like to hear more about number nineteen, Mrs. Stack."

"Call me Sammy," she admonished. "Well, here's the rest of it. She goes on to say, 'But he was so inexperienced! Would you believe it, diary, he was a virgin? And at his age! I had to be as aggressive as a professional hooker with him. As I said, he'd never had a woman before, but he learned fast! When we're together, he simply can't get enough, although I think between our meetings he feels terribly guilty about it. I expect some of the thrill for me is in his innocence, and me, the experienced woman, teaching him. Partly, too, I suppose, I get a kick out of tempting him. In spite of his guilty feelings, he can't resist. It isn't going to be easy breaking off with him when the time comes. There are bound to be more than the usual complications. He wants to marry me, of course, like most of the others. He can't see

167

how utterly unsuitable that would be. What a ridiculous couple we would make! I'm afraid, though, that when I break it off, he'll go to pieces. He's so emotional anyway. So passionate, so grateful to me, so much in need of me. I don't know what he'll do when he finds out it is all over." Sammy slapped the book shut. "And that, chaps, is the end, the last entry. Finis. Thirty and out. She must have kissed him off—number nineteen, that is—and he refused to take no for an answer. But who is he? She never names any of the guys, does she?"

"Just assigns them a number, so far as I can tell," Casey said. "Prompted, I suppose, from a sense of delicacy. An unfortunate omission, though, from my point of view. If she'd only named names. Now I have to track down number nineteen, and I haven't the faintest idea where to begin."

"I have," Randollph said, "because I think I know his name."

"No, I repeat, I won't give you his name." Randollph hoped he didn't sound as testy as he felt. "There is no point in badgering me for it, Lieutenant."

"You could be obstructing justice, you know." Michael Casey, who sounded rather testy himself, Randollph thought, swung the Pontiac into Sheridan Road with unnecessary abruptness.

"Come now, Lieutenant," Randollph chided, "recall if you will your lecture to me on the need for solid facts in police work. I have no solid facts to go on."

Casey irritably touched his siren to break up a clot of traffic which threatened to obstruct him, startling a taxi driver and a fat little man in a Cadillac. "You must have something," he growled with an uncharacteristic truculence. He knew he was transgressing the polite, controlled limits of official behavior he had set for himself, which had contributed so much to his rapid rise in the police hierarchy. "Put Casey on it," the captain always said when a crime involved people of position and importance. "He knows how to handle the nobs." Well, he wasn't handling the nobs very well at the moment, he admitted to himself. He was getting short-tempered over his lack of progress in this damned case of the oversexed choir singer. Why couldn't Marianne Reedman have been some obscure streetwalker? Then no one would care very much if the case got solved in a hurry or even if it ever did. He would care, of course, because a man has his professional pride. But he wouldn't be hounded by newspaper reporters every day and have to read in the evening editions that "Detective Lieutenant Michael Casey, who is in charge of the investigation, is expecting to make an arrest shortly." He was coming in for a good deal of kidding about that from his colleagues and not-very-genial sessions with the captain. The captain, he was pretty sure, was not very genial with him because the commissioner was not very genial with the captain. Sensational murders of society figures, especially when committed in the sacred belly of an important church, needed solving for the good of the department, the peace of mind of the captain, and, most of all, the professional future of Detective Lieutenant Michael Casey.

Randollph twisted sideways in the front-seat passenger space the better to address the morose driver. "I have nothing but a surmise," he said in a conciliatory voice, "a surmise arising from the faintest of indications. No more than a hunch, really. If it is inaccurate, as hunches often are, then I would be doing the person I suspect of being lover number nineteen and possibly a murderer, a terrible disservice to give you his name."

Casey was not comforted. "Then are you just going to ignore the whole thing, forget it, let it go?" It was an accusation rather than a question.

"Of course not."

"Then what are you going to do about it?"

Randollph let Casey maneuver past an illegally parked delivery van before answering. "I'm going to do what I did under similar circumstances when playing football for the National Football League," he said, "if you will pardon an illustration from my misspent youth."

"I don't get it," Casey said. "Do they have murders in the NFL?"

"Patience," Sammy admonished. "Let the man explain."

"Let's say we were playing a team with a rookie defensive back," Randollph said. "You have some information about how he played in college, of course. But you have a hunch he's going to be nervous and unsure of himself. That's the standard hunch about rookies, of course."

169

"Sure. I watch the tube, I even get out to see the Bears once in a while. What you do is test your hunch. You toss a couple in his zone to see how he reacts." Casey still sounded irascible. "And if he falls on his ass—I beg your pardon, Mrs. Stack—and you put six on the board, you have confirmed your hunch."

"Exactly," Randollph said.

"Ooh, you big men are so smart, and I'm just a girl who thinks a pass is what that Neanderthal in TV time sales is doing when he keeps trying to feel my leg." Samantha had no intention of being excluded from the conversation. "Would you please interpret all that male talk for me?"

Randollph obliged her. "I'm going to test my hunch as to the identity of lover number nineteen before I tell the lieutenant his name."

"Well, thanks, I'm glad you intend to tell me his name," Casey said, slightly mollified.

"Only if my hunch is confirmed. Only if I can establish a fact which would make it a genuine possibility."

"Sure. Now tell me how you are going to do it, and how long it will take," Casey shot back. "I had better come up with something soon or it will be my—" He checked himself. "I'll have some unpleasant explaining to do unless we get a break soon."

"Two days at most," Randollph said, "but I hope this hunch is not confirmed."

"Now what does that mean?" Casey demanded.

"I don't think I care to expand on it yet." Randollph used the voice he employed when shutting off an unprofitable class discussion. "I hope I never have to."

22

THE NEXT morning Randollph discovered what every pastor of a busy parish soon learns—that the business of running an institution can be counted on to intrude on the time he sets aside for study and sermon preparation. He was wrestling with an Easter sermon and losing. It was easy for him to prepare classroom lectures because he could select his material from a storehouse of facts, or what history said were facts, and order them and embroider on them as he wished. He was rather proud of his reputation among the student body as a professor who could make a moribund subject dance with excitement.

But preaching, he was finding out, is different, especially for a special occasion like Easter.

"Easter," the bishop had told him when he sought guidance, "is the easiest or the hardest sermon of the year to prepare."

"If you choose to speak in paradoxes," Randollph had complained, "at least you could select them for their qualities of illumination. I don't know what you're talking about."

"What I mean, C.P., is that Easter is the one Sunday of the year when more Christians are in church than any other occasion. Many of them never hear anything but an Easter sermon. Am I not correct?"

"Yes."

"They aren't there to be edified by the sermon. They are performing a rite, and hearing a sermon is a part of the rite. They'll be satisfied if you just tell them what they've always heard on Easter."

"Which is? I confess, Freddie, that I always skip church on Easter. It's one of my religious convictions."

171

"You can get by nicely by stringing the familiar phrases together —'victory over death,' 'immortal life,' that sort of thing. It reassures the faithful and is easy as pie to prepare. Most of our preachers, I'm afraid, take that route."

"And the hard alternative?"

"Really dig into the subject, C.P. Take what is, as you know, a dubious piece of history and make it a relevant article of faith for the modern mind. Think up something fresh to say on the subject. Now that's hard."

Randollph had planned to dig into the subject this morning. He had instructed Miss Windfall that he would be in his study in the penthouse all morning. Would she try to make an appointment for him with the president of the seminary, what was his name?

"Dr. Damon Laudermilk," Miss Windfall had supplied.

"Ask if he can see me late this afternoon," Randollph told her, "and hold all my calls."

The walls began to crumble at breakfast. Mrs. Creedy in customary black (didn't the woman own another dress?) served him a plate of underdone pancakes and said, "I want to thank you, Dr. Randollph, for the pay increase and the better room, not that I don't deserve it, the amount of work I do. You simply must give attention to my responsibilities. Today's my inspection day, and I wish you to accompany me. I start at eleven."

"Ah, yes, I must go into your problems," Randollph said as he doused the squishy pancakes with syrup. "I'm awfully busy today; perhaps next week would do as well."

"No," said Mrs. Creedy.

Randollph knew he could have dismissed a similar demand from Little Bobbie Torgeson with a curt refusal and wondered why he caved in to Mrs. Creedy.

"Eleven, then," he said, regretfully chopping an hour off of his study time.

He was reading a commentary on the Easter story as recorded in the Gospel of Luke which sounded as if the author were writing on papyrus when the phone rang.

"Dr. Randollph," Miss Windfall's rather masculine voice said, "I

172

know I shouldn't disturb you, but Mr. Gantry is here, insisting that he must talk to you."

"Put him on," Randollph said resignedly.

"Boss, I've got that dope you wanted." Dan sounded excited.

"What dope, Dan?" Randollph searched his memory without results.

"You know, about certain financial aspects of our operation you told me to look into."

Light flooded in. "You mean the trustees?"

"Sure. I think I'd better give it to you personally."

Randollph threw in the towel. "I'll be right down."

"Addie wants to talk to you again," Dan said.

Miss Windfall came back on the line.

"Dr. Laudermilk will be pleased to see you at four o'clock this afternoon," she said.

Before going down to his office, Randollph rang Sammy Stack.

"How would you like to see a seminary?" he asked her.

"Not very much," she answered, "but if, as I hope, that is an invitation to go somewhere with you, I'd like that. I'm not very subtle, am I?" Randollph could hear her stifle a yawn. "It's too damn early to be subtle."

"I've never cared much for coyness," Randollph said. "Pick you up about three fifteen?"

"Why don't I pick you up?" Sammy asked. "I've got a car, you know. It needs exercise. I'll be in front of your House of God at three fifteen. Don't keep me waiting. That's a no-parking zone."

"Here's the picture, boss," Dan said. "Little Bobbie's got all the insurance—church, hotel, other real estate, workmen's compensation, hospitalization, the works. He's had it for years. The premiums make you choke. Friend of mine in the insurance racket told me we're paying about double what we ought."

Randollph felt very unworldly. "I always thought there were standard rates for insurance," he said.

"Nope. It's what the traffic will bear. Most businesses put their insurance up for bids, and that keeps the vultures from picking too much of the carcass. But Good Shepherd's never had bids. Little

Bobbie gets the business automatically and bills us what he wants, no questions asked. And that's not all."

"Go on," Randollph said, thinking that this was more than enough.

"Jamie McNutt, he's a CPA, has the contract for all the auditing. I don't know what other auditors charge, but he charges plenty. Gets the business just by being a trustee, no shopping around."

"Anything more?" Randollph asked, unhappily certain that there would be.

"Yep. Those two were easy to dig out. In fact, all I had to do was look at Stinky Smelser's records. The others were tougher, except Ward Reedman. You know about him already."

Not as much as I'd like to know about him, Randollph reflected.

"I figure Bailey and Craft must have fingers in this pie," Dan continued. "That wasn't easy to dig out. Took my lawyer friend to do it. Turns out Bailey is the owner of the real estate corporation that does all the leasing of stores and offices. That's big dough, especially if he gets the contract for the cheaps, which I'll bet my lily-white arse he does."

"And Craft?"

"He owns the company that's got the janitorial service contract for the whole building. Did you ever think how many windows there are to be washed in this dump?"

Randollph sighed. He'd have to do something about it, of course. But a venal board of trustees on top of a lurid murder seemed too much. He'd have to handle it so as to generate no publicity. Another public scandal would be more than the Church of the Good Shepherd could bear right now. He'd likely be less censorious of Freddie's administrative methods in the future, he decided.

"Tell Mr. Smelser to cancel all those contracts and put them up for bids," he told Dan.

"Hot dog! Will those old bastards be mad! Who's going to tell them the gravy train isn't running anymore?"

"Mr. Smelser, I should think. It's his department."

"Stinky'll swallow his choppers! You going to let those old bastards bid?"

"Of course."

174

Dan's disappointment showed. Righteousness always wanted to hare after miscreants, swords drawn, Randollph knew.

"If we don't let them bid, that's as good as charging them with a crime," he explained to Dan. "This way, they have no real comeback. We're just instituting good business procedure. I expect," he added, "that we'll inspect those bids rather carefully. The windfall profits are a thing of the past." He felt a little disappointed himself.

When Randollph came out onto the street, the sun was searching out holes in the clouds to shine through, but the light wind was soft and promised that genuine spring would be arriving soon. Sammy was sitting in a sporty little coupe, bright orange, chatting amiably with a traffic policeman. Randollph tossed his topcoat behind the seat and squirmed in beside Sammy.

"Thanks, Flaherty." Sammy smiled at the policeman. "Thanks for letting me park here." She flicked the stubby floor shift up and squeezed into the traffic. "The things a woman has to do to get by in a man's world!" she said cheerfully. "Where to?"

"Head north on the drive," he instructed. "We're going to visit a seminary in Evanston."

"East Jesus Tech?"

"What?"

"East Jesus Tech. That's what the kids at the university call it. The Episcopalians have a seminary across the street and the kids call it—"

"West Jesus Tech, I'm sure," Randollph said. "Very clever. How do you know about it?"

"I went to Northwestern. School of Speech and Drama. One of the best, the school, that is, not me. Although I did pretty well. Like my car?"

"What is it?"

"A Datsun 240Z."

"It expresses your personality. Cars are supposed to express the personality of the owner."

"How does it express my personality?" she asked, then said: "Sammy, you ought to be ashamed of fishing for a compliment."

"It's bright, colorful, a beauty, peppy, has excellent lines." Randollph was quite conscious of Sammy's legs, scarcely concealed by a very short cream-white skirt.

"Glad I fished," Sammy said. "What kind of car do you drive?"

"I once owned a Ferrari," Randollph answered her. "Red. Made a big impression on the ladies."

"I'll bet! Why didn't you keep it?"

"Perhaps I was unworthy of it," Randolph said. "It was a nuisance. Every now and then you had to take it out and drive it at a hundred and fifteen or twenty or its plugs would foul up. I guess I'm just not the Ferrari type."

"What type are you?"

"I often ponder that question myself. But as for my automobile, like Lieutenant Columbo, I drive an ancient foreign convertible, only mine's a Jaguar."

"Aha!" Sammy exclaimed. "The Jaguar type! That means that you—"

"Sorry to disappoint you," Randollph interrupted, "but it doesn't mean a thing. I bought it because it was cheap, in reasonably good running order, and in California one appreciates a convertible, or drophead as the British would say. It would have made no difference to me had it been a Ford. I look on automobiles as a necessary evil."

"Lieutenant Columbo with a clean raincoat," Sammy said. "OK, so why are we going to East Jesus Tech?"

"I have an appointment with the president," Randollph mumbled. "Something about a guest lecture, I think."

"Liar! All right, don't tell me." Sammy pouted.

Randollph didn't answer her. There were sailboats scooting along the green water of the lake, he noticed. People too long the prisoners of winter dotted the grassy areas on either side of the drive, walking, sitting, playing ball. The liturgies of spring in a northern climate, Randollph thought.

"Chess, who is lover number nineteen?" Sammy asked.

"What? Oh, I don't know."

"You said you did."

"I said I thought I knew his name."

"It's the same thing."

"Not at all." Randollph paused to shift his mind from the contemplation of the arrival of spring. "All I have is a surmise based on very flimsy evidence. The surmise needs corroboration before I can say I know his name. Until I have that corroboration, it would be wrong for me to name him."

"Even to me?"

"Even to you."

Sammy slammed the powerful little car into a lower gear and shot it past a startled chauffeur sedately piloting a Cadillac limousine. "I hate men of high moral principle," she said.

Randollph thought it best to keep quiet.

East Jesus Tech's proper name was Hofnagel Theological Seminary. It was named, Randollph had learned, for Alfred Wolfgang Hofnagel, a German immigrant who combined intense Protestant piety with an aptitude for watering railroad stock. His generous endowment of the small Bible school was looked on by the trustees as a blessing from God and adequate reason for naming the institution after its benefactor.

The school had grown, Randollph saw as Sammy turned into the drive leading to the main building, into an impressive-looking institution. Hofnagel Theological Seminary had co-opted a generous chunk of choice lakefront real estate from the university campus. Several acres of carefully kept lawn led up to a long three-story gray-stone building resembling a medieval college at Cambridge. The architect had been generous with gargoyles and heavy metal-bound doors and leaded glass. The chancel or east end (which was actually the west end) of a chapel poked out from the pile, a massive nose on the great stone face. One instinctively felt, Randollph thought, that inside so solemn a structure ponderous scholarship combined with masculine piety to produce young divines whose characters and theology could be relied on not to trouble the most finicky of congregations. You almost expected to see soutane-clad seminarians strolling on the lawn in meditation and prayer.

There were a dozen or so seminarians on the lawn, engaged not in devotions but a touch football game. Sammy parked, with unnecessary abruptness, Randollph thought, in a small lot labeled "Reserved for Faculty." As they walked toward the huge double doors that looked as if they were designed to shut out the sights and noises of this present world, a weak punt slanted out of bounds and trickled toward Randollph's feet.

"Hey, pops," a sweaty young theologian in a T-shirt bearing the legend "Make Love, Not War" called to Randollph, "toss it back, will ya?"

"If he can throw it that far," a beefy blond youth wearing a bile-green pullover shouted.

Randollph picked up the ball. "You in the ugly green sweater," he said, "see that tree down there?"

"Yeah, so what?"

"You take off, and when you get to that tree, turn around and the ball will be right in your gut."

"You got to be nuts," the bile-green sweater said. "That's forty yards, maybe more. I can't even throw it that far. You'll get a hernia even trying."

"Take off!" Randollph commanded.

"You wanna ruin your arm or something it's OK with me," the youth yelled. He started running, feinting, and dodging imaginary defenders. Randollph, gauging the boy's speed, threw the football in a flat arc. When he reached the tree, the boy turned around and the ball hit him in the pit of the stomach.

"Ooof!" he grunted, doubling up as the football bounded away. "Christ amighty!"

Randollph dusted off his hands. "I'm afraid I threw it too hard for the lad," he said, loudly enough for the players to hear.

"Gawd!" the player in the make love T-shirt spoke in awe. "No old guy should be able to throw a ball like that!"

"Tell that to George Blanda, sonny," Randollph said, walking away.

"Show-off," Sammy chided. But she was smiling, Randollph observed.

"That's right," he answered. "Showing off for my girl. Weren't you impressed?"

"Yes," Sammy said. She hooked her arm in his.

Inside the big doors was a glass cubicle, anachronistic, Randollph thought, containing a telephone switchboard.

It also contained a stringy-haired girl, probably a future pastoress, he decided, reading *Ms.* magazine. After negotiations, the girl made a brief call and directed him to the president's office.

"I won't be long," Randollph said to Sammy. "Perhaps you'd like to wait in the library."

"I doubt if there is any zippy reading in the library," Sammy said. "No, I'll just hang around out here and watch the little seminarians."

"More likely the little seminarians will be watching you," Randollph said.

"Why, C. P. Randollph, you know they have only chaste, spiritual thoughts."

"Hah!" said Randollph.

Damon Laudermilk was waiting at his office door. "Well, well, what a privilege to meet you! The great Con Randolph? I saw that little incident with the football down in the yard, happened to be standing at the window. That ought to teach those young bucks a lesson!" Laudermilk grasped Randollph's hand with both of his. "What do I call you? C.P. all right? Come in, come in! How's my good friend Bishop Freddie? Fine man! Fine bishop! Mrs. Price"—the president spoke to a plump, dowdy-looking woman at a desk in his outer office —"this is the famous Dr. C. P. Randollph, you've heard of him, of course, was an all-pro quarterback with the Rams until he decided to throw those touchdowns for the Lord!" Mrs. Price looked baffled, but there was no need for her to reply. Laudermilk swept Randollph into the inner office, directed him to a chair, then sat down behind a mammoth desk. "Now, tell me what I can do for you? I'd like to show you around our school."

Randollph, who did not like to be overwhelmed, wanted to pronounce a curt no to this big, hearty future bishop. Instead, he reprimanded himself for allowing himself to be irritated by what, after all, was only the meaningless good fellowship of the professional politician. Also, he needed a favor.

"May I set aside a whole day to visit the school?" he asked, trying to sound eager. "I have friends waiting for me now and couldn't devote proper time to a visit. Actually, I've come to ask a favor."

Laudermilk became less hearty. "Anything we can do, of course, we will," he answered guardedly. "How can I be of help to you?"

Randollph told him.

President Damon Laudermilk gazed at the outside world through his office windows as if he found it somehow distasteful. "This could have serious repercussions for the seminary, you know," he said.

"I know."

"You feel this must be done?" The president was not keen on courses of action which could possibly reflect adversely on his institution.

"Yes."

Laudermilk sighed in resignation. "All right. I'll try to have the information for you by tomorrow."

On the drive back Sammy chattered away, but Randollph was mostly silent. The wind had shifted and brushed away the tentative advances of spring. The lake was now frothy with waves, and rain spat at the little orange car. Traffic, lights on, moved ceaselessly through the gray gloom. Sheol, Randollph thought, must be something like this.

As Sammy peeled off the drive into North Michigan Avenue, Randollph said, "I hope you will be my guest for dinner."

"Nope, not this time."

"I am being rejected then?"

"I'm taking you to my pad where I'll feed you. If that Mrs. Creedy cooks as badly as you say, I doubt that you're eating properly." Sammy turned left into Ohio Street. "I live down here, just a couple of blocks now. Expensive as hell, even for my one-room so-called efficiency. But it's almost across the street from the studio, and it does have an underground garage. And security. Twenty-four-hour doorman. Nobody gets raped here unless it's by her regular boyfriend and she doesn't mind." She turned left again and double-parked in front of a blue and white canopy with the street number across the front in script. A huge black man in doorman's uniform opened Sammy's door.

"Put it away for you, Miss Stack?"

"You're a sweety, Claude." Sammy patted his cheek.

"Yeah," Claude said. Randollph wondered how Claude would ever fit himself behind the wheel.

Sammy opened the door of her apartment. "Take off your shoes," she ordered, "like the Japanese. My carpet's white, and I don't want

180

all that gunk from the street ground into it. The john's to the right, where you can go if you want to, right after me."

Randollph sat down on a vivid green sofa which, he assumed, pulled out to make a bed. The room was not large, but cheerful. An oversized abstract painting with too many colors to count half covered the inside wall. The outside wall was glass framed by drapes as white as the carpet. A breakfast bar separated the room from a Pullman kitchen.

Sammy returned and pulled the drapes. "White makes a nice background for a redheaded woman, don't you think?" She crossed to the kitchen and opened a cabinet. "Let's see, you can have gin, sherry or Dubonnet. From now on you have no choices."

"Dubonnet, I think," Randollph said. "Do you have lemon peel?"

"Always." Sammy put ice cubes in two squat glasses, poured them full of the dark red liquid, and twisted strips of lemon peel over them. "Why don't you sit up here at my table and talk to me while I fix things? Now where did I put my apron? Oh, well, this skirt has to go to the cleaners anyway." She took two strip steaks from the refrigerator and displayed them for Randollph's approval.

"Beautiful!" he said. "Well marbled. What are the little green spots?"

"Peppercorns."

"Of course. *Steak au poivre.*"

"Right. Sauce is all ready to heat." She set out two plates of fresh asparagus in vinegar dressing. "That's your salad. Start on it now if you like."

Randollph forked up a dripping asparagus spear and chewed it with appreciation. "I'm amazed," he said. "Does your larder always contain such resources as all this?"

"I think ahead," Sammy replied, smacking the steaks on the grill. "Chess, you're awfully worried about this mess of a murder, aren't you?"

Randollph considered his reply. "Yes. I'm worried. I'm concerned about its remaining unsolved and what that's doing to the Church of the Good Shepherd."

"Can't you just leave it up to Mike Casey? He'll solve it."

"If thorough, efficient police work can solve it, he will. But it's

181

like whenever I wasn't in the game, I still fretted about how the team was doing. I felt responsible even though I was on the sidelines. And Casey isn't getting anywhere. He still favors the absent husband."

"Why?"

"Probably because he had the opportunity. Did you know he was late to the meeting of the trustees that night? He could have been in the choir room during the time span when the doctor said she was killed."

"But did he have a motive?"

"Casey thinks so. He says spouses always have reasons for murdering each other."

"That's a terribly cynical view of marriage." Sammy wrinkled her nose.

"True. But I expect that being a policeman tends to make one cynical about human nature. Also, what you don't know is that Ward Reedman absconded with approximately ten million dollars of the church's money which was in his care."

"Holy— Words fail me, at least words fit for clerical ears," a startled Sammy replied.

"We've kept the lid on it, and you must, too," Randollph told her. "There is reason to think that Marianne Reedman knew her husband was pilfering church money and that she was thinking of turning him in. Casey likes that motive for throttling her."

Sammy dished up the steaks. "Sounds like a good motive to me. Don't you like it? Here, open this bottle of wine. It's not vintage stuff, just good California."

"I'm sure it's delicious," Randollph said, working in the corkscrew. "Yes, I suppose I should like it. What do I know about motives that Casey doesn't? But it's like trying to complete a jigsaw puzzle with a piece that doesn't quite fit."

"Why so? Like your steak?"

"Marvelous steak!" Randollph said. "How thoughtful of you to prepare this superb sauce."

"I can be a show-off, too. Besides, I didn't think you were a plain steak type. Why doesn't Ward Reedman fit? Why did he run away if he didn't do it?"

"He ran away, I think, because I announced at the trustees' meet-

182

ing that I was ordering an inventory of the securities he held for the church and that it would be done immediately. Of course, he had been planning to abscond for some time, I imagine. I just upset his time-table."

"He could still have killed her."

"But to what end? And don't forget that she had had sexual relations shortly before she died. How does Reedman figure in that part of the picture?"

"Chess"—Sammy laughed—"I love the way you talk. Very precise. If you were a drab little bookkeeper it'd sound prissy. 'Had sexual relations,' for heaven's sake! Why don't you say, 'She'd been screwed'? Don't you ever use vulgar language?"

Randollph laughed too. "I have used it. I can use it. I seldom do. Partly because I developed a distaste for banal vulgarities so common in the locker room. Mostly because I have a respect for the English language. It's so rich in resources, and we ought to use them. Do I sound like a fussy old professor?"

"Yes, you do. Say, 'She'd been screwed.'"

"She'd been screwed."

"That's better. Now, who screwed her? Lover number nineteen?"

"Perhaps."

"And you think you know who he is?"

"As I told you, I have only an unsupported surmise."

"And you aren't going to tell me his name."

"Not yet."

"OK. I'm not going to pout. But whoever did it, she was asking for it."

Randollph was surprised at Sammy's vehemence. "Why was she asking for it?"

"It's not that I have anything against sex, mind you," Sammy answered. "Just the opposite. But when a broad like Marianne Reedman rolls over for that many guys, she's almost sure to pick at least one who'll give her trouble. I'll say this for her, though. If she told her diary the truth, she wasn't any common nymph. She sure seemed to enjoy it." Sammy got up to set out coffee cups. "For dessert there's strawberry tart, made by my friendly neighborhood baker."

Randollph munched his way through the rather tasteless pastry.

Who for certain was lover number nineteen? he wondered. What could possibly have motivated him to strangle that beautiful woman? Was Casey on the right track thinking that Reedman had done it, or did he think so because no one else had an apparent motive? Could it have been a tramp or a wino who had just strayed in from the street? Had one of Marianne's earlier and rejected lovers, insane with jealousy, waited concealed in the choir room (where he had, presumably, so often enjoyed Marianne Reedman's favors) until her current lover had loved and departed, then throttled her? Could that rejected lover have been Professor Don Miller, who admitted he was bewitched by Marianne? Was there any connection between the peculations of the Good Shepherd trustees and Marianne's apparent awareness of at least her husband's misappropriations and her death?

"Come back to earth, Randolph, you've been staring into that coffee cup for three minutes."

"Oh? Sorry."

Sammy went over to a closet, got out his raincoat, and held it for him. "It's time for you to go home. Not that I want to be rid of you, but I've got to change before I go over to do my ever-popular TV show and, dear Reverend Doctor, our relationship hasn't reached the stage where I'm ready to undress in front of you—for which I devoutly hope you are sorry. However," she said as she led him to the door, "I think it has reached the stage where a good-night kiss would be in order." She put her arms around him and kissed him with considerable authority. Randolph opened the door and was out in the hall when he heard her say, "Wait, Chess."

"Yes?"

"You forgot your shoes."

23

MARCH, RANDOLLPH observed, was going out like a lamb. From the window wall of Good Shepherd's penthouse parsonage, he watched a brilliant sun chase away the last wisps of the morning fog and wash the surrounding buildings with light. Even the distasteful task he had set for himself this morning could not suppress his rising spirits.

He turned from the window, crossed the living room to the dining room, where Mrs. Creedy, a reed in customary black, was methodically arranging eight place settings on a damask-sheathed table.

"A glorious morning, Mrs. Creedy! Makes one glad to be alive!"

"It's a weather breeder. You mark my words, Dr. Randollph, it's a weather breeder." Mrs. Creedy handed down her somber judgment as she vigorously polished a knife with her apron.

Randollph abandoned his attempts at jollity with Mrs. Creedy. It had become a little game with him, the effort to elicit a laugh, even a smile, or some sign of simple pleasure from Mrs. Creedy. But without success. The Calvinistic personality, he had to keep reminding himself, by assiduously searching for gloom in a bright spring day expects to enhance its chances of dwelling in eternal light.

Samantha was the first to arrive. Randollph heard the elevator and was waiting when it opened. "Up these three steps," Randollph said, taking her arm, "and then into my abode."

"Three steps for the Trinity?" Samantha asked.

"Heavens, I don't know," Randollph answered, taking her light camel-colored coat and stowing it in the foyer closet. Sammy was wearing a navy-blue silk suit with white polka dots.

185

"You are a harbinger of spring," he said. "If you will pardon a cliche."

"What a nice compliment," Sammy said. "Now, let's see this bachelor pad of yours."

Randollph ushered her into the living room with its wall of glass, its huge fireplace, and its air of restrained luxury.

"Wow!" Sammy said incredulously. "Some pad! You mean this is how preachers live? Don't I recall a Scripture verse from my Sunday school days about the son of man having no place to lay his head? Things seem to have improved in the prophet business since then. You could rent this place for more than my annual salary, and I'm quite well paid."

"It is rather sumptuous," Randollph admitted. "I believe I hear the elevator arriving."

They were all on the elevator. Randollph and Samantha greeted them, Randollph introducing her to the ones she had not met. O. B. Smelser, sunk in contemplation of some private misery, acknowledged her perfunctorily. Miss Windfall coolly surveyed her and pronounced, "We've talked on the phone." Evelyn, enchanted at meeting a local celebrity, said fluttery things. Arnie Uhlinger was charming, although with an effort, Randollph thought. Lieutenant Casey was affable. Dan Gantry said, "Mornin', Sam. Early for you, isn't it?"

"I'm sure we're all hungry." Randollph made a stab at playing the jovial host as he herded them toward the dining room. He stood behind the chair at the head of the table, Sammy placing herself at the opposite end. "Take any places you please." He waved vaguely at the remaining places. He supposed ecclesiastical protocol called for a prayer. When all of them had found places, he said, "I shall ask Mr. Smelser to offer our thanks."

Mr. Smelser looked startled, but reacted professionally. "Be pleased to accept our gratitude for these gifts we are about to receive," he mumbled unctuously. He did not sound grateful. Perhaps, Randollph thought, he is acquainted with Mrs. Creedy's cooking.

Mrs. Creedy gloomily offered a selection of orange or tomato juice. "There's grapefruit juice, too, if anybody wants it," she said.

"Friends," Randollph addressed them, "you may be wondering why you were invited this morning. There are two reasons. First, and most

186

important," he lied, "is that I had hoped to have our staff together here before this, but the unfortunate events of recent weeks have forced me to postpone it."

"Oh, I think it's lovely," Evelyn bubbled. "I've never been up here before. Such a keen place! I bet you adore living here!"

Miss Windfall silenced her with a frown. "Never been up here myself. Dr. Hartshorne did not believe in socializing with his employees." Randollph could not tell if she was rebuking Dr. Hartshorne or himself.

"Mrs. Stack and Lieutenant Casey are not of our staff, of course. I have asked Mrs. Stack to act as hostess for this little gathering. You all know Lieutenant Casey and his special responsibilities here at Good Shepherd. He wants to bring you up to date on the progress of his investigations and ask for your cooperation in a plan he has to further them. But that can wait," he added cheerily, "until we've been fed." He was not, Randollph mused as he sat down, the hearty host type.

Mrs. Creedy reappeared with individual plates on a serving cart. They contained, as Randollph feared, grayish scrambled eggs and greasy bacon. The portions were precise and meager, except for his own heaping platter and a similar one for Arnie Uhlinger. Both the larger helpings were forms of judgment, Randollph guessed. In his case, Mrs. Creedy was saying, "Since you insist on being a glutton, let the world see that you are a glutton." As for Arnie, perhaps he triggered some deeply buried maternal instinct in Mrs. Creedy. Any mother would want to put meat on Arnie's bony frame.

Randollph tried to spark gay table talk. Samantha, he noticed, had disappeared toward the kitchen before Mrs. Creedy had finished serving the plates. He did succeed in getting Lieutenant Casey to state that while intellectually he was all for the changes instituted by Vatican II, he sort of missed the Latin mass.

"Lotta crap," Dan pronounced. "You think maybe God talks like a wop? Superstitious crap." Randollph was relieved when Samantha entered with a large platter of puffy yellow scrambled eggs and a hill of crisp bacon.

"I thought there might be a call for seconds," she announced. "Dan, you serve"—she pushed the platter into his hands—"while I see to

187

more coffee and hot toast." Randollph momentarily wondered how Samantha had managed to bypass Mrs. Creedy. He was anxious to get on with it, so when O. B. Smelser, surprisingly, stripped the cellophane hide from a cigar and asked permission to smoke it, he spoke.

"I'm going to ask Lieutenant Casey to speak to you now," he said without preamble.

Casey poured himself another cup of coffee from the silver pot Samantha had placed at his end of the table, tasted it and found it satisfactory, then began.

"I want to thank you all for the help you have given us up to now. I must confess, though, that nothing much has come of it or from anything else for that matter. We are at an impasse in our attempt to find the murderer of Mrs. Ward Reedman." Casey, Randollph could see, was enjoying this. Employing a friendly but formal tone, choosing his words with care without seeming to do so, perhaps he thought of this exercise as good practice against the time he became commissioner, and adroit handling of press and public could make a man. "So what we do in a situation like this," he explained as if they knew it already, "is to cover the ground again."

"I've told you all I know, and that's not much," Miss Windfall protested, lips drawn in a thin line of disapproval.

"Me too," O. B. Smelser chimed in from behind a screen of cigar smoke.

"I wasn't even around that awful evening. I don't know why you think I can help," Arnie piped. He sounded petulant.

Casey was placating. "I understand your feelings. This is a tedious procedure. But solving crimes, contrary to television and the movies, is a dull, boring, tedious business. We have to assemble facts, masses of facts, and hope that one of them or more will point to a solution. And," he added, "they usually do."

"But, Loot," Dan broke in, "you have all the facts we have. We've all spilled the beans to you. I admit there wasn't beans enough to make a good f—" Dan caught himself to Randollph's relief. "Not enough beans to make a meal for a gnat," he amended.

"I know you all have told me everything you think you know," Casey said soothingly. "But people often know things they don't know they know." He laughed at his little joke. "One time there was a murder done in the dark of a theater during the picture—a stabbing it was—and we got nowhere until the third time I questioned a girl usher; she remembered the smell of a certain brand of perfume, and that fact led to the solution. She wasn't trying to hide anything from us, the girl; she just didn't remember until we'd gone over the ground several times." Randollph wondered if this was true or if Casey had made it up out of the need of the moment.

Randollph had decided to use his office for what Casey called a useless charade.

"I don't see why you can't just bring in whoever it is and be done with it," Casey grumbled.

"Because I might be wrong, and then this person would have been singled out as suspect. You can't keep a thing like that secret, and so I would have perpetrated an injustice." Randollph was firm.

But Casey continued to complain. "At least you could tell me which one it is."

"No, you might give it away and put the person on guard."

"Ha!" Casey scoffed. "I'm nothing if not professional."

"Let me tell you a story," Randollph answered. "One of the best free safeties in the NFL, a real terror, a real pro, had a habit of rubbing his hands together when the safety blitz was on—probably anticipating the pleasure of smacking the poor defenseless quarterback. Well, anyway, I picked up his little habit and we made uncounted yards on their safety blitz. He complained that I had ESP or was a warlock or something supernatural, but all it was was his little giveaway."

"Oh, all right, have it your way, you're the quarterback anyway," Casey, unappeased, agreed.

O. B. Smelser came first. Whatever strength and pleasure he had drawn from his postbreakfast cigar had been dissipated, Randollph saw. He looked furtive and unhappy. Seated by Randollph's desk, he began his familiar ritual of polishing his granny glasses.

"Lieutenant Casey knows about Ward Reedman and the church's securities," Randollph told Smelser, "so you can speak freely. We have naturally wondered if there is some connection with his dis-

189

appearance and the murder. We thought you might throw some light on it."

But Smelser couldn't. Yes, he had wondered if perhaps Marianne Reedman had discovered her husband's pilferage of church securities and threatened to expose him. Everyone knew they didn't get along well. Maybe she'd decided to divorce him, and having him up on criminal charges would be a good excuse. Then, to protect himself and in a fit of anger, Reedman had killed her. O. B. Smelser had thought these thoughts. Ward Reedman was not a nice man. Randollph wondered how much rudeness Smelser had endured from Reedman over the years. If Ward Reedman, instead of his wife, had been the victim, Smelser would have been a prime suspect. The human spirit, even one like Smelser born to be affronted, will endure just so much indignity. Meeker men than Smelser had become mass murderers.

"Who's next?" Casey inquired when O. B. Smelser had departed.

Randollph consulted a list. "We are going to take Arnold Uhlinger and Dan Gantry together, then the ladies together. It will save time."

"Chaps like Uhlinger, they bother me," Casey reflected aloud. "We get 'em in the priesthood too, lots of them. Something about the clerical life attracts 'em. Not quite sure of their gender. Too artsy. Too tender."

"I'm surprised at you, Lieutenant." Casey was rebuked by Randollph. "You a college man, a modern man, and you talk like Sergeant Garbaski."

"Now wait a minute—"

"No, you listen." Randollph shut him up. "Is a man a man because he is rough and tough? Am I more masculine because I endured being kicked around on the football field by big oafs in armor? Do only women care for music and painting? Is a high-pitched voice a mark of shame in a male? Is an Arnold Uhlinger an oddball because he is an oddball or because of a cultural bias held by the rest of us?"

"Whew!" Casey said. "I've never seen you so worked up before. You are usually Mr. Cool himself."

"I ought to get worked up more often," Randollph said. "Maybe I've been too long in academia. Academics prize the detached and analytical personality. That's our cultural bias."

"I guess I have my Irish prejudices," Casey said. "My wife keeps telling me that I would be a typical dominating male if she would put up with it, which she won't. She's wrapped up in all this new woman business."

"The point I really want to make is that there is no necessary connection between a deep voice and masculinity," Randollph said. "Now let's have the boys in."

"Arnie and I decided it's got to be Ward Reedman did it," Dan Gantry cheerfully assured Randollph and Casey. Arnie pulled his chair up to the desk and rested his elbows on it while listening to Dan. He plainly didn't like this business at all.

"You see," Dan continued, "everyone knows Ward Reedman's a revolving son of a bitch—"

"Oh, Dan"—Arnie giggled nervously—"what's a revolving whatchama-call-it?"

"That," Dan replied, "is anyone who is a son of a bitch no matter what angle you look at him."

"You have further evidence, I suppose?" Casey smiled.

"No," Dan admitted, "just that whoever did it's gotta be a real mean bastard. Reedman's a real mean bastard."

"My wife says he's not the type to kill someone," Casey said. "She says he only loved himself, and people who only love themselves usually don't kill anyone. And she's usually right."

"Couldn't we make an exception in Reedman's case?" Dan asked.

Randollph estimated that enough time had been spent in establishing rapport. "The lieutenant wants you to think carefully about that night," he instructed them.

"I can't think of anything I haven't told you already," Dan said.

"I can't either," Arnie said.

"Let's try anyway," Casey said pleasantly. "Arnie, you told us that you often helped Mrs. Reedman with putting away the music after choir practice?"

"Whenever I could," Arnie answered. "I liked her company, and it made me feel useful." He fidgeted in his chair.

"This particular night, though," Casey went on, referring to a notebook, "you didn't attend choir practice."

"No, I was at the honors banquet out at school. It lasted too late

191

for me to get downtown here in time for practice. It lasted past ten o'clock actually."

"But, Arnie," Randollph intervened, "I asked President Laudermilk to check on your whereabouts that night, which he agreed, quite reluctantly, to do. Several students are prepared to swear that you disappeared from the banquet not long after eight o'clock and weren't seen again. You couldn't have made it in time for choir practice, but you could easily have been in the choir room by nine o'clock, maybe before."

Randollph was watching Arnie's face carefully as he spoke. It reminded him of those instant replays in slow motion which begin with everything equal and then, bit by bit, the blocking breaks down, the symmetry is destroyed, and it ends in a jumble.

Arnie at first looked at him unblinkingly, then started to speak. Slowly his solemn face began to crumble. His lips trembled; he blinked back tears; the jaw went slack. Then, like a ball carrier scragged from behind, Randollph thought, his head went forward onto the desk.

"*Mea culpa,*" he whispered, "*mea culpa, mea culpa!*" His voice swooped steadily upward to a scream, and he beat the desk with his fists. "Oh, *mea culpa! mea culpa! Mea culpa!*"

24

LIEUTENANT MICHAEL CASEY shot the unmarked police Pontiac into a space labeled "Doctors Only," set the brake, and said to Randollph, "Let's go. I'm anxious to talk to him."

"So am I, of course," Randollph said.

They pushed through the double glass doors and into the hushed busyness of a city hospital. Casey made for a bank of elevators and, finding an empty, took quick possession, jabbing the button numbered nine.

"You got a problem," he said to Randollph as the doors sighed shut. "It isn't going to be easy explaining to the public that one of your pastors is a killer."

"I may not have to."

"Somebody sure as hell has to. If not you, who? You're the boss at Good Shepherd, aren't you?"

"If Arnold Uhlinger did indeed kill Marianne Reedman, of course, it will fall to me to explain to the public, if such a thing can be explained, which I doubt," Randollph said. "But it has by no means been established that Arnie is a murderer."

Casey stared at him incredulously. "What in God's name are you talking about? You were there. You were the one who figured out it was him. You set him up. You heard him confess." The elevator jerked to a stop and Casey irritably punched the "open door" button. Out in the hall, he stopped abruptly. "Let's get this straight. You don't think he's guilty?"

"Of course he's guilty. He kept saying *mea culpa*, 'I am guilty,' until the doctor sedated him and they took him away. But guilty of what? He didn't say."

"Oh, for Christ's sake," Casey exploded, "guilty of murder. What else is there for him to be guilty of?"

"I would guess that he is guilty of being Marianne Reedman's number nineteen lover. That is fairly apparent from her diary."

"Hell, I figured that out. Not until you nailed him, I admit. But you mean to tell me that all that table pounding and screeching, '*Mea culpa, mea culpa,*' was just because he laid this dame a few times? Come on, Doctor!"

"Yes," Randollph said.

"I don't believe it. I just don't believe it."

"Nevertheless, I think you'll find it's true. You see, Lieutenant, you are out of my league when it comes to clues and collecting facts and putting them into a pattern. You understand how to trace overt guilt, the legally guilty. You think of guilt in technical terms."

"So?"

"I'm one up on you, though, when it comes to psychological guilt, especially when it comes to understanding what makes a thoroughly indoctrinated Christian feel guilty. And nothing, but nothing, does the job like indulgence in what our Christian culture calls illicit sex."

"You think I don't know that? I had a Catholic education. The father scared the bejesus out of us about pounding our—about masturbation and getting into a girl's blouse, the whole bit. Sex and sin are practically synonymous to Catholics."

"They are to Protestants, too, believe me," Randollph said. "But there's a difference."

"How so?"

"You Catholics know you are going to masturbate, and get in girls' blouses, and copulate," Randollph explained. "So you provide relief in the form of the sacrament of confession."

"You approve of confession?" Casey was surprised. "I thought Protestants all make jokes about Catholics confessing and then they go out and do it again."

"I approve of it as long as we are going to load Christians with a heavy burden of guilt about their sexual natures. It seems to me absolutely essential for emotional health. When you do something you are taught is sinful, and you know you are going to keep doing it, there

194

has to be some way to peel off the guilt from time to time. That's what Protestants don't have. That's what Arnie didn't have."

"I thought you went directly to God, you Protestants, and received absolution directly from him."

"So we do. But our method lacks the precision and certainty of the confessional. Not many people can be certain that they hear the Almighty say, 'I forgive you,' but no one has any trouble hearing an Irish priest say, 'Three hail Marys and a paternoster.' Anyway," Randollph continued, "Arnie, who I feel certain was raised in a sexually repressive atmosphere—"

"How do you know that?"

"Because he has all the symptoms. Well, we know he lost his virginity to Marianne Reedman. He discovers sex, and according to Marianne's diary, he thinks it's just great. So he goes around half the time in heaven and the other half in a hell of guilt because what he is doing violates his upbringing and his religion. Then Marianne is murdered, right after he had been with her apparently. He probably connected her death with God's punishment of their sin and held himself responsible. That's plenty of reason for somebody with Arnie's hangups to pound my desk and cry, *'Mea culpa.'*"

Lieutenant Casey took a little time to digest all this. "Well, I'll be damned," he said finally. "You make it sound plausible, and you could be right. But I'm not convinced. How could he keep going all this time since the murder and not crack? If he's as sensitive as you say, he should have come apart at the seams before now."

"I thought of that," Randollph answered. "But then, he's an actor, and a very good one. He's had theatrical training, I imagine. I've seen him before the public, and he's almost a different personality. I expect it's taken a formidable act of will to keep going. I asked him to help with Mrs. Reedman's funeral, and he refused. He was very nervous about it. I was puzzled at the time, but now I understand. Actor or no, he knew his limitations, and he knew he'd never make it through her funeral."

"I don't buy it, but I'll keep it in mind when we talk to him, which why don't we do now?"

They walked down the hall to where a uniformed policeman was sitting in a chair reading a paper.

"Hello, Collins," Casey said, "any excitement around here?"

"'Bout to go out of my gourd with boredom, Lieutenant," the policeman said.

"Go get a sandwich or something," Casey told him. "We'll be here half an hour probably."

"Thanks, Lieutenant." The policeman put down his paper with relief. "I have to piss pretty bad."

Inside the room a nurse was on duty. Casey reprieved her for half an hour.

Arnie was lying in a hospital bed with the head cranked up about forty degrees. He stared at them with the disinterested gaze of the partially drugged. But when Randollph offered his hand, Arnie grasped it and said, "Oh, Dr. Randollph, I'm so glad you came to see me."

"How are you feeling, Arnie?" Randollph asked gently.

"Pretty dopey. That's because I've been doped." Arnie giggled. "I guess I made a fool of myself yesterday. It was yesterday, wasn't it?"

"Yes." Randollph paused, then asked, "Do you want to tell us about it, Arnie?"

It was like turning a tap wide open. The words gushed out.

"I've been wanting to tell you for so long! You have no idea what a strain it's been to pretend I didn't know anything." Arnie hitched himself into a sitting position and shook his head as if to clear out the morphine mists. "I'll never be able to forgive myself. I was having an affair with Marianne Reedman. It's probably hard for you to believe that, it's hard for me to believe it, I'm surely not the type to be having an affair—"

"Everyone's the type," Casey said, quoting Liz.

"Oh, hello, Lieutenant." Arnie swiveled his head in Casey's direction. "I guess I hardly knew you were here. I mean, I knew, but it didn't quite register."

"That's OK," Casey assured him.

"What I can't really understand," Arnie rushed on, "is what she saw in me. I'd never have had the nerve to make advances to her. We were awfully good friends, of course. I helped her all the time after choir. You know about that. One night she threw her arms around me—she had these impulsive mannerisms, you know—and she kissed me hard and pressed into me and said, 'Arnie, you're sweet,' and

196

the next thing I knew we were on that couch where"—Arnie stopped and gulped—"well, anyway I couldn't possibly give you the sequence of events or how she got undressed or any of that. All I know is that all of a sudden we were"—he searched for a delicate word—"in a sexual embrace. She must have done most of it, because I didn't really know what I was doing."

"Because it was the first time for you," Randollph supplied.

Arnie was surprised. "How did you know that? Yes, I was a twenty-four-year-old virgin." He managed a weak grin. "Dan would think that was pretty funny, I bet. But you see, Dr. Randollph, my father died when I was just a little boy and my mother raised me to be suspicious of girls and warned me not to do the dirty things other boys did with them. I know I have effeminate ways and people sometimes make fun of me. But that doesn't mean I don't have strong sexual desires, like any other young fellow. It was just that I was scared to try until Marianne. . . ." His voice trailed off.

"Take your time, Arnie," Randollph said.

With a visible effort, Arnie pulled up from the private reverie into which he was sliding.

"I know what we were doing was sinful," he confessed. "She was another man's wife, and I was raised to believe it was just awful to do it unless you were married. I felt guilty all the time, and I prayed for forgiveness. But I just lived for those evenings in the choir room. They were worth more to me than my immortal soul. Is that blasphemy, Dr. Randollph?"

"No," said Randollph. "I'm afraid you have been the victim of some pretty bad theology."

"I never did quite figure out why it all seemed so beautiful when we were together and then afterward I felt damned to hell," Arnie said, with a puzzled expression. The puzzlement gave way to defiance. "I don't care, though. This was the most wonderful thing that ever happened to me in my whole life. She, I don't know exactly how to say it, she confirmed my manhood. Can you understand that, Dr. Randollph? I'd always believed that—well, that an involvement with a woman was a snare of evil, that the lusts of the flesh make a slave of us. But it wasn't that way at all. It freed me from a lot of things I'd been carrying around. Does that make sense to you?"

Randollph said that, contrary to official Protestant dogma, it made a lot of sense to him.

Casey was growing impatient. "Then, Mr. Uhlinger," he addressed Arnie in a severe voice, "if you were so fond of Mrs. Reedman, why did you kill her?"

Arnie turned an uncomprehending face to Casey.

"Kill her?"

"Yes, why did you kill her?"

Arnie stared at Casey, then at Randollph, then back at Casey. "You mean you think I murdered Marianne?"

"I don't." Randollph hastily put himself on record.

"You admit you lied about being at that banquet out at your school all evening," Casey accused him. "You admit you came back to the church and met Mrs. Reedman in the choir room. You admit that you had relations with her that night—"

"You make it sound so dirty," Arnie interrupted. "Yes, I lied. Another sin on my conscience. Once you start being wicked, I guess it's easy to just keep on going."

"Don't overrate yourself as a sinner," Randollph remonstrated. "You're still pretty much of an amateur in the wickedness department, Arnie."

"Not if he's a murderer he isn't," Casey said. "Let's get back to the point. Now, Mr. Uhlinger, you had relations with Mrs. Reedman that night, you admit that?"

"Yes," said Arnie. "It was my semen you found in her. How beautiful it seemed when it happened. Now it sounds ugly and vulgar, and she's dead." He turned his face to the wall, sobbing. When he regained control of himself, he addressed Casey. "But I didn't kill her. I couldn't kill anything. But if I did, it wouldn't be the one best person I ever knew." He blinked back new tears. "It never occurred to me that anyone would think I killed her."

"Then why did you lie about where you were that night? Why didn't you tell us all about it?" Casey, exasperated, asked.

"Because I didn't want Marianne's good name sullied, of course. And because I thought if anyone found out what I had been doing, I would be dismissed from the ministry, and that would mean the end of my life, because all I want to be is a good minister. I'd think you could understand that, Lieutenant."

"Makes sense to me," Randollph said, suppressing a smile that might have further irritated a thoroughly frustrated Lieutenant Casey.

"We'll have to have a police guard until we can evaluate your story," Casey said dourly.

"I don't mind," Arnie said. "I'd just like to stay here a couple of days and rest and pull myself together." He already looked better, Randollph thought.

"I want you to remember everything that happened that night," Casey instructed. "If you didn't kill her, which I'm not convinced you didn't because you fit all the facts, somebody sure as hell did. So try to remember every detail. I don't care how painful it is, I want it all."

"Sure, Lieutenant, I owe you that."

"Begin when you got to the choir room," Casey told him.

Arnie wrinkled his long, angular face in concentration.

"I got there a little before nine. Everyone had cleared out by then, and well, we didn't waste much time."

"What was the big hurry?" the lieutenant asked.

Arnie struggled to explain, his prominent Adam's apple bobbing up and down like a fisherman's cork. "If you had known her, that is, Marianne was a woman of different moods. Sometimes she would, well, tease me for a while. Then she could be very tender and romantic. Other times she was abrupt and, well, insistent."

"And this was one of her insistent nights?"

"Yes."

"Tell me about it."

"You mean"—Arnie was hesitant—"you mean what she said, all the words?"

"I mean everything. What she said, what she did. Everything."

"All right." Arnie sighed. "Well, I had no sooner got inside the door than she was all over me. 'Oh, Arnie, darling, screw me, screw me quick,' is what she said. It sounds vulgar, I know. I wish I could explain it really wasn't. Not from her. I don't use those words, I've always thought of them as disgusting, but when she used them, they weren't. They were terribly exciting!"

"And you followed instructions, I take it?"

"Yes, Lieutenant." Randollph noted that Arnie was blushing.

"Then what happened?"

"Well, usually on those, um, abrupt nights, we'd talk afterward. Maybe an hour. But this night I didn't stay because she said she had to look in on a committee meeting for some charity she was connected with, and anyway, I had quite a bit of studying to do. So I left not very much after nine."

"Wham bam," Casey said.

"What?"

"Nothing. Was it always your habit to leave first?"

"Oh, yes," Arnie replied. "She insisted on that. Said it was fun for a man to watch a woman take her clothes off, but no treat to watch her put them on. Besides, afterward—you know, afterward—she liked to stretch out on that couch and just drowse for a few minutes. I always left first."

Casey snorted in disgust. "That all adds up to a lot of nothing. What you tell us, if that's true, anyone who can't prove where he was from about ten minutes after nine until maybe eleven thirty, midnight could have done it. Including you, Mr. Uhlinger. You're still the best candidate. I've got enough now to book you."

Randollph interrupted. "Let's give it a day or two before you do anything that definite, Lieutenant. Arnie's not going anywhere."

"That he isn't." Casey stood up. "We might as well go."

"Dr. Randollph," Arnie said hesitantly, "could I talk to you for a minute?" He looked at Casey. "I mean alone?"

"If the lieutenant agrees," Randollph said.

"Don't mind me." Casey was disgruntled and wasn't hiding it. "Like Collins, I have to piss. Take about three minutes." He left.

"I think he's pretty mad at me," Arnie said.

"He's mainly angry with himself because he thought he had the answer to this frustrating case, and now he isn't positive," Randollph said. "You should have told us everything right off, you know."

"I know. But I didn't. What I want to talk about is to ask, Dr. Randollph, do you, are you sure God will forgive such awful sins as I have committed?"

200

Randollph was irritated at Arnie's insistence at playing the role of blackest of sinners.

"Look, Arnie," he said firmly, "it was stupid of you to keep all this secret. At the best it was bad judgment. At the worst, it was a selfish desire to protect yourself no matter what the cost to others. That is a bad sin, all right, but certainly nothing to challenge the efficacy of God's forgiving grace. He's had lots worse problems. I tell you again that as a sinner you hold a strictly amateur ranking."

"Oh, I didn't mean that," Arnie said. "I meant the, well, sex."

"Oh, you think of that as a sin?"

"Don't you?"

"No." Randollph wondered if it was his imagination or did Arnie look slightly disappointed? "You said yourself, Arnie, that it was a liberating experience for you, that your times together were moments of beauty."

"That's right. But she was another man's wife."

"Only technically. They'd had nothing to do with each other for years. She must have told you that."

"Yes, she did."

"Well, I can't speak for God, but I consider a beautiful and liberating experience, something that makes you more human than you were before, to be good, not evil. And," Randollph added, "I rather think that God would agree with me."

Arnie thought about it. "I'd like to believe that," he said finally, "but it sounds too good to be true."

"God's grace always sounds too good to be true. That's why so few people ever accept it. Now I want to ask you something. Think back to that night. Did Marianne take her clothes off and fold them in a neat pile?"

"No, she never did that. She just tossed things. Especially when she was, you know, abrupt."

"And this was one of her abrupt nights, you said. Another thing, when you left, was the light on?"

"Oh, no," Arnie replied. "Well, yes, in a way. The light down there's on a rheostat. Tony likes to be able to regulate it to suit him. We always turned it down to where there was hardly any light at all.

She thought it was romantic, and I—and, I guess it made me less embarrassed. When I left, I could just barely see to get my clothes on."

Randollph heard Lieutenant Casey open the door and ask, "Ready?" His mind was like the choir room, dark, dim, but a little light was seeping in. He couldn't see very well yet, only outlines. But if he could just turn up the rheostat a bit. . . .

"Ready," he said.

25

"A CHECKED suit," the bishop said as Randollph led him into the penthouse, "and a paisley tie. My, my, C.P., you look almost gaudy."

"Only by your unimaginative sartorial standards, Freddie. They're very small checks. I put on peppy clothes when I want to cheer myself up."

"Feeling a little down, C.P.?" the bishop asked, selecting a large easy chair with a hassock.

"Attrition of spirit mostly. I never guessed the pastoral ministry would be like this."

"It usually isn't. Many of our pastors, especially the ones in rural areas, complain that it is dull, and that trying to live by the restrictive standards small-town Protestantism prescribes for its pastor is stultifying. Most of them are wildly envious of you—living in the big city with large responsibilities, not to mention your generous income and this grandiose apartment. Even all this trouble you have on your hands appears exciting to a pastor whose big moment of the week is the Kiwanis Club luncheon. Oh, good afternoon, Mrs. Creedy."

"Afternoon." Mrs. Creedy began arranging cups and saucers on the enormous coffee table.

"Well, Mrs. Creedy," the bishop persisted, "I trust this lovely weather finds you in good health?"

"Well as can be expected, considering the burdens the Lord lays on me to bear." Startled, the bishop was searching for an appropriate reply when Mrs. Creedy whisked out of the room.

Randollph laughed. "I can't recall, Freddie, that I ever saw you at a loss for words before," he said.

"It would depress me having that woman around," the bishop said.

"She isn't exactly a ray of sunshine," Randollph answered. "I believe my other guests are arriving."

Mrs. Creedy, at the sound of the door chimes, whisked back in and silently admitted Samantha Stack, Dan Gantry, and Lieutenant Michael Casey.

"Tea!" Casey snorted. "You invite me to tea, or your secretary did. Laverty is on the desk and takes the call because I wasn't there, and Laverty thinks he is a humorist. So he tells everybody, and now it's 'Has the duchess invited you to her garden party, Lieutenant Casey, esquire?' or 'I'm so glad I know someone who takes tea with the upper classes. Could you get me an invitation to tea sometime, Lieutenant Casey, sir?' Oh, they're cards, the boys in my precinct. I'll never live it down."

"I think you have a weak ego structure, Lieutenant, to be bothered by that sort of stupid heavy-handed male humor. They're probably just envious, anyway," Sammy said.

She turned to the bishop. "You must be the bishop. Although you're more cheerful-looking than most bishops I've met. I'm Samantha Stack."

"I know," the bishop said, struggling to his feet. "I watch your excellent show when I have the opportunity. You are very adroit with your questions, I must say."

"I came to eat, not chitchat," Dan said. "Where are the groceries?"

"Coming up." Randollph pressed a button. Mrs. Creedy came in almost immediately bearing two large silver pots.

"Tea and coffee," she announced. "Be right back with sandwiches."

"Will you pour, Samantha?" Randollph asked. "Lieutenant, I'm sorry if my invitation struck your comrades as effete and they joshed you, but your presence here today is essential, and I thought this the best way to go about it."

"Oh?" Casey was interested. "Why so?"

"Because this confounded murder is not only a threat to the well-being of the church, but it is disrupting my life by absorbing time and attention owed to other duties. It simply must be cleared up, and immediately."

"Disrupting your life?" Casey was almost hostile. "Does your bishop call you in every morning and chew your"—Casey looked at the bishop—"and chew you out because you haven't been able to do anything about it? Well, mine does that to me. The captain's my bishop, and he's made some very rude remarks to me lately. All the publicity may be bad for your church, but the pressure's on us. You read the papers?"

"Yes."

"Then you know how nasty they've been lately. Say we're dragging our feet. Say we're incompetent. That means I'm incompetent. You know what that can do to my career?"

Randollph was sympathetic. "Of course I do. I know it isn't fair. I know you're not incompetent."

"Thanks." Casey was slightly mollified. "You say it must be cleared up. How? You got an idea?"

"Perhaps."

"Well, that's just grand! Ideas we've got by the hundreds. What I need is the name of whoever it was that did it. You'll give me that?"

"I plan to."

Casey decided to change his scornful tone. "You're going to tell me it was Arnie after all. I figured that, but you talked me into leaving him alone—"

"Arnie who?" Samantha asked.

"Arnie Uhlinger," Randollph said. "Lover number nineteen. You don't know him."

"Arnie Uhlinger?" The bishop sounded confused. "You mean to say you suspect Arnie of doing this awful thing? Why, that's ridiculous!"

"Of course it is," Randollph assured him. "I'll tell you about Arnie later, Freddie. Oh, Mrs. Creedy, those sandwiches look delicious. Pass them, if you please."

"Aim to," Mrs. Creedy snapped.

"Mrs. Creedy," Randollph said, "Lieutenant Casey would like you to tell him why you strangled Marianne Reedman."

"Oh, my!" Sammy gasped. The bishop suddenly sat upright. Casey slowly put his cup on the coffee table.

"Because she stole my—because she was a wicked woman and the Lord reached out and smote her with His strong right arm," Mrs.

205

Creedy stated calmly. She offered the platter of sandwiches to Dan. "There's cucumber, and tomato, and chicken salad," she said. "You like the chicken salad, Mr. Gantry, you snitch enough of them when we have the ladies' society teas anyways."

Randollph spoke gently to her. "You are saying, Mrs. Creedy, that the Lord reached out through you to punish Mrs. Reedman?"

"I'm the Lord's servant. I do His bidding." Mrs. Creedy offered the platter to the bishop, who didn't look very hungry.

"You mean," an incredulous Casey asked her, "you choked Mrs. Reedman to death because God told you to?"

"Of course," Mrs. Creedy said.

Casey was on his feet. "You'll have to come down to the station for questions," he said.

"Expect to." Mrs. Creedy carefully placed the sandwich tray on the coffee table. "The Bible says we should submit to those in authority over us."

Randollph said, "Lieutenant, why don't you phone for a police-woman? Mrs. Creedy can wait in the kitchen."

"Now just a minute, there's knives in the kitchen, she might—"

"Lieutenant!" Mrs. Creedy's voice was a rebuke. "You don't think I'd do away with myself. The Bible says that's a sin, an awful sin."

"I'm sure the lieutenant understands that." Randollph spoke to her gently. "I think we are all done with our plates and cups. You could wash up while we wait."

"There's cakes and tarts yet," Mrs. Creedy said.

"I don't think anyone wants anything else to eat," Randollph said.

"Just go to waste." Mrs. Creedy took the tray and left.

"All right," Casey said, returning from making the phone call, "I sure hope you know what you're doing. If she does anything to herself, it'll be my neck."

"She won't," Randollph said, "because she doesn't want to sin against God."

"Murder isn't a sin?"

"Not when it was the will of God for her to do it."

"Christ!" Dan said. "Ol' Creepy Creedy knocked off Marianne Reedman. How come? Why?"

"I sure want to hear how come," Casey said. "Assuming that she

206

did it. Religious nuts like her confess to stuff they never did all the time. It doesn't make sense."

"She did it all right. It doesn't make sense from a rational point of view, but from her perspective it was the logical thing for her to do." Randollph hoped he didn't sound smug but thought he probably did. "Don't chide yourself, Lieutenant, for failing to think of Mrs. Creedy. You see, I had two advantages over you. I'm a lot better acquainted with the psychology of religious nuts than you are. It's my business. Church history abounds in them. Also, I knew of Mrs. Creedy's unfortunate experience on the mission field when her husband was seduced by—"

"Oh, I know about that," Casey interrupted. "I checked out the backgrounds of everyone around here. Why, I could tell you things about yourself that you've probably forgotten."

"Please don't," Randollph said. "At all events, we assumed that whoever last, ah, made love to Mrs. Reedman also killed her. But when it turned out that Arnie Uhlinger was the man with her that night, I felt certain some other explanation was necessary."

"Arnie?" the bishop asked. "Arnie made love to that unfortunate woman? That strains my credulity."

"Mine, too," Dan said.

"What's Mrs. Creedy's husband got to do with it?" Casey asked.

"I expect Mrs. Creedy has some kind of fondness for Arnie," Randollph answered. "Did you notice that at the staff breakfast we had here, he was the only one besides me whom she provided with a heaping plate? Now I've nagged at her to do that for me, but why Arnie? And when she discovered that Arnie and Marianne Reedman were making love regularly in the choir room, it is likely that she identified Mrs. Reedman with the native girl who seduced her husband. First she seduced her husband and took him away from her. Now it was Arnie, someone else she was fond of. When I asked her why she had strangled Marianne Reedman she said, 'Because she stole my—' and then stopped."

"Why blame the woman? That's a rotten thing to do. Lovemaking needs mutual consent, doesn't it?" Sammy Stack said.

"Mrs. Creedy looks at almost everything through the eyes of the Bible," Randollph explained. "The Bible has a first-century view of women, which includes woman as temptress, seducer, the occasion of sin."

"The occasion of sin! Oh, my God!" Sammy replied.

"So you figured all this because you understand the psychology of religious nuts? I don't believe it. Something she said or did must have tipped you off." There was an edge of irritation in Casey's voice.

"You're right, Lieutenant." Randollph tried to sound conciliatory. "What bothered me all along was that we had witnesses who testified that Marianne was in the habit of scattering her clothes when disrobing preparatory to—"

"Witnesses?" Casey was alert. "What witnesses?"

"Oh, we'll come to that later." Randollph realized he had some explaining to do to Casey. "But her clothes were found neatly folded. That bothered me. It had to have significance. Now I see Mrs. Creedy every day, both in her capacity as my housekeeper and the church housekeeper. She has a compulsion about neatness and cleanliness. She's almost a fanatic about it. She snatches away the dishes before I'm through eating because she says she can't stand anything messy. She berates me for failing to put my bath towels in the laundry hamper. She's just the kind of person who would be unable to have clothes scattered about, even in the room where she'd just strangled someone."

"What a screwball!" Dan said. "Is that why she turned up the light in the choir room, so she could see to pick up the clothes?"

"Maybe," Randollph said. "Or maybe it was an unconscious desire to let the world see clearly what happens to those who follow dark and evil ways. Perhaps both. I don't know."

"I wonder how she caught on to all the fun going on down in that dungeon?" Sammy asked. "Does she have a dirty mind?"

"I expect that she found plenty evidence during her weekly inspection of the building," Randollph said. "Making love is somewhat messy. There were bound to be traces discernible to an eye as sharp as Mrs. Creedy's."

"The voice of experience speaks," Sammy remarked.

Randollph hastily continued. "She probably hid behind the curtain that divides the choir room one night to confirm her suspicions. Once she knew the routine, that Marianne customarily stayed after

Arnie left and often dozed awhile, it was easy for her to hide behind that curtain, slip up behind Marianne, and strangle her. On a Thursday night no one would notice her coming and going. She was a familiar part of the scenery around here."

Dan spoke up. "I wouldn't have thought the old biddy was strong enough to throttle someone. She's as thin as Bobbie Torgeson's mustache."

"Her righteous purpose gave her strength," Randollph said. "And she isn't so old."

"Sixty-five if she's a day," Dan said.

"Forty-eight. I looked it up," Randollph said.

The door chimes sounded. Mrs. Creedy was there before Randollph.

"You the ladies Mr. Casey phoned for?" she asked the two women. "I'll get my coat and be with you in a minute."

"I asked for two," Casey explained. "That way they won't need handcuffs. Excuse me, I'd better have a word with them."

Mrs. Creedy returned wearing a neat but worn-looking black wool coat and an unadorned black felt hat that, Randollph thought, looked as if it had been purchased in the bargain section at a Good Will store. She was carrying a small plastic overnight bag.

"Everything's washed up, sandwiches wrapped in the refrigerator, cakes put away in the bread box. Don't know what you'll do with all of them, Dr. Randollph. Don't know when I might be back," she said.

"We'll manage." Randollph tried to be reassuring. "We'll be in touch. We'll see that you'll get everything you need."

"Don't worry about me. The Lord looks after His own. I'm ready, ladies."

After Mrs. Creedy had gone, Sammy asked, "What will happen to her?"

"I expect she's certifiably insane," Randollph said. "Perhaps there are private institutions for people like her."

"She ought to pay for what she did," Casey said.

"But how?" Randollph asked him. "When one has no sense of transgression, how are they to be punished? After Tomás de Torquemada finished with torturing and executing thousands in the name of Christ, he retired to a monastery and spent his remaining days in prayer and contemplation. There is no evidence that he ever suffered the slightest twinge of conscience. How can you punish someone like that? I imagine that wherever she ends up, Mrs. Creedy will organize prayer and Bible study groups and be quite content. Don't you think so, Freddie?"

The bishop, resting his chin on the church steeple he had made of his hands and looking gloomy, roused himself. "What I'm thinking, C.P., is that we are still missing ten million dollars in Good Shepherd's endowments."

Casey cleared his throat. "Well, your grace—Bishop—I haven't had a chance to tell you yet, but we've located Ward Reedman."

The bishop put his hands on the arms of the big chair and pushed himself forward. "I say, that's splendid! Where was he? Did he have the—"

Casey put up his hand. "Let me tell you about it." It was, Randollph observed, Casey's turn to look smug. "Dr. Randollph figured out about Mrs. Creedy, and I admit it was very sharp thinking. We probably would have got it sooner or later by our slow, unimaginative methods—"

"I'm sure you would have, Lieutenant," Randollph interrupted. "I hope you won't even need to mention me in your report."

"No, sir," Casey said, "credit where credit is due. I'm going to say you called our attention to Mrs. Creedy and gave us invaluable help. But about Reedman. When we were out at their place looking for the diaries, I took a little time to go over his apartment again. I noticed he had a pile of yachting magazines and a set of tapes for learning French in a hurry. And I remembered he had a reputation for gambling. Now if you put those three things together, what do you come up with?"

Randollph started to say, "Monte Carlo," but thought better of it. "I've no idea," he said.

"Monte Carlo," Casey said with a triumphant grin. "Actually we found him living in Nice—with a French tart. Said she was helping him with his French. He didn't even know his wife was dead until we told him, by the way."

"Interesting," the bishop said, "but what about—"

"I'm coming to that. Our man who went over to get him says he bought a nifty sailboat—motorized, teakwood cabin, the best. Say about a hundred thousand."

"Oh, dear," the bishop said.

"He's dropped maybe fifty at the casino."

"There's lots more," Dan said. "What did he do with it?"

"Stashed it," Casey said. "Secret accounts, safety-deposit boxes. He'll return it if you don't prosecute."

The bishop brightened. "Thank God!" he said. "I never thought I'd see the day when I felt jubilant about losing a hundred and fifty thousand dollars of church endowment, but I do."

"You mean you aren't going to jail the son of a bitch?" Dan asked.

"Dan"—the bishop spoke kindly—"it offends my clerical conscience to permit Ward Reedman to get away with it. But the recovery of ten million in church endowment comforts my administrator's heart more than the absence of punitive justice offends my conscience. I will be soothed by the Scripture which says, 'Vengeance is mine, saith the Lord.'"

"I agree with you, Freddie," Randollph said. "Perhaps that is a measure of how I have been corrupted by becoming an administrator. I don't know. But I shall insist on demanding the resignation of Good Shepherd's trustees. I'll see that Don Miller is renamed, of course."

"Go right ahead," the bishop agreed.

"And what about O. B. Smelser? It's pretty hard to excuse his conduct."

The bishop sank back in his chair. "I've been giving that some thought, C.P. It is hard to excuse his conduct. He's a weak man, and he entertains ambitions beyond his capacities. On the other hand, if we demanded perfect moral behavior from all our clergy, who would be left to serve? And he is useful. No, I deem it best to leave him right where he is. I could move him to a parish of his own, but he is totally unsuited, after all these years at Good Shepherd, to fill that role. He can stay on at Good Shepherd and live with the bitter knowledge that he's never going to be anything else than a glorified bookkeeper. That's justice. But it will save his skin, and that's mercy. It isn't often you can pronounce justice and extend mercy with the same decision, but I think this will just about do it." The bishop looked as satisfied as a well-fed cat.

211

Samantha Stack got up, went over to Randollph, and extended her hand. "Come on, football player. This is take-a-beautiful-television-star-to-dinner week, and you promised, remember?"

"That I do," Randollph said. "If you gentlemen will excuse us. Just be sure to shut the door when you leave."

As Sammy and Randollph were going out the door, Dan Gantry said, "By the way, boss, who's going to fix your breakfast tomorrow?"

Samantha Stack turned in the doorway and gave Dan a big smile. "Why, Danny, I'm going to fix his breakfast." She shut the door firmly behind her.